Betray Me

Willow Heights Preparatory Academy: The Elite

Book Two

selena

Battle not with monsters, lest ye become a monster. And if you gaze into the abyss, the abyss gazes also into you.

—Friedrich Nietzsche

one

Crystal

There's life, and there's life without Royal. But that's too simple. Because life without Royal isn't life. Without Royal... Life. Stops.

"Come on, Crys, you gotta eat," Duke coaxes as we sit huddled over a table at a diner that smells like cheap fryer oil and imitation maple syrup.

"I can't eat," I mumble, dropping my phone into my bag and pushing away my plate of pancakes and sausage.

"Want ice cream?" King asks.

"It's not even noon yet," I point out. "It's not on the menu."

"I bet I could make it appear for you," he says, taking my hand.

The thought of my favorite food makes my stomach cramp, and I nod. I know they're trying to be nice. But I can't bear the thought of just sitting here while Royal is gone.

King appears a minute later with a piece of apple pie topped with a scoop of vanilla ice cream melting down the sides. "You gotta eat, baby sis," he says, setting it in front of me.

"We have to do something," I say, taking a bite. I taste nothing as I swallow the warm, spicy pie and cold, sweet ice cream. I only feel the jagged hole left where my heart used to be, scraped out and hollow as if Devlin reached down my throat with an ice cream scoop.

And then I can't breathe, and tears spring to my eyes. I try to swallow the pie, but it lodges in my throat. Tears spill down my cheeks, dripping into my ice cream.

"Crys," King says, sliding around the table and wrapping a strong arm around me. He knows I'm not a crier, but this… These aren't ordinary circumstances. Today, I'm a crier.

Suddenly, the horror of King's revelation about Royal and the realization that I inadvertently played into it is too much. I bolt out of my seat, fly through the door, and fall on my knees in the bathroom, emptying my stomach and retching on bile until it hurts too badly to go on. When I sit up, all three of my brothers are standing behind me, ready to hold my hair. But all I can think is… *It should be four.*

This time, they can't say the right words to make me feel better. This time, there are no right words, and nothing can make me feel better. Nothing can make me feel at all.

I thought I was numb after finding out a girl I bullied tried to end her life. Every day I fought the demons that whispered in my ears that I'd been found out, that everyone knew I was a fraud. My brothers were still royalty, but I no longer felt like their Dolce Princess. When people found out, they began to fight for my throne. They wanted to take me down. Half of being queen is believing you are, after all. Believing you deserve it. And I knew I didn't.

For six months, I was falling. Falling from grace. I walked around school watching my throne crumble, watching myself tumble from it in slow motion. I didn't care anymore.

But that was nothing compared to this. King could still take me out for ice cream and make me feel better back then. Duke could still be ridiculous and make me laugh. Now… Ice cream makes me puke and the thought of laughing or feeling better is a betrayal.

"This was a bad idea," King says, wrapping an arm around me when I'm done washing my face. "Fix your makeup, and let's go home."

Home. Right next door to Devlin Darling, who used me to keep me out of the way while Preston—

I won't think the word. I won't think about what he did. I won't think about a world where Royal Dolce isn't my brother, my twin, the brave, reckless half that never gets to come out in me. I have to be a Dolce daughter, to cultivate an image, to emulate my mother's effortless beauty and be my daddy's little angel. I don't get to fight and fuck and black out drunk like my brothers.

I have to fix my makeup and tighten up my pony, so even while I'm shattering into a million crystal shards inside, I present a flawless face to the world.

A middle-aged woman with a Karen haircut and an Old Navy wardrobe tries to come in the bathroom, but Baron shoves it closed in her face. "Go on," he says to me, leaning back against the door so no one else will disturb us.

I do as I'm told without question. I can't feel my hands, but they know what to do. Ten minutes later, my face is in place. Unless you look closely, you'd never even notice that my eyes are still a little red from puking and crying.

We leave the bathroom, ignoring the manager and the Karen and her husband, who are all yelling at us. We don't hurry or dawdle. We walk out of the diner like four kids who just ate breakfast like anyone else, on any other day. Like our brother didn't disappear last night.

When we pull up at the house, I jolt forward against the seatbelt, a scream tearing from my throat. In the driveway, lights flashing, sits a police car.

two

Crystal

I can't lose Royal. I can't comprehend that option. Losing Royal means losing myself. Which means that finding my brother means finding myself again.
Doesn't it?

I lurch out the door before they can stop me, forgetting I'm wearing my stupid homecoming heels with the sweatpants I stole from Devlin. I go tumbling out of the Evija and crash to the ground on hands and knees, a second scream lodging in my throat. Strong arms wrap around me, and King lifts me to my feet.

"Not in the yard," he says, cutting his eyes toward Devlin's house. There's something in my brother's eyes I've never seen before, and I know in that moment that none of us will ever be the same. This isn't some stupid high school game of thrones to see who runs this town. This is real.

Daddy comes striding over, his phone in one hand and a pissed off expression on his face. "I've been trying to call you all damn night," he snaps at us, his eyes fixing on me.

"Sorry, Daddy," I say, biting down on my lip when it begins to tremble.

"Okay, everyone else is safe and accounted for," he calls over his shoulder to a fortyish, blond policeman I vaguely recognize from some other lifetime. Oh, yeah. He's the one Dixie said was cute, the one I've seen at the football games. Does he have a kid on the team? Did she say that? No, she said something about him and the Darlings…

"I told you I talked to them," King says to Daddy, sounding irritated. "I told you they were fine. We're all fine. Now where the fuck is Royal?"

My head is spinning, my thoughts coming in fragments. My heart beats in a fragmented rhythm, too, crashing against my ribs like two syllables of his name.

Roy-al. Roy-al. Roy-al.

The officer comes toward us, and I sway on my feet. This time, it's Duke that wraps a strong arm around my shoulders, squeezing me so tightly to him that I can barely breathe.

"I want you to know we'll do everything we can to locate your boy," the policeman says.

Which means he's not dead. He's not. Because if he were, the world might keep spinning, but I wouldn't be here to see it. If Royal were dead, I would know. I would die, too.

"Now, we're just going to ask you a few more questions, and maybe if these kids can add anything helpful, we'll have a little more to go on."

"Isn't that your job?" Duke asks.

The officer smiles and holds out a hand. "It sure is," he says. He's got a strong southern accent, and not the kind the Darlings have. This guy's accent is straight-up redneck. "I'm Officer Gunn, and that's Officer Rosewood, and we're here doing our job, which is to figure out where your brother went. So if there's anything you can tell us that might help us locate him, we can bring him on home."

He's tall and broad-shouldered, filling out the black uniform to perfection. Add to that the hint of golden stubble scattered across a strong jaw, and I can see why Dixie thinks he's attractive despite the accent. I don't give a fuck what he looks like or which side of the tracks he's from, though. If he can find my brother, I'll bow down and hero worship him for the rest of my life.

"Do you think he's okay?" I blurt out, unable to hold in the one question that matters.

"I can't answer that," Officer Gunn says. "But I can tell you that nine times out of ten, when these kids get a wild hair, they're home by dinnertime."

"My son doesn't get 'wild hairs,'" Daddy says icily, which is not at all true. But Royal would have told us if he was going somewhere. He wouldn't have told Daddy, but he'd tell King. We always tell King. He knows everything about all of us.

"So, he's never gone off for a night without telling you where he's going?" Officer Gunn asks.

None of us can deny that Royal's done that—dozens of times. It's only the next morning. I know I should chill, that he'll probably come rolling in any minute with a hangover and a black eye like he has all the other times. But somehow, I know it's not going to happen this time. I know, and Dad must know it, too, because it's only noon, and he's already called the police.

"He's under eighteen," I blurt. "Shouldn't the FBI be involved or something? It's a kidnapping!"

"Now, let's not get ahead of ourselves," Gunn says, raising a hand. "The proper authorities have been notified, but it's only been a few hours. Sometimes teenagers do impulsive things. Trust me, I know. I got a couple of 'em myself."

"He didn't run away," I growl.

"Again, I'm not sayin' he did," Officer Gunn says, raising a hand. "But moving can be hard on a kid. Was he happy to come here? He been getting on well at school?"

"You know the answer to that," Daddy says, stepping forward so he's towering over the policeman, his brows drawn together in a thunderous frown.

"Have you called his mother?" Officer Gunn asks. "Is there any chance he—"

"What?" I ask, gesturing to the house. "Drove back to New York without his car?"

Duke squeezes me against him, his grip tightening. I don't get to fall apart. Even now, I have to keep it together.

"Of course I've talked to my wife," Daddy says, his voice hard.

"I understand how upset you must be," Officer Gunn says. "We have to ask these sorts of questions. Cover all the bases."

We quickly fill him in on the few details we have—an estimate of when we left the dance, when we last saw him, when he last texted each of us. My stomach tightens with each answer, and sickness clutches my insides. It's our fault. We left him there. What kind of asshole am I? I left my twin brother and jumped in a car with someone I don't even like, someone who was nothing but horrible to me every moment up until last night. I rode in his car, having a blast. I was fucking having a party while my twin was being—

Before I can finish the thought, the little red convertible Devlin bought to replace the Bel Air turns into the neighborhood. My stomach heaves, and Duke's arm drops to my waist, wrapping around me as if he thinks I'll go running into the house and hide. I want to. I never want to show my face again. Not to him. He doesn't deserve to see my pain.

King frowns at us, obviously noticing there's something going on that he doesn't yet know. Oh god. He doesn't know what I did last night. And he's going to kill me when he finds out. Because as much as I don't want to, I'm going to have to tell him.

Devlin's car cruises slowly up the drive, taking its sweet time, making sure we see him, see that he's in no hurry to hide from us. My body entire body clenches like a fist, not relaxing until he pulls around the back of the house toward the garage.

"Aren't you going to go talk to him?" I ask Officer Gunn.

Daddy gives me a stern look, but I don't care. I don't care about looking like a perfect princess right now. I don't care about being one. I just want my brother back.

"You know, she's got a point," Daddy grits out, glowering at the Darlings' house. "Mr. Darling's been gunning for me since the day we moved in. He's even got my construction site shut down, claiming some dispute over the property."

"What?" King asks, swinging around to look at Daddy.

"Yeah," Daddy says. "One of those Darling bastards outbid me on the property where I'm building the new offices."

"Devlin's dad?" I ask.

"No," he says. "One of the others. There are seven of the sons of bitches. Each of them more unscrupulous than the last."

"Which one?" Duke presses. "Was it Preston's dad? Because Preston's the only one we didn't see last night."

"That's him," Daddy agrees, the vein in his temple beginning to bulge at the mention of the man who's apparently trying to destroy his business here in Faulkner.

"What does that mean?" I ask, my belly flipping. "Are we going back to New York?"

"No," Daddy snaps. "It means we bid higher up front, and we don't play dirty behind the scenes like that son of a bitch is doing. If my son is hurt, and he's behind it…"

"Don't finish that sentence," Officer Gunn warns, holding up a hand.

Daddy looks him over, and I watch the calculation in his eyes as he debates whether this cop is one who could be persuaded. I don't know much about Daddy's business dealings, but I know having my uncle Benny on the force in New York hasn't hurt our family. At least when it comes to personal issues—like all the times my brothers have been picked up or even arrested—he's been a lifesaver. It's harder here, where the cops are already in the Darling family's pockets.

As if on cue with that thought, the door to the Darlings' house swings open, and the three of them start across the lawn toward us. I try to swallow, but my throat freezes, and I can't force it open. I've never seen Mr. Darling up close, but as they draw closer, I see that he looks exactly like his son with about twenty years added. He's still trim and fit, with a no-business attitude and a tense jawline as he approaches. Mrs. Darling clings to his arm, chatting animatedly as they make their way across the acres and acres of lawn.

God, when did it get so big? It seems like they'll never reach us. All the while, I refuse to give Devlin more than the most cursory glance. He hangs a step back, a troubled expression on his face, his hands stuffed in his pockets and his gaze fixed somewhere on the horizon behind us.

"Question them," I say, flinging a hand toward them. I can hear the edge of hysteria in my voice, but it doesn't stop me. "And Preston Darling. Have you talked to him? Because he wasn't with us last night. He hates Royal. He could have been here. Or Mr. Darling. Isn't he a tall, blond man who lives right next to us? Shouldn't you be questioning him instead of us right now?"

The Darlings arrive at the edge of our drive just then, only a few steps off their property. A few steps past the lilac bushes and the mailbox that has been replaced since Royal wrecked into it. I close my eyes and draw a shaky breath. When I open my eyes, Mr. Darling is looking at me, his mouth pressed into a thin line, obviously annoyed by what he overheard.

Good. I wasn't trying to be sneaky. I think his family is responsible for this, and I won't pretend otherwise, no matter how crazy it makes me look.

But he doesn't speak to me. He turns his attention to my father, every part of him tensed as if waiting for a blow. "It's been some time, hasn't it, Tony?" he asks, holding out a hand.

"I kept telling him to come by and pay a visit to the new neighbors," Mrs. Darling coos in her sugary voice. "But you know how the Darling men can be. So stubborn." She clings to her husband's shoulder as he gives Daddy a quick handshake before pulling away and turning to Officer Gunn.

The officer removes his hat and gives Mrs. Darling an apologetic smile. "I'm real sorry to bother you on a Sunday, Ma'am."

Mrs. Darling titters with laughter and swats his arm.

"It's no bother, Officer," Mr. Darling says, reaching out to shake hands with the policeman. "I'm happy to help in any way I can."

"Then let him search your house," I say, the words bursting from me as I choke back a sob. "He's probably got his body in the freezer. You sick fucks, all of you!"

"Now, let's just calm down here," the officer says, holding up a hand. "We have no reason to suspect a crime has been committed. I understand you're upset, Ms. Dolce, but panicking right now won't solve anything."

"You can search my house," Mr. Darling says, glancing between Daddy and the policeman. "Anything I can do to put your mind at ease. I can't imagine how difficult it is to be left wondering where your child is." If Mr. Darling really did try to steal some of Daddy's ideas, I can see why he'd be uncomfortable meeting him again after all this time. Though I have to say, he didn't look one bit guilty. In fact, he seemed genuine in his offer to help the cops out.

Maybe Devlin's douchebaggery comes from the other side of the family.

"Now, that's not necessary," Officer Gunn starts to protest to Mr. Darling. "And you know your father…" He looks both guilty and nervous, as if someone might be secretly recording his words to use in court against him.

The corners of Mr. Darling's mouth tighten. "We don't mind," he says. "You have my permission. Anything we can do to help."

Right. Of course the police know the Darlings. They know they have nothing to hide because they'll help them hide it. The cops must be in their pockets. They run this town. Everyone has told me as much. Suddenly, I see how hopeless this is, and it's all I can do not to break down in sobs in front of Devlin and his whole family. But I won't. Not because Royal doesn't deserve my tears, but because Devlin doesn't deserve to see one blink of true emotion from me. I gave him everything. I won't give him this, too. I won't let him witness another weak moment from me.

"No need to go searching anyone's property," Officer Gunn says. "But if you don't mind, son, is there anything you can tell us that we might not already know?"

Devlin's eyes snap away from the horizon for the first time, and I know he wasn't as uninterested as he looked. He's alert, even if he was staring off, pretending not to care what was happening. He turns his attention to me. His gaze rakes down my body with obscene thoroughness, as if he's still seeing me lying naked on his bed, offering myself up like a sacrifice.

"I don't know anything about it," he says, a smirk toying with the corner of his lip. "I wasn't here last night. I was with Crystal… All… Night."

Now I see it all so clearly. I sacrificed my virginity to be his alibi.

The weight of his words sinks in slowly, and I watch King and my father stiffen.

"Crystal?" Daddy says.

I nod once, my face flaming with a mixture of embarrassment and pure, incinerating hatred. I stare at the ground, at my feet clad in a pair of designer heels that once meant something to me, even if only an escape, a momentary high when I punched in the credit card number and hit *Pay*. The pointed toe of my shoe aims like an arrow straight at a single drop of blood.

My head swims, and I sway on my feet. Someone's going to pay for this, alright. Maybe all of us. But we won't be the only ones. I won't rest until my brother is back with us, and the Darlings are broken worse than I am, crushed into a thousand tiny pieces, exposed for the filth they are. I will make them wish they'd never heard the name Dolce. If it's the last thing I ever do, I will make them pay.

three

Crystal

Royal is the better part of me. I need him more than ever right now, when it feels like the better part of me is gone, like everything good in me was a lie. What if it was all a lie, the Dolce daughter, the mafia princess, the good sister. What if that was never me at all? Maybe Royal's goodness made me believe, but now I can see clearly. Now I can see the truth. What if I was always bad, so evil that I made another girl's life so unbearable that she didn't want to live anymore? What if this is my punishment?

"Crystal, put your phone down," Daddy says, stepping into the kitchen and closing the door behind him. "You got some explaining to do."

I shove my phone away and fight the urge to cover my face and hide. I've been sitting at the table with my brothers for fifteen minutes, waiting for Daddy to finish with the cops.

Now, I watch as the police follow the Darlings across their lawn. Relief washes over me. I know they're not going to find anything, that Mr. Darling isn't stupid enough to invite them to search his house without a warrant if there's anything even slightly suspicious in there. Still, it gives me a bit more confidence in the police force around here. They're covering all the bases.

And if I'm being completely honest and unbiased, I don't think Mr. Darling is involved. Sure, he seemed tense around my dad, but Daddy can be intimidating. He's tall and dark like my brothers, and he's got a commanding presence that has me sinking lower in my chair and wanting to disappear.

"What'd the cops say?" King asks, watching them enter the Darlings' house next door.

"They don't think a crime's been committed," Daddy says. "But they're going to follow up on any leads we gave them."

"Royal wouldn't run off like that," King says, shaking his head. "Not without telling me."

Daddy sits down at the table and turns to me. "Now what's this I hear about you and that Darling boy? You been sleeping with the enemy?"

"No," I say quickly. "I wasn't—I haven't been… It was a mistake."

"A mistake?" he asks, his glower growing more fearsome by the minute.

"Do you like him?" King asks incredulously. "Devlin Darling? I thought the plan was to replace them, not hook up. What were you thinking?"

"I wasn't," I say, tears threatening behind my eyes. I should have known better than to give in to what I wanted. I should have known that I couldn't stop being a Dolce daughter for even a single moment. That my actions, my choices, would be scrutinized and discussed at the table like it's family business. I should have known that no one would ask how I'm feeling, or what I want now. The only person who would have asked that is gone.

The men in this room are family, and I love them, but they only see how this affects the family. The don't care that it's my body and my decision. They don't agree that it's my decision. All they see is how this will look, how it reflects on the Dolces. Dolce daughters don't spread their legs for random boys. Especially not Darling boys.

Though I can guarantee no one ever sits Duke down and has a talk with him when he hooks up with a different girl every night. No one ever stages an intervention when Royal wants to come dragging home at four in the morning with a black eye every other week.

"Do you like him?" King presses.

"No." I draw a long breath through my nose, staving off the tears that want to fall. "I don't like him. It just happened. Once. Last night. It's never happened before. I swear."

"Last night," King says, narrowing his eyes at our twin brothers. "And where were you when all this was happening?"

"It was a party," Duke protests. "We weren't watching every second."

"You should have been watching," Daddy thunders, slamming a fist down on the table so hard I nearly jump out of my chair.

"She's our sister," King says. "You couldn't stop thinking with your dick for one minute and check on her?"

"We were with Dolly," Baron says, as if that explains everything.

Daddy's face goes even redder, and his voice lowers to a dangerous pitch. "The mayor's daughter?"

"Before you flip out on us, we got her on our side," Duke says, holding up a hand. "She told the Darlings to fuck off this morning, and we drove her home and kissed her goodbye like gentlemen. I even got her number. I'm really going to call her, too."

"Okay," Daddy says, lowering his head and rubbing between his eyebrows with his thumb. "That better stay the case. I warned you not to get involved with her. Since you went ahead and did it, anyway, you're going to have to face the consequences of that decision for the next few months."

Oh, yeah. Daddy's pissed. He knows how fast Duke goes through girls, and if he's making him stay with one for a few months, he knows exactly how severe a punishment that is.

I wait for mine, pressing my hands together and squeezing them with my knees to keep them from shaking. Daddy looks at me for a long minute, a calculating look in his eye that makes me feel less than human, like a commodity. I can see the mafia face that terrifies people into bending to his will. The wait is worse than any sentence can be.

"Did you take a shower after being with that boy?" he asks at last.

"What?" I ask, my face warning under the intense stares of all those boys. Those boys who do this all the time, who have done what Devlin did to me to so many girls I know they've lost track. I suddenly feel dirtier than I did when Devlin told me I was just a pawn in his game. They all know what I did, what he did to me. They'll never look at me the same. I'll never be their sweet little sister again. Now I'm someone who's had a cock inside her.

"Well, you don't like him," King says slowly. "So, you must not have wanted to have sex with him."

"No," I start, shaking my head because it wasn't like that.

"So, he forced you to," Daddy says.

"No," I say again, shaking my head harder.

"Well, which one is it?" King asks.

"Here's what we're going to do," Daddy says. "King's going to take you to the hospital to get an exam, since I can't trust these two boneheads to look after you. I'm going to go talk to that policeman while he's here, and if he doesn't make an arrest, the twins will take care of that bastard tonight. You're going to be okay, sweetheart."

He reaches out and takes my hand, and I don't see disgust and disappointment in his eyes. I see sympathy, and it's addictive. For one second, I think about what Veronica would have done, what they want me to do. It would get me what I want. It would ruin the Darlings.

But just considering it sickens me. Knowing I'm the kind of person who thought about it for even a second sickens me even more. I pull my hand back, hide them under the table, pressing my palms down on my thighs.

"He didn't rape me," I say. "I wanted to do it, okay?"

They all stare at me, and the sympathy disappears from their eyes. I drop my gaze and swallow hard, unable to look at them.

"You were wasted last night," Duke says. "We all were."

"It—it wasn't last night," I say, my face heating at having to give any detail to a room full of men when it's none of their damn business. "It was this morning."

Baron reaches over and takes my elbow, giving it a reassuring squeeze. "I know it's scary, but we'll get through this, Crystal. We've got your back. You can do this."

"I don't want to do this," I say, yanking away and balling my hands into fists. "Don't you get it?"

They all stare at me again, obviously not getting it at all.

"Why the fuck would you want to have sex with Devlin Darling?" King asks, his voice hard. I've heard him use that voice before, but not with me. Never with me.

"I'm sorry I'm not your perfect little angel," I say. "I'm sorry I'm not your little girl anymore, Daddy. But I'm not. I'm not a kid, no matter how much you all treat me that way. I'm the same age as all of you. And none of you are anywhere close to pure, so why do you expect me to be?"

No one speaks. I sit there another minute, fighting to get myself under control. When it's clear that no one has anything to say to me anymore, I stand. I take a deep breath and start for the door. In the doorway, I stop and turn back.

"I'm not pressing charges. If the Darlings did something to Royal, I will personally bring them to their knees, but I'm not going to lie and say something happened when it didn't. Because it didn't. And if any one of you can tell me you've never hooked up with someone and later realized it was a mistake, you can come and lecture me some more. Otherwise, I'm done talking about it."

In my room, I cross to the door and step out onto the balcony as if drawn by some invisible, magnetic force. I stare across the space between our houses, my eyes fixing on a figure standing at the black railing of their balcony. For a second, neither of us moves. We're too far apart for me to read his expression, but I swear I can feel the caress of his heated gaze on my skin.

I turn away, step back into my room, close the balcony door, and pull the curtains all the way shut.

four

Devlin

"We've got a problem," I say into my phone, watching from the window as Dad walks Officer Gunn to his cruiser.

"Is it something that can be cured by six to eight weeks of antibiotics?" Preston jokes.

"Not now," I snap.

"What's up?" Colt asks, yawning through the phone.

"The cops are here," I answer.

"The cops?" Preston asks, disdain in his voice. "What do they want?"

"They want to know where Crystal's brother is," I answer. "You wouldn't happen to know anything about that, would you?"

"Now he's *Crystal's brother*?" Preston asks. "Damn, man. Say it ain't so."

"You got the hots for your dog?" Colt asks. "I mean, shit, I don't blame you. She's hot. I'd do her."

"Focus," I growl.

"Whatever you say, Captain," Preston says, but I can hear laughter in the bastard's voice. "I'll let my dad know, and he'll tell Gramps."

"Are you sure that's a good idea?" I ask, hooking a finger in the curtain and pulling it back to see out the window. This time, I'm not looking down at the policeman and Dad chatting like old friends. Officer Gunn is solid. I'm not worried about him doing anything shady. What I'm worried about is the fact that I have no fucking clue what angle the Dolces are playing this time. Fucking Crystal was supposed break them, and send them slinking back to Manhattan like they did the last time.

I thought it would be over, that we'd win, and I could stop doing this shit. But we didn't win. And now they've upped the stakes to a whole new level of fucked up, going further than we dreamed they'd go—further than we're willing to go. I don't know if there's anything we can do to protect our family but fold.

The heavy stone of dread in my gut tells me Gramps would not agree.

five

Crystal

It's Monday, but there's no school for the Dolces today. How can I go back to school, walk those halls, face the people who have hurt me, without my strength, my comfort, my anchor? Without him, I'm untethered, unmoored, a ship lost at sea.

The next morning, Royal has not returned. Our property, as well as every property in our neighborhood, has been scoured by policemen and volunteers and dogs. There is no sign of Royal except the single drop of blood.

"Until we know it's his, we still don't know there's been a crime," Baron points out.

None of us speak, no one wanting to admit his words might be true. If it's not the Darlings, we have no leads. No hope. If there wasn't a crime at all, that means Royal left us. He wouldn't do that.

Would he?

I mean, he couldn't have been happy we ditched him at the dance, even though he had a ride home. He was probably pissed. And I know what my brother does when he's pissed.

He fights.

If he found a fighting ring around here…

What if they were rougher than the one in New York? What if he didn't know what he was getting into? And shit, how many times have I told him he's going to get himself killed? One wrong hit, one person who gets carried away…

What if he's lying in a hospital somewhere with amnesia? In a coma?

What if he's the one who got carried away, and he beat someone to death, and the locals at the fight retaliated and killed him?

The front door slams, making us all jump. I swear I smell her perfume, lavender and jasmine, light and sweet, a second before she steps into the room. "There you are, darlings," Mom crows, throwing her arms around King first.

"Mom," I say, surprised at the lump in my throat. "What are you doing here?"

"Well, your father tells me Royal's gone and got himself into some mess again," she says. "I should have known he couldn't keep you kids out of trouble by himself. Why, a month into the attempt and he's *lost* one of you."

She laughs, and suddenly, the sentimental fantasy that Mommy is here to make it all better evaporates at the rude reminder of what my mother is really like.

"It's not funny," I grit out. "He could be dead."

"Oh, don't be dramatic," says the woman who kept her visit a secret so she could surprise us by walking through the door. She probably wants us to fall all over ourselves with joy. Because of course this, like everything, is all about her.

She turns her cheek to collect kisses from my brothers as they embrace her, then steps over to pull me in for a hug and an air-kiss, as if there are hidden cameras on us at all times.

Welcome to being a Dolce Doll, I think. The Darlings might use that term to denote their fangirls, but our family embraces it like that's what we are. Especially my mother. I can feel the bonds of my name tightening around me like corset strings cutting off my breath. But I smile and return her air kiss, my programming roaring back to life at full force. Never lose face. Never lose control. Never cry or show real emotion. Emotion is a currency, always calculated, shown in exact proportions at the correct times to get what one wants.

"Now, what are you four doing home in the middle of a Monday?" she asks, giving two quick snaps of her fingers behind her as the housekeeper struggles through the door, heaving her oversized Louis Vuitton luggage inside. She's breathing hard, as she must be over seventy years old.

"Where should I put these, ma'am?"

"Oh, just leave them there for now," Mom says. "I'll have one of the men bring them up. Now, I'll need a gin and tonic, and my purse. Where's the rest of the staff?"

"Mom, it's just her," I say.

"I'll take your bags up," Duke says, snagging them before turning to our mother. "Which room should I put them in?"

We all wait, holding our breath, for the answer to that question. Are she and Daddy getting back together? Is this stay permanent, or just until Royal shows up?

"Just set them in the guest room," she says. "And Crystal, make me a drink. We're going to have to get some more help here for you kids. Have you been cooking your own meals? Your father tells me the Darlings have three servants, and they've only got three people living there."

Here we go with the whole *Keeping Up with the Joneses* routine. If they have three servants, we'd better have four. Sometimes I think she had five kids because she had to make sure she had more than any of the other Manhattan moms in her circle.

"There are six of you, so we're going to need six," she says, turning to the housekeeper. "Do you have any friends looking for work? We need a cook, a cleaning lady, a butler, a groundskeeper, a gardener, and a driver. And I guess you'll do for the seventh, since I'm here."

Before the poor woman can respond, Mom is back to us. Despite her faults, Mom knows how to get shit done. "Go get dressed. I'm taking you to school."

"But Royal—" I start before she waves a hand.

"The police are looking for him. Your father's made some calls as well. We'll find your brother. In the meantime, there's no use sitting around here stewing in misery. Being with friends will take your mind off things."

"Okay," I say, going to the liquor cabinet. "But let me get your drink before I go. You must be exhausted from traveling."

After a couple martinis, Mom relaxes, and we manage to stay home the rest of the day. I pace the floor until I think I'll wear a track in it. My brothers go out searching and come home drunk. Mom passes out on the couch, and Daddy never comes home at all.

I find myself sitting alone on the balcony just after dark, listening to the eerie sound of falling leaves skittering down the roof and over the eaves. And then I hear it—the familiar sound that sends a chill racing up my arms. Devlin is out back, throwing the football like he does every night. Like nothing happened.

No, that's not exactly right. He hasn't done that in a while, since he got suspended from the team. But now all must be good in his world, because he's back at it.

I want to kill him. I want to hurt him more than he hurt me, but it's not possible. Because to hurt someone the way they've hurt me, that person has to care about someone besides himself. They hurt me by hurting the person I love more than anyone else on earth. Devlin doesn't love anyone. A heart can't break if it doesn't exist.

I stand and go back into my room, drawing the curtains again. I lie in bed for a long time, listening to the smack of leather across the lawn and the skittering of leaves above. He has to have a weakness. Everyone does. I just need to find out what it is.

six

Crystal

How to survive day 3 without your twin. Dive deep into it. Swan dive for style points. Don't embrace it—attack it. Wallow in it. Get drunk on it until you can't even remember who you are or that you have a brother. Overdose on it. Sink to the bottom and let it swallow you like a chlorine pool in summer. And don't come up from the depths.

Tuesday morning, we head down the front steps while Duke goes around back for the Hummer. I hear men yelling, and my heart clutches. I turn toward the Darling house, even though I know it's not my brother. Mr. Darling stands on his porch in front of the front door, his arms crossed over his chest and his feet planted wide, as if blocking the other man from entering. I can't see the other man, but he's tall and broad with a full head of silver hair. I remember the policeman saying something about Mr. Darling's father, and I take it he's not too happy about the search conducted without a warrant.

Duke's Hummer pulls up, and I turn away from the Darlings and climb in with my brothers. I have enough troubles of my own without prying into other people's. Apparently, the feeling is not mutual. At the gate to our neighborhood, a news van sits idling. A woman with a schooled, tragic expression is talking earnestly into a microphone while a cameraman films.

"Hold on," King says, and Duke draws the Hummer to a halt. I can see the reporter nearly cream herself as King and Duke climb out of the car, probably thinking she'll get an exclusive, the first interview with the family. That, or all the muscles and dark good looks have her knees clenching.

Baron, who stayed in the car with me, hops over the console and into the driver's seat, a grin on his face. "Watch and learn, baby sis," he says. King goes for the camera, and Duke goes for the microphone.

"Our family's not your fucking circus," I hear King snap as another guy comes running from the news van. It's too late now, though. The camera's twisted and smashed beyond repair, and the mic dangles from Duke's hand as he jogs back, slides in next to me while King takes shotgun. Baron takes off, laughing his ass off with Duke as we speed away. For a second, irritation flares in me. But I push it down, knowing we all grieve and cope the best we can, even if it's not in the same way. Their laughter doesn't make their pain less real.

We make plans on the way to school. Preparing for what waits for us for the next seven hours. I feel guilty for thinking of myself right now, when Royal is still missing. But I have to survive, and Mom was right. It takes my mind off him, as much as that's possible.

We pull up to the school, and I take a minute to try to calm down. Royal, my rock and anchor, isn't here to ground me. But after a few minutes, I get my anxiety under control and climb down from the Hummer. I float toward the building on numb legs. At least I know now that they can't hurt me worse than I'm already hurt. They can't break me, because I'm already broken. Sure, they can taunt me, but what are a few ugly names when my brother is gone?

They must think that doing it all at once, ruining me and taking Royal, will send us packing. That it'll be too much. But in truth, it only makes having sex with Devlin meaningless. I might have been humiliated and crushed that he lied and took my virginity. But now it doesn't even register on the scale of what's important.

When we walk into school, the hall falls silent. Everyone is staring, whispering. Wondering why we're here, judging us for coming to school when Royal is missing. They'd judge us if we didn't come, too. I know it's human nature, but I can't help but tense up at the unwanted attention. At our last school, I was feared and revered because of my brothers. But this is different. Here, it feels more like being an oddity, a circus freak.

They can stare all they want. I'll never give them what they're after. I'll never fall apart in front of them. I vow that to myself as I walk. I can shatter into a million fragments when I'm alone, or even with my family. But for these people, who have done nothing but gossip and stare since the moment we got here, I won't perform.

My brothers escort me to my locker, then split off when I'm within sight of my next class. The moment they disappear, Colt appears at my elbow as if from thin air. Anger claws at my skin from within, but I ignore him and keep walking. If he has one shred of decency in him, he won't start with me today, even if he has nothing whatsoever to do with Royal. He knows what happened. The whole fucking town knows.

In New York, kids disappear every fucking day. No one bats an eye. Here, it's a fucking circus.

Okay, so Royal's disappearance would have been noticed in New York. People like us can't help but be noticed wherever we go, whether or not we like it.

Colt nudges me with his elbow, but I notice a difference in the way he's looking at me. I can't tell what it is yet, but it's there. Smugness, maybe. He thinks I care that Devlin used me like a condom and threw me away. He thinks my hymen matters to me.

"Hey, Sugar Crystal," he says, all dimples and slow-as-molasses charm.

"Don't start," I say, my voice clipped.

"Oh, come on, Sweetie Pie, you can't be mad," Colt says, giving me those puppy dog eyes that melted my heart one too many times.

"Try me," I snap.

"Ah, baby, don't hate the player, hate the game."

"It's so much easier to hate both," I say with a saccharine smile, shoving past some people to escape him. But I can't shake him. I may have to fight through the other students, but they part for him like he's fucking royalty. And today, they're not just watching him. They're watching us. Waiting to see if we'll give them a show.

Well, fuck them, and fuck Colt, too. They got all the show they're going to get at the party where I walked around shirtless. I'm done playing their fucking games. Royal's disappearance has made one thing clear. Life is not a game. It's all too real.

The appearance of Preston on my other side only reminds me of that.

"Leave me alone," I say to them, refusing to even look their way.

"Don't be mad at me because of my cousin," Colt says. "I treated you right on our date."

I snort but don't dignify that bullshit with an answer.

"Okay, okay, play hard to get," he says. "But you're like an M&M. I know you're still sweet underneath that crispy shell."

"I told you, I'm anything but. And if you don't stop pushing me, you're going to find that out."

Preston leans closer and lowers his voice, speaking into my ear with that voice. "That's not what I hear," he purrs. "I hear that pussy's real sweet and juicy."

"Not for you," I shoot back. "I don't get wet for lying little bitches who hide behind their grand-daddy's big name."

Preston's eyes harden for just a second, but just as quickly, it disappears behind a grin. "That's okay, Manhattan," he drawls. "Devlin can keep that pussy wet until you're ready for the real fun to begin."

Ignoring his words, I turn over the implications behind that flash of anger. I saw it before he slammed that door in my face and returned to the easy smile that can't touch his eyes, the gaze that's all apathy and boredom, like he can't be

bothered to care. But he cares. I saw it. He's sensitive about…
What? His name? His grandfather? Being called a little bitch?

Colt slides into the seat next to me with an easy grin, an easy grace. The weightlessness, the carelessness of his movements speaks of a boy who's never had a trouble in his life. We have nothing in common. This boy can't begin to understand my life. And any naïve notion I had about us being friends before is gone.

"Why are you here?" I ask, turning to Preston, who followed us into class and sat down on my other side. I try not to notice how close they are, the two of them caging me in like they think I might run.

"Because you are, Sweet Thing," Colt says.

"So, what? You're going to harass me until I run back to Manhattan?"

"This one ain't too dumb after all," Preston says, looking me over with an appraising glance. "Needs to dress a little more slutty, but I'm not complaining. This leaves something to the imagination."

I roll my eyes. "Why do you care so much? Aren't you supposed to swagger around like a big man, gloating to everyone that you fucked me, you're done, and I'm a used up old slut?"

"Oh, I will," Preston says, sitting back in his chair and tilting his chin up to look down at me with those fierce blue eyes. "After I fuck you."

A weaker woman might melt for him, but I know him for the sociopath he is. No matter how dominating and commanding he looks, no matter how sexy it is when he gets all possessive, I know the truth. There's nothing inside his chest but toxic black rot.

"Then you'll be waiting a long fucking time," I say. "Because it won't happen in my lifetime."

"Oh, Sweetie Pie, don't be naïve," Colt drawls. "All three of us fuck the dogs at this school. How else are you supposed relieve the stress of being the Darling Dog? It's an important role at this school."

"Trust me, I can relieve my own stress just fine."

Preston grins, but his eyes are colder than a snake's. "I'd like to see that," he says, taking my hand. I try to pull away, but his grip tightens around my palm. He strokes my fingers with his free hand, a light touch of his skin against mine that makes my hand curl into a fist around his. He runs the pad of his thumb across the knuckles of my fist. "I'd like to see these sweet little fingers knuckle deep in the pink."

I can feel my face heat, unused to a guy talking to me like this. Sure, my brothers say shit like that about other girls all the time, but Preston is gazing into my eyes, talking about the most personal thing a person can do.

"Yeah, well, like I said, never gonna happen," I mutter, glancing at the teacher who strides into the room just then.

"I think it is," Preston drawls, releasing my hand and sliding out of his seat. He leans down, resting his hands on the edge of my desk and getting right in my face. "And you'll be grateful when we throw you a bone, because there's not another guy in this school who'll fuck his own dog, Sweetheart. And they sure as hell won't try to fuck ours."

I turn to Colt. "So, what's your game? You all want to fuck me? Why? Just to humiliate me? Devlin said it wasn't about me."

Colt grins and shakes a finger at me. "Oh, no," he says. "You don't get to ask the questions, Sweetie Pie. You don't make the rules in this game."

"It's not a game," I grit out, feeling the throbbing ache in my heart at the thought of my brother.

"Everything's a game," he says. "You gotta play, or you gotta pay."

Is that it? Royal wouldn't play their game, by their rules?

No, that can't be it. My brothers have been playing that stupid game with them since the moment we walked into this school. They love the game. And yet, somehow, Royal lost. How?

That's not even the most frustrating part. The frustrating part is that I can't keep up with the game, where I'm never told the rules, and just when I think I've figured them out, they change. Or maybe there are no rules at all. Not for these boys. These boys make the rules, and break their own rules, and rule the town. Only the Darlings know what game we're playing, who's a player, and who's a pawn.

seven

Crystal

How can I sit through class with this boy, a boy who pretended to be my friend, a boy who came into my room and made a truce with me, who kissed me like he meant it—my first kiss. And all along, it was all a ploy? How can I look at that boy in the eye and know he's laughing at what a sucker I am, that I could believe he cared about me? And worse, so much worse, that he might have planned it all so he could hurt my brother? There's only one way.
Revenge.

When I step out of class, Colt on my heels, all heads turn our way. A pause ensues, where the hall goes quiet, the air crackling with anticipation. And then the first deep *woof* comes right behind me. Colt. That fucking bastard. The sound echoes down the hall, but not for long. After a single second, twenty more voices join in. Their football team, guys I don't know, girls. I swallow the sick feeling in my stomach, duck my head, and plow forward. I can't look at them. I won't look because today, I'm not sure I can hide behind the Dolce mask. Today, my eyes would give me away.

I make it to my next class, my heart thundering in my ears. I slide into my seat, ready to let my guard down, to breathe, to have a moment of relief.

But then Devlin slides into his seat beside me.

Fuck. My. Life.

"I'm going home," I mutter, grabbing my books and standing.

Devlin grabs my arm and pulls me back down beside him. "No, you're not," he says in an even voice, his eyes straight ahead.

"What do you care?" I ask. "You already won. You wanted to break me, and you did. Congratu-fucking-lations. You win, I lose, and we all live happily ever after. Now leave me alone."

"That might be all well and good for you," he says. "But you had to go and call the fucking cops, spreading your lies around."

"I didn't lie," I say through clenched teeth. "I had to fucking tell my father that I wanted to have sex with you. I'm sure that makes you real fucking happy."

Devlin's mouth twitches, and I can tell the bastard is trying not to laugh. "Why would you tell your dad that?" he asks, sounding genuinely curious. And also like he's still amused. The bastard.

"Because *you* told him we fucked," I point out. "And the cops. And your family."

"In hindsight, not my best decision," he admits with a grimace.

"Why?" I demand. "I didn't lie to the cops about it, despite Daddy's encouragement to tell them otherwise."

Devlin's eyes narrow. "Your dad wanted you to tell the cops I raped you?"

"It doesn't matter," I say, wishing I hadn't said anything. I cross my arms over my chest and slide down in my seat. "I didn't lie to the cops."

"Yeah, well, you called them," he says. "And now our grandfather is involved. Which means no one wins."

"I don't care about your family drama," I snap. "You kidnapped my brother."

"I didn't fucking kidnap your brother," Devlin says. "What's wrong with you?"

"What's wrong with me?" I ask incredulously. I notice other kids quieting to listen, but I don't even care anymore. "You fucked up Royal's car, dragged me around a party on a leash letting guys grope me, and fucked me just so you could high-five your buddies. What's wrong with *you?*"

"Stop. Talking." Devlin's voice is low and commanding, his glare trained on mine with barely restrained fury.

But I'm tired of playing by his rules. If he gets to publicly shame me, I get to tell my side of the story. I'm not some cowering dogs who's going to take it lying down. I'm done being quiet about it. He doesn't get to write this narrative, make a joke around the school of how obedient his Darling Dog is. There's another side to this story, and he clearly doesn't want it told.

"Why?" I challenge, lifting my chin to stare back at him. "What are you afraid I'll say, Devlin? Are you afraid I'll reveal the Darlings for the cowards you are?"

"I said, shut up," Devlin says, his blue eyes blazing, his hands clamped around the edge of his desk.

"And what if I won't?" I ask. "What are you going to do? Are the three of you going to hold me at knife point again?"

Devlin jumps up, grabs my wrist, and drags me toward the door. I know I should shut up, but I can't stop. Maybe I want the punishment. The pain. The humiliation. Some fucked up part of me thrives on it.

"Mr. Darling," the teacher warns, but Devlin shoves the door open with his palm. He turns back as he drags me out into the hall.

"Shut up and teach the class," Devlin growls, and then he lets the door fall closed behind us. His grip around my wrist is punishing, but I don't care. The pain only fuels me. I want to hurt again. I want him to rage at me like a storm. I want the obliteration left in the wake of Hurricane Devlin.

"What the fuck are you going on about?" Devlin asks, sounding more annoyed than angry.

I yank at my wrist anyway, making him squeeze even tighter, until I'm wincing with the pain. "You're all fucking cowards," I growl. "That's how I know you kidnapped my brother. You can't just fight him like a regular bunch of punks. Because you're scared. You're scared of them, and you're scared of me."

Devlin smirks, keeping his cool even as I blow apart in front of him. "I'm scared of you?" he asks, his eyes shining with amusement.

"That's right," I say. "You're afraid of someone challenging the status quo, taking your place. But instead of fighting like a real man, you play dirty."

"All's fair," Devlin drawls, his voice all honey and seduction.

"Yeah, well, maybe you should fight my brothers like real men instead of tying up a girl and parading her around to show your power. All that does is make you look weak. Too scared to face my brothers, and too weak to defeat them without going after their little sister."

Devlin's eyes narrow, and he gives me a long, calculating look. He glances around, then drags me down the hall and pushes me into the girls' bathroom. "Go on," he demands.

"Figure it out yourself, dumbass," I shoot back.

Devlin gives me one look, then grabs me by the throat. "You like to run that pretty mouth, so run it, or I'm going to think of something else to do with it."

"Fuck you, Devlin," I manage as his fingers cut into the sides of my neck. I grip his hand, adrenaline charging through my veins.

"Been there, done that," Devlin says, his grip tightening as he gives me a little shake. "Now talk."

"Fine. It took three of you and a knife to get a girl half your size to do what you wanted," I say, spitting the bitter words at him. "You wanted to humiliate me, and you did. Of course I was fucking humiliated. You treated me like an animal. But you're the animal. You're the one who should be humiliated. Every one of my brothers is ten times the man you'll ever be."

Devlin pushes me backwards, and I suck in a deep breath of air, my lungs grateful of the lack of restriction. "Your brothers are nothing but thugs," he says. "You want to talk about playing dirty, why don't you look a little closer at your own family ties?"

"Don't you dare question my brothers' character after what you did to me," I say, stepping forward and shoving Devlin, hard.

He stumbles back, a look of surprise flickering across his features. He whips out a hand and grabs me, shoving me against the sink. His fingers wrap around my throat again, bringing his face so close that I have to close my eyes to keep from seeing the hatred burning in his eyes.

"If you ever disrespect me like that again, see what happens," he growls against my lips. I can't tell if it's a threat or a dare, but my knees go weak with fear at the menace in his voice.

"Let me go," I whisper.

"When I'm ready," he says, his head tilting, his hips pushing me back against the sink. Suddenly, all I can feel is the thick ridge in his slacks, and fear spikes through me along with an erotic charge. He's hard. Fuck. I'm still sore from three days ago.

I grip the edge of the cold porcelain behind me, fumbling for a weapon, but there's nothing. I reach up and grip his wrist, digging my nails into his skin. Devlin sucks in a breath and rocks his hips against mine. "Make no mistake," he whispers. "If you put hands on me, I'll put mine all over you. And not just your pretty face."

"Stop," I gasp, struggling to free myself.

When I open my eyes, Devlin's gaze is on mine, blazing with lust that's close to madness. My core throbs with heat at his gaze, and my head spins with dizziness from his hand choking off my air.

"Not until I've got you down on all fours, reaching back to spread yourself open for me, begging like a dog for me to plow your tight, wet cunt."

"Never," I manage, my core trembling with fear at his words even as my body obeys, and wetness springs to life between my thighs. I'm so confused by the sensations running through me, pain that brings pleasure, terror that turns me on, that I can't decide if I want to kiss him or kill him.

Devlin's fingers tighten on my throat, and his lips caress mine. "Tell me you don't want my bare cock buried balls deep inside your sweet little snatch."

"You said you didn't want it," I point out, desperate to keep my wits about me, grasping for straws. "Why should I want it if you don't?"

"I never said that."

"You said you'd ruin me for other guys," I remind him. "That you've already been there, done that."

"I want to ruin you," he growls, releasing my neck and burying his hand in my hair, yanking my head back. "I want to wreck you, body and soul. Every fucking day until there's nothing left to ruin."

I reach up with both hands, gripping his wrist and trying to free my hair. He pulls harder, until I cry out with pain. Devlin wrenches his belt free, shoving his jeans down over his hips.

"Stop," I gasp. "You're hurting me."

He jerks my dress up around my waist and wrenches my underwear free of my body, ripping them off without bothering to push them down. His cock throbs huge and hot and wild against my trembling thighs. He yanks my knees apart and drives upward with one quick, sharp thrust, burying himself inside me.

eight

Crystal

"Don't lie, Crystal," Devlin rasps, his breath labored and his strong hips pinning me to the sink. "I know you want this. Your cunt's as wet as a slut's creampie."

"I want this," I whisper, closing my eyes and throwing my head back. I don't want him to see my eyes when I say the words, not because he'll know I'm lying, but because he'll know I'm not. "I want you."

I suck in a deep, shuddering breath, inhaling the smell of him until it makes me dizzy with lust. He grips the back of my head and buries his tongue in my open mouth, claiming it as thoroughly as he's claimed the rest of my body. His tongue is as rough and dominant as his thrusts, demanding my surrender. A helpless whimper of pleasure escapes me, and I give in. I give in to what I know I wanted all along, what I knew would happen if I goaded him long enough. He fills me with what's missing, with a feeling of rightness and completion, with pain and sweet relief. He blocks out everything else in the world. I want every part of that and more. And he gives it.

He wraps his arm around my waist and buries himself to the hilt inside me, his cock full and thick and hot as it burns into the soreness left from the last time. Every protest flies from my mind and my body takes over. My hands grip his head, pulling it to me violently until our teeth clash and our tongues battle. My knees give way as he lifts me onto the edge of the sink, grabbing my ass with both hands and driving deep enough to send an arrow of pain through me. I arch my back and open my knees wider, letting him fill me until I think I'll split in two.

"Tell me what you want, Sugar," he says through harsh, quick breaths. "Tell me how you like to be fucked."

"Hard," I whisper. "Punish me."

His cock throbs inside me, and he bends his knees and then drives up with all his strength, plowing into me so hard my head smacks the mirror behind me. Devlin catches me, keeping an arm around my waist and bracing the other hand against the mirror. He buries himself in me over and over, pounding me until I'm gasping for mercy.

He yanks me off the sink, spins me around, and drives into me before I have time to catch my balance. I cry out in surprise and pain as my hips collide with the sink. Devlin yanks me back, letting me grab the edges of the sink before he begins thrusting into me again.

He pounds into me in a frantic, wild rhythm, and I know he can't stop himself any more than I can stop him. I wanted this, and now I'm getting it. Devlin doesn't do anything halfway, and he sure as hell doesn't fuck halfway. He grabs a handful of my hair with one hand and my hip with the other, driving into me hard and fast until I can't hold back.

"Now, Devlin," I gasp out, trying to push back from the sink. "Pull out."

"Never," he growls, thrusting into me so powerfully I have to brace my hands on the mirror. He slams his hips against my ass, and a groan tears from his lips, his eyes falling closed and pure bliss erasing everything else from his expression as he cums. His fingers clench reflexively, cutting into my hip with bruising force, pulling me harder against him as if he can't get close enough, as if we could crash together with such force that we combine to become one, a superstorm that nothing could survive. I watch him in the mirror, steam forming around my fingers, until the sight of his face lost in such pure pleasure pushes me too far. I cry out, my own climax spiraling through me in pulses of pure magic as Devlin sucks in a shuddering breath, throbbing inside me as he gives me every last drop of himself.

Neither of us moves for a long minute. At last, I open my eyes, and my gaze locks with his in the mirror. My cheeks are flushed, my lips swollen, my hair a wreck. But Devlin must see something else. The look in his eyes is the furthest thing from the one my brothers get when I'm a mess. Devlin looks like he's ready to eat me alive.

"You're so fucking beautiful," Devlin says, his voice rough, almost accusatory. "I love watching you cum."

I love watching him, too. I've seen the animal in his eyes, the one I unleash when we're together. I've seen the boy who held me after, the one who was sweet and real. And now I've seen the pure, blissed-out oblivion I bring him, too. I wonder what demons Devlin Darling has to escape, what he's using me to forget.

He draws away, pulling my dress down over my hips. He picks up my torn panties, balls them in his fist, and shoves them into the pocket of his blazer just as the door opens. Two girls I've seen before step into the bathroom, give us one look, and pause. One of them looks me up and down, my rumpled dress, wild hair, and smudged lipstick giving away exactly what we've been up to. Her lip curls in disgust, and she mutters something under her breath and turns around and walks out.

I swallow hard, wishing she couldn't hurt or humiliate me so easily. I've never been called a slut because I've never been one. Now, apparently I'm the kind of girl who fucks guys in bathrooms. Guys I don't even like. Guys who might have killed my brother.

The thought hits me so hard I can't breathe. I haven't thought about it once in the last ten minutes. And when it hits, it's like finding out for the first time.

My stomach rebels, and I dash into one of the stalls, fall to my knees, and get sick. When I'm done, I stagger to my feet and turn to find Devlin still there. I expected him to bolt at the sight of a girl puking. Instead, he frowns down at me with those damn, inscrutable eyes.

"What?" I snap, wiping my mouth with the back of my hand.

"What was that about?" he asks.

"Like you'd care," I say, moving to the sink and turning on the water. I clean my face and rinse my mouth, ignoring Devlin. When I turn back, he's still there, looming over me like a bodyguard.

"I might," he says, watching me warily. "Has that been happening a lot?"

"What?"

"You're not pregnant, are you?"

"Fuck you, Devlin," I say, tossing a handful of paper towels into the trash. "It has nothing to do with you."

"Are you sure about that?" he asks, following me out of the bathroom.

"I'm sure," I snap. "Now leave me alone."

"Where are you going?"

"Not your problem," I say, heading for the doors. I don't know where I'm going. I don't care, as long as it's far away from him. I can still feel him on me, the tenderness between my legs throbbing with each step. What the fuck am I doing?

"Maybe it is," Devln says, falling into step next to me.

"It's not." I feel like a wounded animal, one that needs to crawl under a rock to be alone, to lick my wounds and either recover in peace or die trying. But Devlin's on my heels, refusing to let me.

I stop and turn to face him again. "Look, you got what you wanted," I say. "I'm not naïve or arrogant enough to say all you wanted was to get laid. You could do that with any girl in this school. You told me it wasn't personal, and I get it. But now you've fucked me, and proven your point, and ruined my family just like you wanted. So leave me the fuck alone."

"You still don't get it, do you?" he says, taking my arm. His grip is commanding, even possessive, but I know how much more he's capable of. I know the violence of Devlin Darling, how quickly his mood can change.

I roll my eyes. "Apparently not, King Devlin. So why don't you explain it to me, since I'm such a peasant?"

"You're ours," he says. "You belong to the Darlings. You don't get to say when we leave you alone and when we don't. We decide when we're done with you. We decide where you go and when. And you're not leaving school right now."

"Oh, so now you're the morality police? I don't get to skip school unless you say so."

"Now you're catching on," he says.

"Fine," I say, crossing my arms over my chest. "So, what do you have for me next?"

"You'll know when you need to know."

"Seriously?" I throw my hands up in frustration. "You humiliated me, showed everyone I'm under your thumb. You fucked me and laughed about it with your buddies. And I'm still here. I'm not going anywhere. So, either tell me what else you want from me, or just put another notch in your belt and move on like you do with every other girl."

Devlin gives the slightest smirk and shakes his head. "Cute. Now if you're done with your tantrum, let's get back to class."

I could keep fighting, but I know he'll never give up. I know that if I tried to walk out the door, he'd stop me. He's clearly done with this conversation, and I'm not keen on being dragged back into class by the wrist like he dragged me out. I sigh and push past him, back toward the classroom. I know when I'm beaten. I may have fought my way to the top of the social ladder in Manhattan, but I can't fight a guy. Boys fight dirty in different ways, and I'm not sure how to fight back against Devlin.

I walk into class, doing the walk of shame back to my seat. I can feel their eyes on me, the snickers and knowing looks, but I don't look up. Today, I'm beaten. I give up. There's no more fight in me, and I know I'd never win even if there were.

I make it to lunch and walk into the cafeteria, barely hearing the barking around me. I feel numb, stumbling forward on numb legs. And then strong arms link through mine on either side, and I nearly sob in relief as I look up to see the twins on either side of me.

"What the fuck's going on?" King asks, glaring around.

I shake my head, not trusting my voice to tell him that this has happened before, that I'm a dog to this school. As soon as my brothers show up, the cowards shut up, everyone going silent and watching to see what we'll do.

That gives me strength, and I find my Dolce strength somewhere inside, the steel spine I was born with that's been twisted by the Darlings and their sick games. I may be twisted and broken, but I'm still made of the same stuff. I'm still stronger than they know. I stand tall between my brothers, sucking strength from them like a starving man, feeding off their confidence and energy and power like some kind of vampire. They feed me willingly, holding me up and conveying me to the table in the corner where Dixie sits, her head bent over her plate.

King sits next to me and grips my knee under the table. "What's going on, Crys?"

"Nothing," I say, swallowing hard. Duke and Baron, who slid in across from me, gape at something behind me. I spot a couple guys making subdued woofs, but that's not what has my brothers' eyes glazing. A striking figure makes her way toward us, curves that should be illegal hugged by a dress that appears to be made of hot pink vinyl. White go-go boots complete the ensemble, and her hair is so high I'm pretty sure every 80s pageant girl alive would sigh with nostalgia at the sight.

Dolly flicks her razor-clawed fingers towards the table with the barking guys. "Don't y'all think it's funny that you're the ones obediently barking?" she asks in her sugary, slow drawl. "Maybe you should look in the mirror and see the real dogs around here."

She minces over to our table, sets down her giant white vinyl purse with huge gold grommets and rhinestones that looks like a nightmare sold at a gas station, and smiles.

"How you two holdin' up?" she asks, nodding at me and Dixie. "Any word on your brother?"

"Not yet," King says. "I'm sure he'll be home by the time we get back."

I know my brother well enough to see the worry etched into his face, though, the tightness of his jaw and the hard set of his eyes. Royal disappeared Saturday night. It's Tuesday. He's never been gone this long before, even in Manhattan where he had lots of friends to crash with if he was pissed at one of us or got trounced in a fight.

Dolly nods and pulls a can of Dr. Pepper from her handbag, popping the tab with her baby pink manicure. "And you two?" she asks me and Dixie. "Getting the Darling treatment?"

"If by that you mean completely shutting me out like I don't exist, then yes," Dixie mumbles. I suddenly feel like shit for not checking in on her. I was so caught up in worry about Royal that I barely thought of her all weekend. The past few days have been like walking through a nightmare where nothing is real except the pain of waiting.

I reach out and cover her soft hand with mine. "I'm sorry."

She shrugs. "I'm okay. Preston called me Winn-Dixie this morning, so I guess I'm back to being a dog to him. You?"

I take a deep breath and glance at my brothers. I could tell them about being the Darling Dog, and they'd go apeshit and start another fight. Someone would get hurt, and the cycle would continue. I'm not about to lose another of my brothers.

"Same," I lie. Whatever the Darlings do to me, it won't hurt worse than what they've already done. I can take it. The only thing I can't survive is the loss of my family. I would trade anything in the world for Royal. If they leave my brothers alone, I'll take every bit of their wrath, play their sick games, endure the shame and humiliation.

I can feel King's eyes on me, the cloud of doubt around him, but he can't read me like Royal can. And Royal's not here to tell him.

"Did any of them say anything to you?" King asks.

"Yeah," I say with a shrug, like it doesn't matter. "They were assholes, but I handled it."

"You handled it?" Baron asks, looking skeptical.

"Yes," I say, widening my eyes at him. "Believe it or not, I can do some things without you holding my hand."

"Like jerk off Devlin?" Duke asks.

Baron reaches over and pops him on the back of the head with a scowl. "Too soon, dude."

"Sorry," Duke says, grinning at me. "If you don't want us to treat you like our little sister, and you're one of us now, you're going to have to take the abuse."

I smirk at him. "You want to hear about Devlin's dick?"

"No!" comes a chorus from all three of my brothers.

I can't believe I'm capable of laughing, but the next second, I'm joining Dolly and Dixie as they giggle at our banter. My brothers glare.

"I'm older than you two, anyway," I say to the twins. "Which makes you my little brothers."

They groan in unison. "Trust me, sis, there's nothing little about me," Duke says, slinging his arm around Dolly. "Is there, sweetheart? Tell her who's the big man on campus."

"I thought you didn't want to hear about Devlin's dick," she says.

This time, we all crack up so hard that people turn to stare. As I wipe my tears, I see Devlin watching, his eyes dark and a frown creasing his brow. I swallow hard, and guilt twists inside me. I can't help but wonder if I'm dying laughing while my twin is really dying.

nine

Crystal

There's a say by Confucius that goes, "Before you embark on a journey of revenge, dig two graves." I know I might get hurt, but there's something Confucius didn't take into account. And that's what happens if the person you're seeking revenge against has already dug your grave. There's nothing left to do but lie down in it. And fuck if I'm going to lie down in my grave before there's someone lying in that second grave, too.

When the door to the six-car garage slides open, all the spots are filled. A tiny, cherry red convertible with rental plates sits in Duke's spot.

"What the fuck," he mutters. "Dad brought his girlfriend over when Mom's home?"

"Daddy doesn't have a girlfriend," I snap. But my mind returns to all the long nights, the nights when he hasn't come home at all.

Because he was at the office, though. My father would never cheat.

Baron snorts, but he shuts up when I cast a glare at him. We park and climb out, entering the house through the garage.

"Who the fuck took my parking spot?" Duke yells as the three of them tromp in like a heard of wildebeests.

"Shut up," I hiss, elbowing him. "It could be the mayor or—."

"Who the fuck's using that language to their beloved grandmother?" says a voice so heavily accented with Italian bravado that there's no mistaking it. Grandpa Dolce steps out of the kitchen with a spatula in one hand looking like he's ready to raise hell—and welts on all our thighs for using that language around his wife. Ironically, his cussing would put a ship full of the saltiest sailors to shame.

"*Nonni*," I say, running forward and wrapping my arms around him. He's as tall as dad, though his shoulders are now stooped, and his hair is steely grey. Ten minutes with him, and it's easy to see where the mafia rumors came from. Trade the full head of hair for a mustache, and Grandpa Dolce could have taken Marlon Brando's role in *The Godfather*.

"My little sugar crystal," he says, wrapping his strong arms around me and squeezing. Though he's no bigger than the other men in my family, I feel small and protected in his arms. His aura is larger than him, larger than life.

"*Mi bambini*," Nonna cries, bustling in from the kitchen to fuss over my brothers. They take turns picking her up and spinning her around while she fawns over their muscles and how big they've gotten.

When they set her down, she takes my hands in hers and looks me over, her eyes crinkling at the corners with more wrinkles than the last time I saw her. Her hair is still raven-black and wound into a thick bun at the back of her head, but at sixty, she's anything but feeble. Our grandmother a force to be reckoned with, all four feet and ten inches of her. Five minutes with her, and it's easy to see where the Dolces get our steel spines.

"More beautiful every day," she says, patting my cheek. "We have so much catching up to do. I can't wait to hear all about your new school, your friends, your classes. Do you have a special boy in your life?"

Her eyes sparkle, but I shake my head. "Any word?" I ask, gripping her hand and anxiously searching her eyes.

Her lips tighten, and she shakes her head. "No, *bambina.* I'm sorry."

I nod, having figured as much. "Where's Mom?"

"Oh, you know your mother," she says with a scowl of disapproval. "Spends more time in bed than a bride on her honeymoon, and there's not a man in sight."

"Yeah," I say, biting my lip. I had hoped that maybe things would be different for her here, too. Maybe she'd get herself together, for Royal if nothing else.

"Oh, I shouldn't complain about your mother," Nonna says with a dismissive wave. "She's making it easier on all of us by taking her rest when she wants it. I know you've got enough on your mind without having to worry about us fighting."

"You're here to help?" I ask, watching my brothers disappear into the kitchen with Grandpa Dolce.

"Of course," Nonna says. "We'll find him, *bambina mia*. You know that, don't you?"

I nod, my throat aching as I swallow.

"You don't believe me," she says, patting my cheek hard enough to sting a little. "Don't you dare give up on your brother, girl. We're going to find him. You can trust me on that."

"Oh, *Nonna,*" I say, wrapping my arms around her and hugging her hard. I don't know what else to say, so we just stand there for a minute.

Then she pulls back and smiles. "Such a big house! Show me your room, *'tina mia.*"

In my room, Nonna strolls around, running her fingers along the walls with a faraway look in her eyes. "I always wondered what lay hidden behind these walls," she says, pulling aside the curtains to gaze out the window.

My heart does a funny little flip in my chest. "What?"

Surely my *nonna* isn't going senile. She may be small, but she's strong as an ox and twice as stubborn. She always jokes around about aging, flexing her muscles and saying "I'd like to see old age try to get me."

She turns away from the window and sighs. "I guess your father finally got his dream. To live in the big house where he was shunned so long ago. I think he was born with a vengeful bone. Couldn't talk him out of it no matter how hard I tried. I can't say it's ever hurt him, so maybe it's not such a bad thing after all."

"What are you talking about?" I ask, my head spinning and my heart hammering. It's one thing for her to say something bad about Mom, but Daddy is her own son.

"Don't tell me your father didn't tell you about the time he was thrown out of this very house," she says. "Buying it outright must have been one of his proudest moments."

"No," I say slowly. "He mentioned he lived around here for a while when he was in high school. That's it, though. Why? What happened?"

"Oh, look at that, you have a chair outside," Nonna says, looking out onto the balcony.

"Yeah, I sit out there sometimes," I say. "Or… I used to, anyway."

"Well, after that long flight, I could really use a cigarette break," she says, winking at me. "Don't tell your grandfather. I told him I quit."

I can't help but smile back at her. Without another word, she opens my window and ducks out onto the veranda. I grab the little white wooden chair that sits at my vanity and climb out the window to join her as she plops into my deck chair and pulls a pack of Virginia Slims from the pocket of her light jacket.

She lights up and sighs, leaning back and closing her eyes as she lets out a slow trail of smoke. "Ah, there's nothing like that first drag."

"Nonna," I prod. "How come you never told me you lived here?"

"Not *here*," she says, gesturing vaguely to our surroundings with her cigarette. "We weren't made of such rich stuff. You know your grandpa and me don't need all this."

"But you lived in Faulkner."

She nods. "I suppose we don't talk about it much because it didn't last long, and it wasn't the happiest time in our lives for any of us. You know how proud your father can be. Just like his father."

"What happened?"

"Well," she says, taking a delicate drag on her skinny cigarette. "Your grandfather had made a few bad business deals, and he got himself into some debt. Long story short, he ended up owing money to the wrong people."

"The mob?" I whisper.

"Well, certain people thought it would be best if we left town for a while until the dust settled, and this seemed like a good place to live a quiet life."

Shit. No one has ever talked to me like this, like it's something I have a right to know about my family. Like our connections aren't unfit for my delicate ears.

"Are you saying… What I think you're saying?" I ask.

"That our family is anything but quiet?" she asks, laughing as she taps her cigarette on the arm of her chair. "I suppose it was naïve to think we could blend in here, but we didn't know anything about this town, or the south in general. It was… An adjustment for everyone."

"What happened?" I ask, leaning forward in my chair. Nonna has always been open with me, but I've never stuck my nose where I was told it didn't belong. But now… I don't know. Things are different. I'm not as content to be sheltered and safe under my brothers' wings as I used to be. Lately, I've wanted to peek my head out of the nest, see what's hidden behind those broad, protective wings.

"Well, we moved here, that's what happened," she says. "You've been here a few months. You know how this town is. We'd heard all about southern hospitality, but it turned out, people weren't as welcoming to outsiders as we'd hoped."

I imagine my brothers starting at Willow Heights, with all their brag and bravado, but without money. It's not a picture I want to dwell on. Before I can ask more, a door on the veranda opposite ours opens, and Devlin Darling steps out. He's wearing a pair of low-slung grey sweatpants and a t-shirt with the Willow Heights crest on the front. His blond hair glints in the last rays of the cool, wintery sunlight as he stares across the way at us.

"Well, hell," Nonna says, sitting up straighter in her chair. "Who is that?"

"That's Devlin Darling," I mutter, fighting the warmth that threatens to creep up my cheeks at the sight of him. I turn my face toward my grandma, refusing to be drawn in by the magnetic pull I can feel all the way across the expanse of lawn separating our houses.

Nonna examines him through narrowed eyes as she drags on her cigarette. "He's quite a looker, isn't he?" she asks at last, shooting me a sly grin.

I shrug. "He hates us."

"I bet," Nonna says, settling back in her chair. "Isn't that what men do to women they can't have?"

"What?" I ask.

"He's a Darling," she says. "Your father would never allow it."

"So, what happened back then?" I ask. "Mom said Mr. Darling tried to steal his ideas or something. But that can't be right if he was only in high school. Daddy didn't even have the company until after I was born."

I know, because he always tells me how he named the first candy after me, the company's signature sparkling clear hard candies, *Dolce Crystals*.

"The Darlings ran this town back then," she says, speaking to me while openly admiring the sexy neighbor boy on his deck. "Mr. Darling and all seven of his sons. I can't remember how many were in school with your father, but there were quite a few. They even had some secret society in the school, I can't recall the name of it, but I think even Mr. Darling senior was involved somehow. Your father would never admit it now, but he was dying to join. Of course they wouldn't let him in, being a scholarship student and all. We didn't come from money or have a big name in the town."

My grandparents live comfortably, but they've never been rich. Daddy did that all on his own. He's always been proud of being a self-made man, always worn that like a badge of honor. I never questioned what gave him those lofty ambitions, why he wanted so badly to succeed. I sure as hell never knew he was rejected for being poor compared to a powerful family I'd never heard of until a few months ago.

I glance across the way at Devlin. I wonder if he knows all this. If he knows my father came back here to rub his success in the faces of Devlin's father and all the Darlings for snubbing him back then. Now he's just as rich as all of them, and he did it all himself.

"Your father's a proud man, Crystal," Nonna goes on. "Always was. It was hard on him, and hard on us as parents to see him being scorned the way he was, the way all the scholarship students were back then. The Darlings had big fancy parties, and he wasn't invited. One night, he and Benny and Angela got together all the scholarship kids and decided to crash one of the parties, thrown right here in this house. They were told their kind wasn't welcome here. There was quite a brawl over it, let me tell you."

"Damn," I say, trying to imagine Daddy and Mr. Darling going at it in the yard. That's way more exciting than some argument over a patent.

"To be honest, I think your father's been trying to prove something to himself ever since then," Nonna says. "Seeing your kids struggle and knowing you can't do a damn thing to help them is the hardest moment of being a parent. At some point, you can't protect them anymore, and they learn the truth—that the world is a hard, unforgiving place for all of us."

I think of Daddy and my brothers trying so hard to shelter me, and my resentment towards them thaws a bit. I know that's all they've ever wanted. To protect me.

"I'm sorry, Nonna," I say, leaning over to wrap an arm around her and lay my head on her shoulder.

"Well, you know your father," she says with a chuckle. "He sure made the best of it, didn't he? Look at all this. From the other side of town to buying a Darling house right out from under their noses."

"That's a long way to come in only twenty years," I agree, marveling for a moment over how fortunate our family is. Because of Daddy's hard work and determination, we have all of this.

Nonna nods. "To be frank, the night of that brawl changed him, and I'm not sure it's always been a good thing. You see, that's the moment he decided to become rich. We left town after that, but from that moment on, nothing came before his ambition, even when it should have. I'm sure there have been plenty of nights when you kids and your mother experienced that firsthand." She turns to press a tobacco tinged kiss to my temple.

"And moving back here was… What? His big chance to rub his success in their face?" I ask, straightening. It seemed so random, Daddy deciding to move to the middle of nowhere. It hadn't made sense. Our lives were set in Manhattan. He had no reason to come here. Now, it all makes sense. All along, he was building his Dolce Sweets empire as some kind of revenge. Which means that all along, he knew one day he'd come back here. Nice of him to let us know ahead of time, to prepare us for the big change.

"I suppose it was, in a way," Nonna says. She finishes her cigarette and searches for a place to snuff it out. "I'd better go wash up and brush my teeth, so your grandfather doesn't smell this on me when he kisses me goodnight." She gives me a wink and rises from her chair to stash her cigarettes.

"TMI, Nonna," I say, shaking my head.

"I'll leave you two alone to make eyes at each other." She nods toward the Darling house and flashes a grin before ducking in through my window and disappearing into my bathroom.

I can feel Devlin's gaze on me, the weight of it, the heat. But I don't look at him, the boy from the family that drove my father out of town. I don't blame him for coming back to the town that didn't want him, that said he wasn't good enough. I don't blame him for returning to throw his success in their faces by building a branch right here in the town that rejected him, on a piece of land that must have been theirs since they're disputing whether they still own it. I just wish he'd told us, that he'd given us some warning. I wish he'd told us what this town meant to him instead of letting us find out about the Darlings ourselves.

But now it makes so much sense. Why he wants us to take over the school, why he wants my brothers to take the Darlings' spots on the football team, why he wants to impress the mayor and buy a house that once belonged to the Darlings, right next door to one of the boys who told him he wasn't good enough to attend a party in this house. It must feel really fucking good to come back and buy that very house, to show them that "our type" does belong in this neighborhood, as an equal to any of the Darlings.

Now, more than ever, I know that the Darlings are nothing but entitled assholes from one generation to the next. I know that I will never be anything to them but a dog, a piece of trash, just like my father was before me. And they will never be anything to me but a family that tried to destroy mine and failed. Daddy came back from that and made millions. He came back to show them what Dolces are made of.

And I'm going to have to do the same thing. Without a backwards glance at Devlin, I stand, climb in my window, and pull the window closed except for a crack to let the cool fall air in. I pull the curtain closed, erasing Devlin and his beautiful house with one sweep of my hand.

ten

Devlin

Crystal. Fucking. Dolce.

She blew into my life like a fucking hurricane. Hurricane Crystal, with those curves all hidden under her mommish dresses like some kind of proper society lady when I know better. I know what's up. I know what's under there. That waist I could almost wrap my hands around, tits that make me want to bury my head between them and an ass that makes me want to bury my dick in it. One taste, and I'm standing out on a balcony waiting for her like some pathetic, pussy-whipped puppy.

I've been doing this shit since I saw her out on the balcony that first night wearing next to nothing, a flimsy little nightgown that made her look like a ghost.

I didn't know she'd be haunting me for the rest of my fucking life.

eleven

Crystal

Day 4 without Royal. I'm beginning to understand the Darlings. I know what makes their family different from mine. My family taught me love, loyalty, the strength of our backbones, the way our blood runs thicker than chocolate. But now I know a new truth. The Darling's truth.
Love makes you weak. Hate makes you strong.

"Get out of my house."

"Your house?" Mom's shriek slices through the remaining drowsiness in my mind.

They're fighting. Typical.

I sigh and climb out of bed, pulling the covers up and arranging the pillows while their voices continue.

"You think because you left me to run down here and prove what a big man you are, that this house is yours? Well, guess what? We're still married, Tony! That means this house is half mine, just like everything else you own, you selfish bastard."

When she gets going, Mom's Jersey accent starts to slip out, no matter how many years she spent training it into hiding. I swallow hard, glancing at the window when I realize their voices are coming from outside. I left my window cracked to let in the fresh, fall air, not to let in the voices of my embarrassing parents. I really hope they go inside before they start making up.

"Then get out of *our* house," Daddy barks.

"Oh, you'd like that wouldn't you?" Mom asks. "Well, I'm not going anywhere until my kid shows up. Got that? You'll just have to have your little underage whores meet you at the office for a while, now won't you?"

"You don't know what you're talking about."

"Oh yeah?" she asks. "Maybe the police should be questioning you, Tony. Maybe he found out you were fucking his little girlfriend, and you're the one who got rid of him. You'd do anything for a piece of teenage ass, wouldn't you?"

I hear his heavy footsteps stomp across the wooden floorboards of the downstairs veranda. Now he's going to grab her and tell her she's gone too far, and she'll slap him, and then they'll start fucking.

I shoot King a text telling him to get our parents off the porch, and then I head into the bathroom to shower. I hear a few more words before I close the door. "I may have done some stupid shit in my life, but I've never lost one of our kids. This one really takes the cake, Tony."

I slam my bathroom door as hard as I can and slide under the spray of hot water, wanting to disappear into the steamy cocoon of oblivion. A bath would be better, but I don't have time for that this morning. Instead, I sing Halsey and force myself to think of anything other than my parents' latest argument.

The water shuts off abruptly, and cool air hits my body at the same moment. My eyes fly open, and a cry escapes me. Devlin stands in my bathroom, so close I could reach out and touch the hard planes of his chest and abs through his grey T-shirt…

So close he could reach out and touch me—slippery wet, completely naked, and still steaming from the hot water trickling over my skin.

"Get out," he says, his voice hard and sharp.

But his eyes are molten on my skin, burning into me with a desire that terrifies and excites at once. My nipples harden under his gaze, and I can see his Adam's apple bob as he swallows. He yanks his gaze back to mine, grabs a towel, and shoves it roughly into my hands.

"Get out," he says again, and this time, the businesslike tone in his voice makes it to his eyes.

At last, I find my own voice. "You get out," I snap, wrenching the towel around my body. "In case you hadn't noticed, I'm taking a shower in *my* bathroom, in *my* house."

"I don't care what you were doing," he says, grabbing my arm and dragging me out of the shower. "Now you're coming with us."

"Us?" I ask, balking. "I don't think so."

Without a word, Devlin drags me out of the bathroom into my bedroom where, I'm relieved to see, there's no one else waiting.

"Get dressed," he says.

"Yeah, because that's really going to happen with you standing right there."

"We've gone over this," he says, sounding slightly annoyed. "I've seen you naked. I've seen plenty of other tits and asses. Now, get dressed."

"Way to make a girl feel special," I mutter, turning away from him and yanking open my dresser.

"I'm not trying to make you feel special," he says. "I'm trying to make you stop thinking that you are."

"Well, you're doing a bang-up job of it," I snap. "I guess you've got what you were after. I'm nothing but another hole for you to wet your dick in. Got it. Loud and clear."

He grunts in response.

"The real question is," I go on, dropping the towel and shoving aside piles of lace and satin to choose a pair of white cotton panties that he can't possibly think are sexy. "If I'm so very, very unspecial, as you like to say I am, then why are you here? Because I'm not the psycho stalker who broke into your house and climbed in the shower with you."

I slide on a white bra, adjust my breasts inside it, and turn to face him. He doesn't say anything. He's staring at me with such complete indifference that I almost believe him. Almost.

"You know what I think?" I ask, prowling toward him.

If he wants to play this game, I'll fucking play it. I may not have experience with guys, but Veronica taught me a thing or two about fucking with people's heads. I swore I'd never do those things again, but here we are, and it's the only weapon at my disposal. He started it, but two can play this game. As he said, all's fair in love and war.

And this is fucking war.

"Aren't you going to play along?" I ask, stopping in front of him. I rest my fingers against his chest and lean up like I'll kiss him, but he stands tall, his chin rising a bit so he can look down at me with bored, hooded eyes.

God, why is he so fucking hot when he's being a dick?

I let my fingers slide down from his chest, over his abs, relishing the way they tense under my touch. I want to go lower, to wrap my fingers around his thick hardness. But I won't. I have to keep my head in the game, just like he is, even though my heart is hammering and my mouth waters at the thought of touching him. Would he let me taste him this time?

Heat surges between my thighs, making my knees clench together to relieve some of the ache.

Devlin stands like a statue, his whole body tensed, waiting for my next move. I stop at his belt, run a fingernail lightly along his abdomen right above the waistband of his navy uniform slacks. I can feel the goosebumps rise on his skin through his dress shirt.

"I think I should be thanking you," I whisper.

For a second, he doesn't move. Then he smirks the tiniest bit. "Yeah?" he says. "I bet most girls don't get to say they had a massive orgasm their first time."

"No, they don't," I whisper, going up on tiptoes so my lips can brush along his jawline. "But that's not all. I want to thank you for showing me exactly how much it meant to you." I drop back to flat feet, turn, and walk to the dresser. I know I'm playing a dangerous game with a dangerous man, but I'm in too deep to walk away now. I was already playing the game, long before I knew it. At least now I know that I'm part of it.

And what can he do to me now? Throw me down and fuck me? He already did that. Hurt someone I love? Done and done. He made an irreparable mistake by taking away the only thing I had to lose.

Just as I reach the dresser, his hand wraps around my elbow, spinning me to face him. Damn he's quiet, stalking like a predator instead of clomping around like an elephant like my brothers do, always wanting people to know when they're coming. Devlin's sneaky as fuck. He pushes me back against my dresser until I'm leaning backwards just so our faces won't collide. I'm afraid if I let them, I wouldn't be able to stop myself. Devlin is the devil himself, sly and sneaky, and irresistible. He slides a hand up to the front of my throat, lifting my chin and staring back at me, his eyes blazing.

"Don't try to fuck with me," he growls, not touching me except for that one menacing hand wrapped around my throat like a warning. "You won't walk away from that game a winner."

"Choking's not going to work on me, big shot," I say. "Apparently I like that shit."

His fingers tighten a fraction, and my traitorous body shivers with desire.

Whoredom confirmed.

"You do, don't you?" he asks with a smirk, leaning closer, his nose brushing gently across mine, his grip just tight enough that it's hard to swallow. I want him crushed up against me, slamming into me like he did before. The tease is too much for me, and I nearly swoon into him.

There's no use denying his words, so I try to nod. He's holding my head back, so I can't move my chin, but I drop my gaze to his lips. His tongue slides out to wet the seam of his lips, and my core trembles at the memory of that tongue in more intimate places. He hooks his free hand around the back of my thigh and slides it up… Up. My breath catches. He stops when his fingers brush my ass. The sensitive skin sings at the touch of his warm, rough hand.

I close my eyes and inhale his intoxicating scent, almost hidden behind the clean, soapy smell of his skin in the morning. I want to fucking eat this boy.

"Are you wet?" he purrs, his voice low and silky, doing things to my body that I can't prevent. His lips brush against mine, then follow my jawline back toward my ear. Chills explode through every inch of me, and there's no use denying that I'm aroused. He's going to feel it in a minute, anyway. I drop my head back, my lids fluttering as Devlin's nose brushes my ear, his lips teasing, his hot breath caressing my neck. I sigh and arch up, but he sways back, keeping our bodies separated by a just enough space to make me want to scream in frustration.

"Yes," I whisper, my hands rising to wrap around his thick biceps. "I'm wet."

God, those big, muscular, farm-boy arms. How did he get muscles like this?

"Then you'd better clean that shit up," his murmuring voice taunts against the side of my throat. "No one likes the smell of wet dog."

My eyes snap open, and heat rushes to my face. What the fuck is wrong with me?

I press my palms to his chest, trying to push him away, clear my head of the intoxicating, toxic effect he has on me. Instead, it makes me notice the hardness of his chest as he presses forward, his body meeting mine at last, when I no longer want it.

"Sugar, don't forget this," he says. "I could have you if I wanted you. But I don't." His voice turns cold, but I'm not so easily fooled. I can feel his hard cock pressing against my belly.

"Liar." His mind may not want this any more than I do, and his heart may be even colder and blacker than mine, but his body... His body wants it as much as mine does.

"You think you're the first whore who creamed her panties for us and thought that meant we felt the same? You're common, Crystal. Pathetic just like every other dog begging for a bone."

I shove at his chest again, but he doesn't even budge. "Fuck you, Devlin Darling," I say, my voice nearly cracking.

Devlin chuckles and leans closer again, forcing my eyes to his riveting blue gaze. He speaks slowly, the smirk never leaving his lips. "Not... Even... If... You... Beg."

"Then what are you here for?" I demand.

"Not for your cunt, as sweet as it is," he says, opening a drawer and tossing me a T-shirt. "Now stop stalling and let's get the fuck out of here. This place gives me the creeps."

"Me, too," I say. "Maybe it's because there's a creeper standing in my room."

"You have thirty seconds to get some pants on before I take you as you are."

I yank on a pair of sweats, wishing I had a pair of ugly, stained, baggy ones to hide my curves. But my mother would never allow me such a luxury. Even my sweats are designer brand, fitted to my ass, and stylish. According to Mom, it's important to look cute at all times. After all, you never know when someone at the gym will snap a pic, or a friend will want a selfie while lounging in my room during a sleepover.

Thirty seconds later, we're climbing out my window. "Is this how you got in?" I ask as we start along the veranda toward the front stairs. This guy's got balls. He's not even climbing up the trellis. Nope, he waltzed right up the front steps and along the side of the house to reach my window.

He doesn't answer, but I guess I don't really need him to. There's no way in hell he went in the front door past my family. He keeps hold of me and hurries me down the set of stairs that swoops up the front of the house to the second-floor balcony.

"Is this how you kidnapped Royal?" I ask, yanking to free myself.

"Don't be stupid," Devlin answers, arriving at the bottom of the stairs.

A whiff of smoke catches my attention, and I turn to see Nonna standing at the corner of the house, a Virginia Slim clutched in one hand, looking as startled as I feel. Devlin drops my elbow and instead slides a possessive arm around my waist as if we're a couple. I could puke at the phony display, but I don't have time for that. If my brothers come out and see Devlin's hands on me, there's going to be a literal murder on this lawn.

And I shouldn't fucking care, I remind myself.

"Well, if it isn't the boy from the family who ran us out of town," Nonna says, looking Devlin up and down with clear appreciation. "You're the spitting image of your father."

"Thank you, Ma'am," Devlin says, tipping his head and reaching up, like he's about to tip a ballcap to her. But his hand drops when he must remember he's not wearing one. "And… I'm sorry."

He reaches out a hand, and Nonna transfers her cigarette to her left hand to shake. "I'm Crystal's grandmother," she says. "You must be the neighbor boy."

"Devlin Darling," he says. "'Fraid I'm going to have to borrow your granddaughter. I'll bring her back in one piece, I promise."

She looks to me, and I nod. "I'll be right back," I say. "Tell the others I went for a run."

She puts her finger to her lips, a twinkle in her eye. "If that's what you kids are calling it these days."

"Nice to meet you, Ma'am," Devlin says in such a courteous way even I'm fooled for a second. I can almost forget he's the devil himself when he turns on the charm like that. I've seen him at school, but he's pretty much a dismissive dick to everyone there, teachers included. I wonder what he's scheming for this time, why he's being polite and charming to my grandmother. Surely his family isn't scared of ours. They ran my grandparents out of town the last time they were here.

"What was that about?" I ask as Devlin marches me quickly past the lilac bushes and onto his property.

"Nothing you need to know," Devlin replies in typical, infuriating asshole fashion.

"Oh, right," I say. "I'm supposed to be a good dog and sit by the door until you call me to come play fetch."

"Do you ever get tired of your own voice?" Devlin asks, shoving me forward into the shadows of his open garage.

twelve

Crystal

"Oh, fuck no," I say, balking when I see Colt leaning against the trunk of Devlin's car and Preston sitting on it, scrolling through his phone. Three other cars sit in the garage as well as what looks like a fourth covered by a black tarp.

"Oh, fuck yes," Colt says, that deceptively easy grin breaking over his face. Damn him and his beautiful, lying face.

"Not going anywhere with that asshole," I say, cutting my eyes to Preston.

"You are," Devlin says, grabbing the back of my neck. "Now, this game is boring me. You can ride in the back seat and shut up, or you can ride in the trunk like you did last time. Your choice, Sugar."

Everything in me wants to be a brat, to turn around and stomp away, refusing to give up my pride and forcing them to strip it from me. But memories of that cramped, terrifying ride invade my mind, and I nod mutely. Better to climb in with any pretense of dignity that remains to me than be stuffed into a trunk kicking and screaming like an animal.

I climb into the back seat, where Colt grins and lays an arm across the top of the seat like he's going to do that stupid guy move and put his arm around me.

"Touch me, and I'll nut-punch you," I warn.

"And then I will," Devlin says, giving his cousin a warning look before opening the driver's door and climbing in. "We're just going for a little ride, Sugar. Things don't have to get ugly unless you make them. That one's your call. What happens when you make things ugly, that's our call."

I shiver at the bored drawl in his voice, like threatening to rape and murder girls is just an everyday thing for him. Which, let's face it, it probably is. His vague threat is even more ominous than what my mind conjured. Probably something worse than rape and murder. Probably more like dismemberment and torture. At least Nonna knows I left with the Darlings. There are witnesses. Maybe that means they're not going to murder me after all. Or maybe it means they're going to kill my grandmother.

Fuck. This is bad.

"Where are we going?" I demand as we pull out of the neighborhood, turning away from the school. Yep. They're going to take me to the middle of nowhere and do something unspeakably horrible.

Preston turns in the passenger seat and opens his mouth like he's going to answer, but one look from Devlin, and he closes his mouth and turns away. But not before I catch a glimpse of something… human in his eyes. Sympathy? Empathy?

Is he even capable of that? Or is that wishful thinking on my part?

Devlin shifts gears and accelerates, and cold November air burns along my cheeks and tears at my wet hair. I wrap my arms around myself, huddling down in the seat. Colt glances down at my chest, where my nipples are quite apparent through my unpadded bra and the T-shirt I had time to slip on before Devlin dragged me out. Then he checks the front seat, where Devlin and Preston are talking, their words torn away by the wind before they reach the back seat. Colt slides off his letterman jacket and swings it around my shoulders. I huddle into it, soaking up the warmth and inhaling the boy smell of it before I can stop myself.

"Why the fuck is our dog wearing your jacket?" Devlin growls from the front seat.

Damn it. Of course I can't expect a simple human kindness from him.

"She's cold," Colt says with a shrug and that disarming, sloppy smile of his.

Interesting. I wouldn't have thought he used that on his bros. I thought that was just for everyone else, the face he showed the world.

Even more interesting, Devlin doesn't push it, just shakes his head and mutters something under his breath that I can't make out over the rushing wind.

Not sure why I fucking care what these guys are like around each other. I care about staying alive. I clutch the jacket tighter around me, as if it's armor that can protect me. As if I could keep Colt from taking it back if he wanted to.

Devlin pulls up at a black, wrought iron fence and punches a code into his phone. The gate swings inwards, and we follow a narrow asphalt drive as it winds along the edge of an enormous lawn that could double as a golf course. On our other side are manicured bushes and shrubs flanked by shade trees. Finally, we pull up to a house that looks pretty much like all the plantation style houses in our neighborhood, though the landscaping is more involved, as there is so much land around us.

Devlin stops the car and stares at a little black Prius parked on the gravel in front of the house, muttering curses under his breath. Maybe the help isn't supposed to park near the front steps.

"What the fuck's she doing here?" Preston asks, climbing out of the car.

Devlin shakes his head and climbs out, too, so I follow suit, along with Colt. I start to ask what the fuck *I'm* doing here, but I stop myself at the last second and watch them, impressed despite myself, as they silently communicate. I can't speak their language, the one made up of shared glances, frowns, and subtle eye movements. These guys aren't just cousins. They're *brothers*.

Maybe not in the biological sense, but I know brothers when I see them. I've seen my own brothers do this shit. Why am I always on the outside?

Without a word spoken between them, Devlin turns to me. "You need to get your parents under control," he says, crossing his arms and frowning down at me. "Ours isn't the kind of neighborhood where people have screaming matches on their front porch. Go back to the trashy part of town if you want to act trashy."

"Seriously?" I ask. "That's what you brought me here for? To lecture me?"

"Well, we couldn't very well trust you not to throw a hissy fit in the middle of the yard like your Jersey Shore mother," Preston says with a disgusted look.

"Is that right?" I ask, planting my hand on my hip and squinting up at Devlin, pretending to ponder something. "I seem to recall a couple guys fighting on your porch a few days ago. We're just trying to keep up appearances. I mean, if the Darlings are doing it, it must be the *in* thing to do."

"That's different," Devlin snaps.

"Oh yeah?" I ask. "Why's that? Because that was two men?"

"That has nothing to do with it."

"Really? Then what is it? Because I don't see the difference otherwise. They were both family matters. Domestic disputes, if you want to get all technical."

"The difference is that my father was standing up to the most powerful man in Faulkner," he says, glaring at me.

"And?"

"And your mom is screaming about your dad cheating like some kind of trailer trash that belongs on the other side of town."

"You're really something," I say, a laugh forcing its way out. "I see your family hasn't changed a bit. Well, guess what? Mine has. Just because you're too backwards to recognize change, that doesn't mean it doesn't happen. Your family might have run the Dolces out of town twenty years ago, but we're back, and we're here to stay."

"Don't count on it, Sweetie Pie," Colt drawls.

"Didn't you learn anything in history, or were you too busy skipping school to bang girls in the bathroom?" I ask, making eyes at him. "You either change with the times, or you become part of history."

"If changing with the times means letting a bunch of mafia thugs take over this town, then I guess we'll go down in history as the last assholes to make a stand in Faulkner," Devlin says. "Sorry, Sugar, but we're not going to let that happen."

"Fine," I say, crossing my arms over my chest. I don't miss the way three pairs of eyes land on my breasts, probably ogling the way my nipples are poking out because I'm so damn cold. "Keep on being rednecks and refusing to admit what's happening right under your nose. That's why my brothers will be the royalty in this school by next year, and you'll be standing over the ruins of your fallen empire."

"You didn't tell me she was a nerd," Preston says with a smirk, studying me like a wolf eyeing a juicy piece of meat he's about to devour. "They're always freaks. What should we have her do?"

One glare from Devlin silences him, but I catch the keen interest in Preston's eyes. He watches Devlin even as his cousin turns to the house when the front door opens. A girl steps out, already turning to pull the door closed as she appears. She's two steps down the stairs before she halts, her blue eyes going wide when she sees us. She looks vaguely familiar, so she might go to Willow Heights, but I can't remember where I've seen her. She's slight, waifish even, with a pale blue buttoned shirt tucked into a pair of stylish, fitted khaki slacks that sit low on her narrow hips. Her blonde hair is pulled back into a no-nonsense ponytail, and zero makeup highlights her best asset—a naturally pretty face. I feel a ridiculous pang of jealousy when all the guys turn to watch her make her way down the steps, her dainty hips swaying with each step.

She visible cowers when she sees the Darlings in the drive, though.

"What are you doing here?" Devlin demands, taking a step closer.

"I…" She trails off, her gaze skipping from him to the other Darlings and lastly, to me. "I was doing a favor for Gramps."

I've never even met the girl, and I can tell she's lying. But I'm more interested in how she fits into this family dynamic. She's either a Darling, and she's talking about the patriarch of their family, or she's familiar enough with them that they know her grandfather. The blonde hair and attractive features lead me toward the first conclusion. Family resemblance must be why she looks vaguely familiar. This town is fucking crawling with Darlings. They just keep popping up like pimples that won't go away no matter how many expensive facials you get.

Devlin's eyes narrow. "What favor?"

"I was… Picking up something." She raises her chin to him, a move that must take a lot of balls even for a member of the family.

"What?" he asks, quirking an eyebrow at her, his arms still crossed over his broad chest.

I want to hate him, but I can't stop staring, watching, absorbing everything they do. I have a sick fascination with their entire family. It's so much like mine, and yet, so very different.

The girl glances up and then holds up her hands, which have nothing in them but the keys she just used to lock the door, along with a handful of other keys on the ring.

"Your keys?" Devlin asks, obviously not believing her, either.

"Yeah," she says. "I forgot them here."

"Then how'd you drive over?"

"I used a spare," she says, seeming quite pleased with herself.

"You were picking up your keys," Devlin says slowly. "As a favor to Gramps."

"That's what I said," she says, circling the Prius and climbing in. I'm guessing by the car she drives and the fact that I haven't seen her around that she must be one of the Darlings who goes to Faulkner High. She slams the car door and drives away before anyone can stop her.

I give her a silent cheer, despite being an enemy.

"That was fucking weird," Colt mutters.

"Yeah," Devlin says, turning to me. A cruel glint enters his eyes that I don't like one bit. "Now, we've delivered our message to this one. What do we do with her now?"

"I'll fuck her if you're done with her," Preston says, slipping his hands in his pockets and assessing me with vague disinterest. "If the pussy's too loose, I'll stick her in the ass. The freaky ones love that."

"No," Devlin says, his psycho eyes dragging down my body. "Let's show this one where her family belongs."

I shrink back, but there's no use fighting them. There's nothing I can do but get in the car and go where they want me to go. I take comfort in the fact that Nonna knows who I'm with. Maybe she'll have told my brothers by now, and they'll be out looking for me. I no longer care if they murder these assholes. They've got it coming.

"Why don't you just take me wherever you have Royal and throw me in that cage?" I ask, crossing my arms and pouting in the back seat like a spoiled princess who isn't getting her way. I wouldn't care if they really did that. Not if Royal was there. I'd rather be kidnapped with my twin than free without him.

"Why do you keep bringing that up?" Devlin asks.

"Because you're obviously responsible for his disappearance." My chest tightens at the thought, and I can't continue even though I have a hell of a lot left to say.

Devlin snorts. "Instead of crying to the cops every chance you get, why don't you ask your dear old daddy if he owes someone money before you come in here accusing my family of that shit?"

"What are you saying?" I demand, sitting forward in my seat.

"I'm saying it probably wouldn't be the first time your dad made someone disappear," Devlin says. "You said he was in the mob."

"You don't know shit about my family," I snap.

"Maybe he faked his own death," Colt says.

I roll my eyes. "I've heard a lot of stupid things in my life, but that one takes the cake."

"People have done worse to get away from their families."

"Royal doesn't want to get away from his family," I say, though I can't help the flood of memories that come with that half-truth. Royal never bought into the whole Dolce image thing. He can't stand Daddy. He's always gone along, like me, but he's never embraced it and become it the way my other brothers have. If there's one person who wants out of this family, it is Royal.

Fuck. Now they have me questioning my own brother instead of them. They have me doubting what I know, that Preston was the one talking to him the night of homecoming. Royal may not love playing the part, but he would never leave without saying goodbye.

"Ask yourself this," Devlin says, turning onto a narrow street lined with small, rundown brick houses. "Why hasn't your father filed a missing persons report? Why isn't the FBI involved, if it's really a kidnapping?"

"Because he's not under twelve," I retort with the answer Daddy gave me.

"If he was in danger, they'd still get involved," Colt says in a reassuring tone. "He's a minor."

"Yeah, well, you probably fucked that up by paying off the local cops or something."

"I can't tell if you're stupid, lying, or living in a pretty little bubble of denial," Devlin says. "But the only reason the FBI isn't involved is because your father told the cops that your brother ran away. You can think about that while you take a nice walk on the wild side."

He pulls up at a cracked curb in front of a tan brick house with dirt darkening the bottom quarter of the walls.

"That house we just left?" Preston says, turning in the front seat to give me a pointed look. "That's where our great-grandfather lived. That's where our family comes from. This is where your family lived when they came to Faulkner."

I take in the house, a seed of dread forming in my belly. Sure, Nonna said they'd fallen on hard times, but damn. The house is shit. The whole street is depressing. There's a car parked in the next driveway with a trash bag taped over a missing window. An old guy two houses down sits on his porch in pajama pants, smoking a cigarette and resting a cheap beer on his shirtless, round belly. He looks me up and down with slimy eyes.

"This is where you came from, and this is where you belong," Devlin says. "Now get out of the car."

"What? No fucking way."

"It wasn't a question."

"Wait, give me back my jacket," Colt says. "And…. Anything else you have. Phone, keys, all that shit."

"No," I say, sitting back in the seat and crossing my arms.

Colt hops out of the convertible without bothering to open the door and hauls me over the top. He drops me on the ground on my back, and my head hits the concrete. Blackness swims in my vision. I can hear Preston laughing.

"Flat on her back where she's most comfortable," he says as Colt wrestles the jacket off me. "I bet you can use that skill to get yourself a ride out of here if you want it so bad. But you'll just end up right back here in the end. The whores are always from this side of town."

When Colt's done, he jumps back into the car, and I scramble to my feet and lunge for the car. Devlin accelerates, and it shoots forward, just out of my reach.

"There are a few gangs on this side of town," Preston says, his arm dangling over the top of the door as he grins at me. "I bet they'd pass a tight little body like yours around a few dozen times before they got tired of you. You could make some dirty money—the only kind your family knows."

Devlin mutters something, and the car jerks onto the street and speeds away, leaving me standing there in sweatpants and a T-shirt, feeling grossly exposed as the man on the porch continues leering at me.

thirteen

Crystal

Fuming, I stomp along the street. I have no fucking clue where I am, but I know it's a bad part of town. I have nothing on me, no phone and no money, nothing for anyone to steal. The only thing I have is my body, and Preston's parting words circle in my head, increasing my panic each time I replay them. When I hear voices behind me, I turn to see a couple rough-looking guys standing beside a car set up on blocks. They see me looking and whistle, one of them grabbing his junk and catcalling. I flip them off and keep walking, but a few minutes later, I glance over my shoulder.

They're about a block back, low-key following me. Well, shit. They're not outright harassing me yet, but I have no clue where I'm going, and I'm betting they do. They probably know exactly where to corner a girl as obviously lost and defenseless as I am. Real fear replaces the anger that's been brewing inside me since the Darlings ditched me, and I walk faster, glancing around in desperate hopes of seeing anything that looks like a slightly nicer neighborhood, one where someone might help me instead of wanting to drag me down to the bottom with them.

And then I see an old white church that makes my heart flip with relief. I'm not on the best terms with the higher power, but surely those assholes won't bother me in a church. I'm almost running by the time I reach the gravel parking lot with dying grass poking up through the gravel at the edges. That's when I realize I've been here before. I know this church, this lot with one car in it, the cemetery inside the low, chain-link fence. I came here with Dixie right before homecoming.

I run up the steps and try the door. The fucking church is locked.

I hear the crunch of feet on gravel, the triumphant snickering of the men coming closer. I hop down off the steps and run around the other side of the church. There's nothing on this side but more fence and some huge shade trees. Fuck. This is worse than the parking lot. They've finally gotten me to a secluded spot.

I start climbing the fence when I spot someone inside the cemetery.

"Hey," I yell, waving like mad even though the guy has his back turned. He spins toward me, and I wave harder, smiling like a maniac. He stares at me. I can't really blame him. I'm perched halfway over the fence, trying not to impale myself on the pointy little triangles of wire that extend past the metal bar on top of the fence, frantically trying to get inside the cemetery before the two guys get close enough to grab me. Instead of looking scared, though, I'm grinning and waving like a lunatic.

"Oh my god, I've been looking for you everywhere," I yell, making sure the creepers can hear me, hoping they'll believe that I know this guy and get lost.

I jump off the side of the fence, stumbling but managing to keep my feet. I run over to the blond guy and throw my arms around him. That ought to convince the assholes I know this guy.

"I found you," I crow. When I pull back, I realize with a start that I do know this guy. Or, I've met him, at least. He was here the last time I came. He was with Devlin. Dixie said something about him… Maybe he's another Darling? Every hot blond in this town seems to be one of them.

"Yeah, you definitely found me," the guy says, setting his hands on my hips and holding me at arm's length. He's looking at me like he might call the cops, or a mental institution, at any moment.

"Sorry," I mutter, too scared to be embarrassed. "Those guys were following me. I was hoping you could pretend to know me." I realize as I say the words how insane I sound. For all I know, this guy is as psycho as the other Darlings. They're all probably worse than a couple regular creepers following me into the bushes. What if this guy is friends with the creepers? What if he's one of them?

But his eyes widen as he glances back at the guys and then at me. "Shit," he says, sliding a protective arm around my shoulders and pulling me in. He kisses my forehead and glares back at the guys. When I look back, they're slowly strolling out of the parking lot like they weren't up to anything sketchy at all.

"You don't know them?" asks my savior.

"No," I say. "And I don't have a phone to call for a ride, or any money, or—" I break off, nearly hyperventilating, and to my horror, the adrenaline draining out of me leaves me close to tears.

"Hey," the guy says. "Hey, don't cry. It's cool. I'll give you a ride. Wherever you need to go."

"Don't you have to get to school or something?" I ask, sniffing. I remember Dixie saying he went to Faulkner High. I think.

He grins and tosses his hair out of his eyes. "Yeah, but I think they'll forgive me if I'm late this one time."

"You play football," I say, squinting at him, trying to remember. Broad shoulders, killer smile, golden hair he's sweeping out of his eyes again. Definitely Darling caliber.

He shrugs, still grinning. "I might be on the team."

"No," I say slowly. "You *are* the team. Aren't you? You're the quarterback who slaughtered us during our last game."

His smile is half pride, half self-consciousness. "I don't know if I'd use the term *slaughtered*…"

"Well, get ready for my brothers to be starters at Willow Heights," I say. "Then you'll know what a slaughter looks like for sure."

"Aren't you supposed to flatter me a little more?" he asks. "I'm basically your knight in shining armor. I expected my damsel in distress to be a little more… Reverent."

"I'm fresh out of reverence," I say. "I think I spent it all on your cousins. They require a lot. It's kind of like a toll when you enter Willow Heights every morning."

He laughs and shakes his head. "I'm sure you're talking about the Darlings," he says. "But I'm not one of them. I'm Chase London." He holds out a hand and shakes mine.

I feel weirdly self-conscious as I slide my hand into his, realizing as he smiles at me with dimples and squinty-cornered blue eyes that I'm not wearing any makeup. My hair is a crazy, damp, wild mane after riding in a convertible, and I'm wearing sweats and a T-shirt over an unpadded bra that does nothing to hide the fact that my nipples aren't shy about reminding the world that it's cold as fuck out here. He, on the other hand, looks like a freaking god. Arkansas sure knows how to grow 'em, as Duke would say.

Chase's eyes drop to my chest, and he clears his throat and pulls his hand from mine after the longest handshake in history. Fuck. I'm staring.

"My girlfriend, however, is," he says, scratching the back of his neck and possibly blushing. "A Darling, I mean. Do you, uh, want my jacket?"

"Thank you," I say, accepting his jacket. I feel kind of like a traitor as I slide my arms into the warmth of his sleeves. I'm wearing a Faulkner High letter jacket. If his girlfriend is anything like the rest of the Darlings, I'm going to pay for this, but right now I'm too grateful to care. He looks pretty grateful that I'm covered, too.

"You need a ride somewhere?" he asks as we start for the gate, walking side by side down a row of headstones.

"Yeah," I say. "Thank you. You must be my guardian angel or something. I didn't expect anyone to be here at seven in the morning on a school day. I was thinking I'd take refuge in the church, but it's locked."

"Yeah, they don't have a lot of staff," he says.

I want to know why he's there, but it would be rude to pry. He obviously has someone in this cemetery he cares about, or he wouldn't be here this time of day. And if he doesn't want to talk about it, I don't know him well enough to ask. Besides, he's not asking me why I'm alone without a phone or wallet or a jacket, so I decide we'll just leave each other our mutual dignity and pretend there's nothing strange going on here.

"So, Chase London," I say as we step out the gate. "Tell me about this illustrious football career of yours."

"Just Chase is fine," he says, smiling and opening the door of his car for me. "And I'm not about to tell you my secrets so you can give them to your brothers. Not that they could kick our asses, anyway."

"Is that right?"

"That's right."

"We'll see," I say, smiling as I turn to the window.

"Want me to take you home to get your stuff, or what?" he asks, turning up the heat as we pull out of the lot.

But another thought has climbed into my mind, a petty, evil plan that Veronica would have concocted in her moments of cunning and social domination.

"Can you take me to school?" I ask.

"To Willow Heights?" he asks, his brows rising. "Don't you need to get your stuff first? And change? Not that there's anything wrong with what you're wearing. Girls at my school where that shit all the time. Not that it looks like shit. It looks good. Really good. I mean, girls at my school don't look like *that* when they wear what you're wearing. Damn, that still came out wrong, didn't it?"

I interrupt him with a laugh, and he laughs, too, sounding both relieved and nervous. "I don't usually wear this to school, since it's not exactly dress code approved," I admit. "But I think I'll be okay this one time."

"Okay," he says, giving me a doubtful look.

I want to bask in this guy's admiration for the whole ride to school. This is exactly what I wanted when I moved here, what I imagined I could have. Flirting with a cute boy with nothing promised. To be wanted would be enough.

But I can't do that now. I owe it to Royal to find out anything and everything I can that might help him. So, I take a deep breath, hide my smile, and turn away from the window.

"So, you must be pretty close with the Darlings, huh?"

"Just the one," he says, smiling in a casual way that none of the Darlings could pull off. Colt fakes what this guy has for real—in spades. Damn it. Maybe I should have gone to public school. The thought makes me shiver, though. I've never gone to public school a day in my life. They'd eat me alive. At least I know how to play the game at Willow Heights.

Sort of.

"How come she goes to Faulkner Public?" I ask. "Your girlfriend."

He shoots me a grin that's half pride and half embarrassment. "Because I go there."

"Ah," I say, nodding. "So you've been together a while?"

"Yeah," he says. "Pretty much all our lives."

I can't tell how he feels about that, as he's looking at the road ahead again. And I need to get info about the Darlings from him, not worry about his relationship. "Oh," I say, forcing a laugh. "How does her family feel about her dating a guy from this side of town?"

This time, he laughs. "I think they've come to terms with it."

I know there's something more, that he's laughing at me for some ignorance, but again, I don't have time to worry about him.

"Well, that's good," I say. "Does she have any brothers at Willow Heights? Maybe I know them."

"Oh, I'm sure you know him," he says. "Isn't that why you're asking? You've got a thing for one of them?"

I shrug. "Every girl at Willow Heights has a thing for the Darling cousins."

He glances at me, and I can tell he's deciding whether to give me what I want. Then he turns back to the road, resting his palm over the top of the steering wheel. I notice the muscles running up his tan forearm, the bulge of his bicep against the sleeve of his black T-shirt, the way his shoulder knots with muscle. I can see why he'd be good enough for a Darling.

"Her brother's Preston," he says. "I'm sure I'm breaking 'bro code' by telling you this, but if you're looking for something serious with him, I'd keep right on looking. Don't get me wrong, he's not a bad dude. If you just want to score for the bragging rights, I'm sure he'd be all over that."

He checks me out from the corner of his eye, not trying to hide his appreciation.

"You are, huh?" I ask. "What makes you so sure?"

"Well, he's a seventeen-year-old guy," Chase says, shifting in his seat and shooting me a smile. "And you're a pretty bangin' chick from out of town."

"Who said I'm from out of town?"

"You did," he says, laughing. "It was the first thing out of your mouth."

I can't help but laugh. The fact that he's still interested even though I'm in sweats and wearing no makeup makes me all warm inside. It's nice to be flattered. And after being around Devlin, where I can't tell where I stand from one sentence to the next, this guy makes it so sweet and simple. If only he weren't dating a Darling. If only I felt something for him, instead of just nice that he thinks I'm hot.

"I'm not after a hookup," I assure him. "I'm just curious."

"Good," he says. "Because dating a Darling is like opening a Pandora's Box filled with generations' worth of family drama and trauma. Trust me, not worth it."

"Says the guy dating a Darling," I remind him, rolling my eyes.

"Exactly," he says, laughing. "So, you know I'm not full of shit. Not all the Darlings are like the ones who go to Willow Heights, but those three..." He breaks off and shakes his head.

"How many Darlings live in Faulkner, anyway?" I ask. "Every time I turn around there's another one."

"Oh, yeah, there's a lot," he says with an easy chuckle. "There's Grandpa Darling, who basically runs the show behind the scenes. I think they pretty much have to check in with him every time they wipe their asses. He's got some secret society shit going on over at Willow Heights, too, so he's still controlling even his grandkids. It was probably worse for his own kids."

"And there's... How many grandkids?"

"Well, he has seven sons, and they all have kids… Basically, you can't throw a stick without hitting a Darling in this town. And if you hit a Darling, well, you better hope it's not the wrong one."

Damn, I need this boy in my life. He's told me more in one breath than everyone else has told me in over a month of living here. Of course that's when he turns onto the long street that runs past Willow Heights, and I know I only have a minute left.

"He has favorites?" I ask, immediately picturing our neighbor blocking him from entering, and the three cousins at Willow Heights who must be in this secret society that's been mentioned twice now, and the preppy girl who was on his front steps of Grampa Darling's childhood home acting all shady.

"For sure," Chase says, pulling me out of my thoughts. "I guess back in the day he disowned, like, half the kids because they wouldn't do his bidding. Took them out of his will and everything. I think some of them are back in his good graces, but I don't keep up with the adult drama around here. I got enough drama of my own."

He flashes me that smile again as he palms the steering wheel and turns into the parking lot of Willow Heights, where I spot Devlin's car in the primo parking spot, the three boys sitting on it like it's their throne. I wonder if losing his car hurt Devlin more than he showed. Did he even care? He showed up with a new convertible just days later like nothing happened. It certainly didn't make him lose the esteem of the other students. He still reigns supreme.

For now.

fourteen

Crystal

"What about you?" Chase asks, his gaze following mine before he whips into a parking spot. "You come with any drama?"

I laugh at that one, a real laugh for the first time in what feels like days. "Sweetheart, you couldn't handle me," I say. "Every damn day of my life is like a soap opera."

I swing the door open and climb out, and just like I hoped, he climbs out, too. I know I'm doing something shitty to a boy who's been nothing but sweet to me, but sometimes sacrifices have to be made. Using him to get a little attention isn't the worst thing I've ever done by a long shot. And I don't think they'll hurt him. He may not have Darling blood, but he's one of them by association.

"Wait," Chase says. "I didn't catch your name."

"Crystal," I say, meeting him at the back of his car, where I'm sure the Darlings can see us. I haven't looked their way, but I know they're watching. I can feel Devlin's gaze crackling across my skin, making the hairs stand up on the nape of my neck. My belly flips, and a delicious shiver of anticipation works its way through me, sinking into a well of want between my thighs.

God, I'm so fucked up.

I step between Chase and the Darlings' line of sight, turning my back on them so Chase has to turn his back to his car. He rests his hands back on the trunk and smiles down at me. "Hey, Crystal," he says, his voice dropping an octave when he sees how close I am. I step even closer, so close that I'd have to straddle his thigh to be any more obvious.

"Hey, Chase." I smile up at him, slowly sliding my arms from his jacket, as if anyone might not have noticed the navy and white jacket in a sea of black and gold.

"I don't guess you'd want to keep that," he says, accepting the jacket from me. "I mean, you could probably use it, but I guess that wouldn't go over too well here."

His eyes flick to something behind me, and I know the Darlings are on the move. Triumph swells in my chest. This wasn't just about proving something to the school. It's about proving something to myself.

"No," I say, reaching out to toy with the buttons on his jacket before glancing up at him shyly. "Thanks for the ride, though."

He clears his throat. "Always happy to rescue a damsel in distress."

I stand on tiptoes, resting my palms on his thighs to steady myself, and let my lips brush over his cheek. "Maybe I'll see you around sometime."

Chase tenses, and I'm yanked backwards so hard I would lose my footing if I wasn't being held flush against a rock hard set of abs. "What the fuck are you doing with our girl?" Devlin asks, not releasing me even when I squirm against his hold.

"Whoa, there," Chase says. "Is that any way to treat a lady?"

Devlin's hand spreads open across my belly, his long fingers splayed, pinning me tighter to him. "Now you're telling me how to treat my girl?" he asks, his voice low and deadly. "After you had your hands on her?"

Jackpot. This fucker can pretend I don't affect him all he wants, but this shit was too easy.

Chase lifts his hands from where they were resting on the edge of his trunk. "No hands," he says. He doesn't sound scared, though he should be. He's not being a smartass about it, at least. He sounds guarded and direct, just stating the facts. A few other students have crept over, anxious to see the fight, I'm sure. Good. The more people see, the more they'll talk. For once, I don't mind.

"This isn't a lady, anyway," Colt drawls, gesturing lazily in my direction. "It's our dog."

Preston steps forward, getting right in Chase's face. "My sister, though, she's a lady. Which is why we're wondering what you're doing feeling up our dog when you have a girl like that at home."

"Just giving her a ride," Chase says, holding up both hands when Preston steps in like he's about to deck the poor guy. I'm starting to regret what I did, even though my heart is racing in my chest. I got what I wanted. I got Devlin to show his hand.

All's fucking fair.

Preston grabs Chase by the front of his jacket and hauls him forward from where he was still leaning on the car all casual. "What are you playing at, London?" Preston asks, giving the guy a shake. The handful of onlookers has turned to a crowd, and they strain forward, ready to see the beatdown.

"Not playing," Chase says, sounding a bit annoyed by the harassment.

"And you won't be for a long-ass time if you fuck around on his sister," Devlin drawls, nodding toward his hand.

Preston grabs Chase's right hand and twists his wrist around. Chase's eyes go wide, and he starts to turn to take the pressure off his wrist. Fuck. I can't let anyone mess up a guy's football arm. Not even for this.

"Leave him alone," I cry, jerking forward in Devlin's grip. "He didn't do anything. I asked him for a ride. That's it. He was just being a gentleman and dropping me off."

"Then why were you kissing him?" Devlin growls in my ear.

"To make you jealous," I admit, my voice barely above a whisper. I hear the defeat in it, but I'm not sure who else heard. Maybe just Devlin. Or maybe they all heard, and they'll go around school gossiping about what a pathetic loser I am.

Like I fucking care.

All the triumph is gone from me. That lasted all of five minutes. He called me his girl, but only his cousins heard. And he forced my hand, so I had to admit that I'm just a scheming bitch like probably every other girl who's ever tried to land a Darling boy.

No one moves for a minute. Preston's jaw is clenched, but at last he shoves Chase back against the car. "Pussy," he says, spitting the word at the public school guy. Chase pops up, flashes a grin at the small crowd, throws a two-finger salute, and hops in his car. The next second, he's driving off, and the crowd wilts with disappointment. Chase is in the Darlings' pocket. He's not going to give them a good fight.

They want something else. They want what my brothers give them. As Duke's Hummer comes roaring into the lot, a collective intake of breath grips the crowd. They're about to get what they want.

"Get in the car," Devlin says, grabbing me by the back of the neck and hurrying me across the lot. "We're going for a drive."

He shoves me into the passenger seat and slides across the hood like some action hero stuntman, opens his door, and is pulling out of his spot before I've even gotten my door closed. I barely manage to slam the door to keep from falling out as he peels out of the lot.

"What the fuck was that?" he yells, pounding his palm on the steering wheel.

I twist around to see if my brothers are on our tail. They're not. The crowd is blocking them from coming after us. I twist around to Devlin. "Are you fucking crazy? I could have fallen out the door, and you'd just have driven over me, wouldn't you?"

He glances at me, his nostrils flared and his jaw still clenched. His eyes burn with rage. "What are you trying to pull?" he asks, his voice controlled now. "Make me jealous? What kind of bullshit lie is that?"

"You think I was lying?"

"Yes," he says. "So, what were you trying to gain from that little display? What are you after, Crystal Dolce?"

I cross my arms over my chest. "Are we negotiating?"

"No," he says. "Fuck no. Darlings don't negotiate."

I've heard a line or two like that before. It strikes me that we're both alike in that way. Stuck in our family's web, bound by expectation of what we should do and be.

"Maybe you should," I say. "You might get what *you* want."

Devlin smirks, the asshole thinking he's back in control, no doubt. "I already get what I want."

And there it is. There is the one problem I can't seem to solve. Devlin gets everything he wants, including, apparently, me.

"Where are you taking me?" I ask, glancing around at the familiar streets.

"Home."

"My dad will kill you."

He snorts. "Your dad's a joke. He's weak, and he will cave."

It's my turn to snort. "Trust me, my father is not weak."

"Any man controlled by what's in his pants is easily controlled," he says.

"First off, gross, and second, why are you taking me home?"

"You can't go to school looking like that."

"Are you fucking serious?" I ask. "You drove me to the ghetto, left me to fend for myself without a phone or weapons in sight, and now you're worried what people will think of me without makeup?"

"I took you there to prove a point," he says. "That's where you belong. If it wasn't, you wouldn't have figured out your way around so fast."

"Yeah, well, if I'm so trashy, why don't you just humiliate me by making me walk around school looking like trash?"

He pulls up our driveway, all the way around the back to the garage. "You don't look like trash," he says, leaning over to slide a hand behind my head. He pulls my face around toward him, his gaze dropping to my lips. "You look like every guy's wet dream."

"What?" I ask, my heart hammering as I wait for the punchline.

"You look like you just got rolled in the sack," he says, a rough edge creeping into his voice. "Only I get to see you like that."

I pull away, shoving his hands off me. "Now you're trying to tell me what to wear and how to do my makeup? What the fuck, Devlin. I'm not wearing dog ears for you."

"My school, my rules." He smirks as he unbuckles his seatbelt and hops out of the car, heading for the back door.

"You think you're just going to waltz in through the door now?" I ask. "You've either got the biggest balls in the world or a death wish. I can't tell which one yet."

"No one's home," Devlin says, sliding a key into the lock and pushing the door open.

"How the fuck do you have the keys to my house?"

"I grew up here," he says. "I know this house as well as my own." He ushers me through with a light touch on my lower back. I try not to let it affect me, try not to notice that it does. Every touch from him is electric, even when I'm baffled by the audacity of this boy.

Trying to calm my racing pulse and jittery nerves, I stomp upstairs and into my room. I don't even bother telling him to leave while I change into a red pencil skirt, a cream silk blouse, and a pair of pumps. He sits there watching me like some kind of overbearing creeper while I flatiron my hair, pull it back, and secure it into a smooth, low pony draped forward over one shoulder. He doesn't say a word as I smooth down every last flyaway. He stares at me in the mirror while I do my makeup like he's trying to memorize my routine.

I ignore him the entire time.

Finally, when I'm done, I turn and give him a curtsy. "Everything up to standards, Father Darling?"

"Don't call me that," he snaps.

Whoa. Okay, then.

"Want me to call you Daddy instead?" I tease in my most sugary voice.

"That's fucking creepy," Devlin says. "Now let's go."

"I would have thought you liked that," I admit as we start down the stairs. "With all your nasty talk about my brothers when we were hooking up."

"When you have a grandpa like ours, who girls are throwing themselves at with that line, it kills the appeal real fucking fast."

"You don't like your grandpa very much, do you?" I ask as we step out the back door.

Devlin doesn't answer.

"Are you sure this passes your inspection?" I ask when we get to the car. I hold out my arms and gesture to my outfit.

His eyes rake down my body and back up with blank indifference. "Yes."

"Wow," I say, sliding into the front seat of his car. "You didn't make a single disparaging comment. Why do I get the feeling we're going to get to school only to have you change your mind and drag me back here yet again?"

I halfway expect Devlin to tell me to get in the back, but he climbs in the driver's seat without a word. Then, he turns and smirks at me with real humor in his eyes this time. "Are you fishing for compliments?"

"No," I say, sitting back and crossing my arms. "Okay, maybe. My ego can only take being told I'm trash so many times in one day."

"I would have thought that asshole just about coming in his pants when you kissed him would have done the trick," Devlin says. He twists around to reverse the car, laying his hand on the back of my seat. And my stupid body reacts to his nearness, electricity crackling up my spine even though his hand is inches from touching me.

But he must not feel it, because once the car's straightened out, he takes his hand away without touching me. I remember this morning again, when he had me up against my dresser and ready to do anything for him. He can turn it off like a switch, walk away from me without a backwards glance.

Why can't I do the same?

"I don't care what some random guy thinks of me," I admit, turning my face away and staring out the window. Suddenly, I don't feel like toying with him, trying to get what I want out of him. If he liked me, he'd give it without me having to beg.

Don't be a dumb bitch, I scold myself.

Devlin Darling does not like me. I'm nothing but a toy to him, something to treat as roughly as he can to see how much it can take before it breaks. I went to all that trouble to make a scene at school, to prove that I could make him jealous. But what did it prove? That I was no better than any other desperate girl trying to hold the Darlings' attention, trying to make them see what they'd be losing. Just because it worked doesn't prove anything. He's possessive because I'm his fucking dog. Not because he feels anything. His heart is too hard to feel anything, too cold, just as his icy blue eyes told me the very first time I met him.

"Chase London isn't some random guy," Devlin says. "He's the most quality dude in this town outside our family. You could do worse."

I could do better, I think.

"Maybe I'm not willing to settle for second best," I mutter.

Devlin doesn't answer. Shit. I can't believe I just said that. As if his ego isn't big enough. I'm sure girls are throwing themselves at his feet and telling him what a god he is night and day. But it's not just that. I basically just told him I liked him. That I want him.

But as we pull up to the school, a crazy idea starts to form. What if I *could* do better? What if I could get a Darling? What if I could get him to trust me enough to tell me the truth about Royal, what happened to him? Maybe he's still alive. Maybe they know where he is.

I know I've fucked things up with Devlin already. I gave in too soon, let him fuck me for his game. He probably thinks I'm easy. And for him, I am. I would never win that battle. He makes me weak, strips back my defenses with one touch and leaves me bare and aching for him. I want Devlin too much, need him in a way that's too raw and real, too powerful.

But he has two cousins. I know Colt a bit. He's burned me a few times, well enough for me to know not to trust him. Preston, on the other hand, is still a mystery to me.

fifteen

Devlin

I tell her to go in, and she obeys. I watch her walk away, her slender figure clad in something a lawyer would wear to work, her curves only hinted at. She doesn't scurry or hurry even though she's late. She doesn't sway her hips to make sure I'm checking out her ass. And even though I know she's carrying a lot with her brother being gone and her world upside down, you'd never know it. Her spine is straight and tall, her gait measured and confident. She walks inside without looking back.

I sit in the car trying to get my shit together. What the fuck is happening? I squeeze my hands around the steering wheel until it creaks in protest.

I did what I was supposed to do. I had to get her out of my head, so I fucked her. It always works for my cousins. Fuck a girl, she's as good as invisible afterwards—she's used up and done. But I don't go around fucking random girls, so I didn't know. I sure as fuck didn't know when this poised and polished, straight-laced virgin cried my name over and over like a chant when she came, that it wasn't just the hottest thing I'd ever heard. My name rolling off her tongue… It's enough to make me hard just thinking about it. I didn't know she'd laid a fucking curse on me with that chant.

A curse so I can never get it out of my head—the sound of her voice softly panting my name, the sight of her lying helpless under me, her pillowy lips parting in ecstasy, my name tearing from them as if it's the only word she can remember, the only thing that matters in her world, the only person who exists to her. This calm and collected girl, who refuses to obey, to fall in line or follow the status quo even after what I did to her, who is so fucking unbreakable it's driving me out of my head… This girl goes to pieces, completely loses control, when I so much as touch her. It's addictive as hell.

I press my forehead to the steering wheel and try to come to terms with this. Is this what addiction feels like? Like a craving for more, for the softness of her body under mine, so vulnerable, completely powerless and yet somehow trusting me enough to open herself completely, to give herself fully to me, to let me make her cum. The feeling of her cunt squeezing around my cock, needing *me* to get her there, to make her cum, to fill her with my cum as if it's the only thing that can quench her thirst.

And now I'm fucking hard as a rock.

I sigh and lean back against the seat, trying to stop thinking about fucking her and think about my job—breaking her. I'm not supposed to want more than that.

I'm used to girls falling all over themselves when we walk in a room. My cousins love it, and our fathers before us, and the truth is, I did, too. Before her. Now… The fawning annoys me. It's starting to bore me. What good is it to have everyone kneel if she's shown the whole thing to be a charade? I don't care about being everyone's king. I want to be *her* king.

And yet, she's the one girl who won't kneel for me. She'll obey outwardly, when we force her to, when she has no choice. But she's just biding her time, waiting to be out from under my thumb, before she goes on being just who she is. Because that's the thing about her, the same thing Dolly has, but in a different way. Crystal is just going to be who she is, and she won't change or apologize for anyone. She doesn't care that her best friend is a fat freshman who wore dog ears to school. She doesn't care that everyone in the entire school calls her a dog.

She's not a bitch about it, either, like those girls who stomp around threatening to cut people and confuse being rude with being a badass. She doesn't have to be loud and cuss and wear slutty clothes for attention. When those girls trashed her locker, she didn't have to get revenge to prove she was bigger and badder. I know that pissed off Lacey and her crew as much as losing their status. They wanted to start a feud with Crystal, to stay relevant, to have everyone back them up.

But Crystal just moved on like they weren't worth the effort. She's above all of it. And that drives the other girls nuts because it just shows them that they're not above the pettiness and bullshit drama. And she is. She's what they want to be, and she doesn't even try. She doesn't rise to the bait when we taunt her. She's unapologetically cool.

I'm in awe of her. And if I'm being honest, that pisses me the fuck off.

She's not in awe of us. She doesn't care who we are. She walks right by the kings of the school like she'd rather sit with our dog. And it's not an act. She is genuinely unimpressed, and it's fucking up everything we've got going. And more than that, it's fucking up the way this town runs, the way things have always been. We're supposed to keep people in line, to make them remember who they look up to, who their families work for, who they worship.

And then the Dolces blow into town with their daughter who looks as delicate as a fucking flower ready to be crushed under the first bootheel that even brushes against her. But after all the bootheels have stomped on her, she's still standing.

Why won't she fucking kneel?

sixteen

Crystal

There's a special place in hell for people who torment a girl who just lost her brother. And that place is going to be filled with assholes from Willow Heights.

Barking follows me down the hall as I make my way to my locker before lunch. I hold my head high and march through them all like I don't hear them. But I do. I fucking hear them loud and clear. I'm a dog, and they don't want me here.

But it's not because of me. It's not because I'm ugly or stupid or mean or don't look like them. It's because Devlin said I was a dog, and they have to play along. Which means it's a kind of *Emperor's New Clothes* test. I am not defective. I am good enough to score a Darling. I just have to get them to think so, too.

I arrive at my locker, fully expecting to have it filled with dog food again now that it's apparently open season on me. But there's not so much as a can of Alpo inside.

I shove my books inside, ignoring the snickers coming from behind me. Are they really so immature as to stick a sign on my back? After closing my locker, I turn to see Lacey and all her bitchy, former Darling Dolls standing there with arms crossed, making disgusted faces at me.

"What's your problem?" I ask. "Got bored of sticking your finger down your throat and came out here to see if I had any more dog food for you?"

"Slut," Lacey hisses, looking me up and down like I'm every bit as trashy as the Darlings think I am. I wonder what the bastards are spreading around school now.

"I may be a lot of things, but I can guarantee you've had more dick in you than I have," I say.

Her friend rolls her eyes. "I doubt it."

"It's not about how many people you're with," Lacey says, jutting her lower lip out and making an ugly face, as if she can't bear to look at me without twisting her face into a troll expression. "It's about how you act."

"You'd know," I say, turning and starting down the hall.

The bitches follow me like annoying little mosquitos. "You can't just go around blowing guys in the bathroom," Lacey snarls at me. "I don't know what you did in New York, but this isn't that kind of school."

My stomach drops, and I hold back the urge to vomit. So that's what he told them. Not about dropping me off in the rough part of town, but about letting him fuck me in the bathroom. Just what I want everyone in school to know. Well, I guess there goes any chance at ever being anything but a whore to this town.

"It's so unsanitary," her friend says, nearly gagging aloud. "Right next to the toilets. Gives a whole new meaning to word *dirty whore*."

"That's actually two words," I say with my sweetest smile. "And I wasn't blowing anyone in the bathroom. I was fucking him."

I flip my ponytail back over my shoulder and stroll into the cafeteria like I own the damn place. Fuck those girls and their petty gossip. If Veronica taught me anything, it's how to spin any story to fit the narrative you want. And if Devlin's going to spread rumors about me, I might as well own it. So, now I'm a slut who gives blowjobs in the bathroom. I wonder what I can get out of that before everyone figures out it's not true. For a rumor that juicy, I'm guessing it'll take a while to be disproven. Which means I need to get as much as I can for it.

I march over to the Darlings' table before I can talk myself out of it, while I'm still fueled by adrenaline and anger. Preston's the only one there, holding court with his fangirls and ass kissers. He sees me coming and leans back in his chair, that look-at-my-dick pose he likes so much.

I walk right up to him and slam my palm down on the table in front of him, leaning in close to his face so he knows I'm not afraid. "What did you do to my brother?" I ask, my words slow and deliberate.

"Aww, there's my little lap dog," Preston drawls, amusement dripping from his words. "Com'ere and sit on my lap, little doggie."

"Don't fuck with me," I say. "If you have a shred of decency anywhere in you, you'll tell me where he is."

"Oh, darlin', I ain't got a single shred of decency left," he says. "But you sit right here on my dick, and I'll tell you just what I told the police."

I stare at him, the hatred inside my heart burning it to a brittle crisp as I stand there. This boy isn't going to be the one to help me. He's the worst of them all.

"I don't want to hear what you told the police," I say through gritted teeth. "I want the truth. What happened to Royal that night, Preston? I know you know."

He pats his thigh in a slow, relentless rhythm until I look down at his lap. "All right," he says. "Sit on my lap, and I'll tell you the truth."

"Just tell me."

He pops a cherry tomato in his mouth and chews slowly. "Them's my terms," he says. "You can take 'em, or you can walk away."

"Fine," I say. "I'll sit like a good dog. But keep your hands off me."

"Don't flatter yourself," he says. "I have no interest in feeling you up like a horny thirteen-year-old. There's only one part of you I have any use for, and you'll just have to wait until I'm good and ready. But don't worry, pretty puppy. When the time comes, I'll wreck that pussy right."

"Don't count on it."

Preston lets out a low, slow laugh. His eyes are cold and sharp, a predator ready for the killing strike. He leans forward until his face is just inches from mine, letting his gaze caress my face and skim over my lips before returning to mine. "If I wanted to, I could bend you over this table and bust one in your ass right now, and not a person in this room would stop me. No, baby. They'd cheer me on. I'm a Darling. Don't underestimate what that means in this town."

My heart is hammering in my chest as I stare back into those piercing blue eyes. There's a warning there, and it's not just to scare me. Preston wants me to know what I'm dealing with. He's not being sneaky. I begin to lower myself toward his lap, but he swings his legs around, sliding both feet between mine and pulling me forward onto his knees. The crowd around us breaks into excited murmurs as I straddle his knees. Preston silences them with one glance.

I never look away from him. "You might think you're untouchable," I say, my voice barely above a whisper, though it stays steady as I speak. "But even a Darling won't get away with murder."

"It's already been done," Preston says, his hands landing on my bare knees. He doesn't squeeze. He doesn't hurt me. But their presence is a threat, a promise. "Learn your history, Dolce. This town lives and dies by it."

His eyes flicker to something behind me, and his hands move higher on my thighs, pushing my skirt up further.

It takes everything in me not to grab his hands, not to slap them away, not to show him how uncomfortable I am right now. Instead, I stare him straight in the eye. "What did you do to Royal?"

"You want to know what happened?" Preston says. "I was at Devlin's, and I saw the limo come up, and I thought you were all in it. Royal got out alone. He taunted me about being at Devlin's, waiting for him like a little lap dog. He said I should be the Darling Dog, and that he knew where Devlin was. I knew where he was, too. I always know where my boys are."

I wait, knowing he doesn't have to tell me this. That he could pretend in front of all his buddies that no one ever challenged his rule.

"He was running his mouth like a bitch, so I punched him."

The crowd around us sucks in a breath. They know Royal's missing. They know Preston's incriminating himself to me. They just don't know why. And neither do I, which scares me more than anything.

"You hit him?"

"Yeah," he says. "I hit him. And he hit back. I wasn't looking to get arrested again, and I knew that little bitch would squeal to the pigs if I did any damage. I wanted back on the team, so I wasn't going to give him what he wanted. So I left him there."

He slides his hands further up my thighs, stopping just before he'd be flashing my underwear to the crowd.

"That's it?" I ask.

"No," he says. "A few minutes later, I was out on the porch, and I saw a shitty old pickup drive up to your house. Royal got in, and they left."

"What?" I ask, my heart pound so hard I think I'm going to pass out. "Who was it?"

"I don't know," he says with a shrug, like it doesn't matter. "No one from this school."

"How do you know?" I demand.

Preston smirks. "I know what everyone here drives."

Before I can poke a hundred holes in his bullshit story, someone grabs the base of my ponytail in a firm grip. "Can I get in on this lap dance?" Colt asks, his voice a silky-slow purr in my ear that sends a shiver through me. The next second, something cold and wet pours over my head, giving me chills for a whole different reason. I gasp, barely holding back a cry of shock.

Around me, everyone breaks into laughter. Cold, white liquid runs down my scalp, trickling down my face. And then they're surrounding me as Colt grips my ponytail, holding my head. Preston grabs my hands and pins them behind my back, forcing my body to bow toward him.

"Whore," Lacey says, throwing a glass of milk in my face.

"Get 'er done," a guy yells, holding his glass up and letting the milk pour like a waterfall over my tits. Everyone jostles to get closer, to drench me further. I blink and sputter, aware of my clothes clinging to my wet skin, the sweet stink of milk drenching me, and the blur of faces laughing as they throw their drinks in my face. Milk cascades over me, rushing down my back, my chest, my face. Half the crowd is barking, and the other half is jeering and catcalling as my silk shirt is soaked, clinging to my body, and my nipples pebble with cold.

Suddenly, an enraged shout goes up, and people go crashing into tables around us. Colt releases me the same moment someone grabs me from behind, dragging me off Preston. King smashes a fist into Preston's face, and he crashes to the floor beside his chair. Duke tackles Colt, and Baron's arms wrap around me, holding me hard against his chest.

"These cunts are going to pay," he says, his voice flat and harsh in my ear. "No one fucks with our sister."

I press my face into his shirt, trying to blink the milk and mascara from my eyes. Is this why Devlin wanted makeup on me? To humiliate me further in front of the whole school?

Suddenly Preston shoots out from under my brothers, his face purple with rage, his arm clutched to his middle. "You broke my fucking arm," he screams, his eyes blind with rage. I cower back against Baron, and every single other person in the audience shrinks back from the insanity written in his eyes, across his face, in his voice and every ragged breath he draws through the pain.

King's on his feet in seconds, his fists up, ready to take another swing. He's the only person in the room who looks unaffected by Preston's raw pain. King speaks, his words like a decree in the silence around us. "You touch my sister again, it'll be your neck."

"I'm going to fucking kill you," Preston growls, his breathing labored as he holds his right arm in his left. But for once, his words don't carry the weight of royalty. His threat sounds empty, weak next to King's. Because at last, we've won a battle. At last, we've broken a Darling.

seventeen

Crystal

I miss home, my old home. I miss the numb pain of guilt. I miss thinking that my words, my lack of actions, made a girl hate her life so bad she wanted to throw it away. I miss being the disgraced queen, the girl who sat in bed and ate ice cream and shopped like the pathetic human she was. I'd give anything to be in her place again. That life seems like a fairytale now. And I'm too old to believe in fairytales.

I can't sleep. I lie in bed staring at the darkness, a darkness deeper and thicker than anything Manhattan had to offer. A darkness so thick it threatens to drown me, to swallow me like it swallowed my brother, leaving nothing but the shape of me sinking into my mattress.

I throw off my blankets and sit up, breathing hard. Where is my twin? Shouldn't I be able to tell, to feel him through some psychic twin bond? I press my fists to my eyes and try to think. Preston claims to know what every student at Willow Heights drives, but he described the truck that took Royal as "a shitty pickup." Not a model or even a make. And what was he doing on Devlin's porch, just hanging out alone, when this truck supposedly came? Would a guy like that really walk away from a fight just because he wants to get back on the team?

One flash of Preston's glassy, insane eyes in my memory answers that question. Football might be the only thing on earth he cares about as much as his family. And now he might never play again. I shouldn't be shocked. This moved beyond pranks and games the moment my brothers totaled Devlin's Bel Air.

Oh god. My heart clenches like a shock. If they have Royal somewhere... Oh my god. What will Preston do to my brother to punish him for what King did to him?

The thought sends me spiraling, and I race to the bathroom and get sick. I sink down against the wall, shaking so hard I can't stand. I know I'm not pregnant because I started my period last night, and I'd had the signs it was coming for a few days. But amid my blur of anxiety, I close my eyes and make a bargain with god. I'd rather get pregnant by a Darling than lose Royal. If he's somehow still alive, I'll be so careful from now on. And if I'm not careful, I'll pay for it. I won't even pray for mercy. If somehow he's still alive...

I rest my head back against the wall, only to hear the sound of girlish giggling in the room next to mine. Ew. When we got home from school today, my three uncles had arrived to help with the search, along with all the male cousins in the family, but none of them brought women. Sick as it is, I know my parents' sex noises, and those aren't them. If there's one thing worse than listening to my parents go at it, it's listening to my grandparents.

I drag myself up from the floor and slide back into bed. But there's no rest for the wicked.

Outside, I hear the familiar smack of Devlin's football. I sigh and pull the pillow over my head, but I can still hear it. It goes on and on, that sound that won't let me sleep, that reminds me he's out there again, that he's on the team again. He's on the team because my brother is gone.

I flop onto my back, too frustrated to sleep. Too pissed at him for acting like everything is fine right now. Too irritated by the incessant reminder that he's right fucking there, just across the lawn. Too mad to admit the truth of what he said today, that Daddy must have told the cops Royal had run away or the FBI would be involved. Too scared to think about what's keeping me awake, about what Royal is going through if he's alive. I won't think about the alternative.

Four days have passed.

At last, I can't take it any longer. I throw off the blankets and climb out of bed, pull on a pair of yoga pants and a hoodie, grab a pair of Uggs, and climb out my window. I tiptoe along the balcony, my heart thudding in my ears, past Duke's room. When I reach King's window, I see a soft glow behind his curtains.

Fuck.

He's awake in there. I wonder what he's doing in there, what penance he believes he owes. I know my brother. I may be Royal's twin, but King is our protector. Yes, I ache for Royal, the boy who grounds me and calms me, the boy whose silent looks understand my soul. But King… King blames himself. And that's so much worse. King hates himself for not being there, for getting suspended, for letting me go to Homecoming with Colt. He blames himself for me sleeping with Devlin, for the shit I'm going through at school, for Royal disappearing.

He blames himself, even though he isn't to blame for any of it, and that makes pain bloom deep inside my chest, an ache for him that hurts every bit as much as the ache of my own heart missing Royal. My soul hurts for my oldest brother, for the way he's changing. For the hardness in his eyes now, for his ability to break Preston's arm without remorse. King will fight to protect any one of us, but he's not violent by nature. This place is changing all of us.

That thought turns my irritation and frustration into anger, and I hurry past King's windows, tiptoe down the stairs, and pause. I slide my feet into my boots and start across the lawn. Dew splatters the toes of my boots, and when I look back, I've left a trail that's plain to see for anyone who might look out a window of our house.

Good.

If I disappear, they'll know who's to blame.

As I step past the row of lilac bushes, I realize I've never set foot on the Darling's property before. Not intentionally. I pause in the shadow of one of the huge bushes. Across an expanse of damp lawn, Devlin's masculine figure is illuminated by a single light bulb hanging from a big shade tree. He's wearing a white undershirt and a pair of sweatpants slung low on his hips. As he rears back to throw the football, the light glimmers against the outlines of his body, illuminating the muscles in his inked arms, his shoulders, his butt. I have to swallow against the pulse that flutters in my throat. Why does he have to look so fucking good?

I shake my head and start across the lawn. It doesn't matter what he looks like, if the silhouette he cuts against the night makes my chest ache, if the arch of his back and the V below his hips makes heat pulse somewhere lower than my throat.

He releases the football, and it sails through the air in a long arc, at last finding its target. It drops through a tire hanging from a sprawling oak tree, hitting the trunk with a familiar *thwack*.

Devlin jogs up to retrieve the ball, which has rolled a few feet back toward him. I swallow hard as I look at his setup. It's so plain, so unpretentious, even a little redneck. I'm sure he could afford something fancy, something to spit the ball out at him like batting cages do a baseball. He could afford a target that's not an old tire swing. Something about the simple swing, the light bulb hung in the tree above it, brings a sad smile to my face.

I don't know what kinds of football contraptions they have for lonely boys. My brothers don't need a tire swing or even a fancy setup. When they want to throw a ball around or practice plays, they have enough players to run them, practically a whole team. Devlin's out here all alone, every night.

When he turns, he spots me and pauses. I step out from the shade of the lilacs and hold out my hands.

"What?" he asks, sounding wary. We're at least fifty feet apart, but his voice is quiet. The neighborhood is silent around us, even the insect noises having quit for the season.

"Throw it," I say.

Devlin works his jaw back and forth once, and then then he draws back and throws. It's a soft pass, like he's afraid he'll hurt me with a real pass, but it's perfect, landing right in my hands.

"Nice catch," he says, not moving.

"The only way I could have missed that is if I threw my hands up over my head and hid when I saw a ball coming toward me."

He shrugs. "What do you want?"

"To get some sleep without having to hear you out here throwing a football by yourself all night." I draw back and throw the ball to him. It spirals high and long, and he has to backtrack a bit to catch it.

"Damn," he says, jogging toward me. "You got an arm on you."

"Don't sound so surprised," I say. "I have four brothers."

Three.

The thought tears at my heart, and it's all I can do not to sob out loud. I'm relieved that Devlin tosses the ball back, and I have something to distract me from the staggering pain. At night, when there's nothing to distract me from it, I can barely keep breathing.

I pick the ball out of the air and toss it toward where Devlin is heading, making him run for it. "Yeah," he says, glancing behind me at the house before returning the pass. "Is one of them out here with you?"

I scowl at him. "No. Just me."

"You know that was a really fucking stupid thing to do?"

"What?" I ask, a taunt in my voice. "Coming out here alone? What are you going to do to me now, Devlin?"

"Whatever I feel like," he says with a smirk.

I throw the ball without warning, but he picks it out of the air like it's nothing. Then he grins at me like he knows exactly how much that pisses me off.

"Are you threatening me?" I ask. "Because I have a house full of guys you really don't want to fuck with right now."

"Yeah, well, you really don't want to fuck with us," Devlin says, tucking the football under his arm and approaching me. "See, that's the thing you don't understand about the Darlings. You can't win against my family, Sugar. No matter what you do, we'll come back twice as hard."

His words send a shiver of desire straight to my core, and it's all I can do not to press my knees together right in front of him. Because if I'm honest, didn't I come out here for that? I want him to want me. To be as unable to resist me as I am him. I walked out here to make him stop making noise, but also so he'd show me more of what he did yesterday, when he called me his girl. I want him to consume me, to take away the thoughts, the pain, if only for a few minutes.

"But you like it hard, don't you, Sugar?" he purrs, lifting my chin with gentle fingers. "You like to be pounded nice and deep."

"So deep," I whisper. I swallow, unable to catch my breath. Damn. He does this to me every fucking time, but I can't stop myself from wanting more. I'm just about begging for it.

His lids drop halfway, and his hooded gaze dips to my lips. His hand moves lower, from my chin to my throat, his long fingers wrapping around my neck gently, like a caress.

"You're a sick little girl, you know that, Dolce?"

We stare at each other a long moment, and then Devlin drops his hand. And my stupid heart aches for it to be back around my throat. I can't quite quell the disappointment that he didn't squeeze this time. He's right. I am sick.

"Who's at your house?" he asks, turning away.

He lifts his arm and throws the football, a casual pass, not one he'd throw in the game. I watch the muscles in his shoulder slide under his golden skin wrapped in tattoos, and my fingers twitch to touch them, to grip his hipbones, to feel the flex of those muscles as he drives into me. I am so fucked up.

"Family," I say with a shrug.

"So you brought your whole mob family down here to lean on my family," he says. "Because you think we had something to do with your brother disappearing."

"I know you did," I growl, all the lusty feelings vanishing with one thought. Guilt and sorrow war inside my chest, but I won't let Devlin see it. I'll be as heartless as he is, and then some.

"And you never stopped for a second to consider that maybe we didn't," he says, shaking his head in disgust. "Because we're the evil, evil Darlings, so it must have been us."

Before I can respond, he turns and jogs over to his tree to retrieve the football.

"No one else here wants to hurt my brother," I say to him, knowing he can hear me even when he doesn't respond. This time, he winds up properly, his back to me as he readies the ball and then hurls it toward the tire swing.

"It seems to me that if your dad came down here to escape some trouble he got in with the mafia, maybe they'd want to hurt your brother."

"You're wrong," I say to his back.

He wheels around to face me. "Why are you out here, Crystal?"

I retreat a step when I see the pure fury blazing in his eyes. He might have indulged me a little, teased me a little, but he doesn't want me out here. He doesn't want to be around me. The realization twists painfully inside me. Devlin still hates me. I might feel something different for him now, but he doesn't.

"I don't know," I mutter, shaking my head and taking another step back.

"I think you do," he says, striding over to me and grabbing my chin. "Don't be shy now. Tell me. Tell me you want me to throw you down on the ground and choke you so hard you black out while I cum inside that tight little pussy. If that's what you want, stop fucking around and just say it."

"That's not what I want," I say, slapping his hand away. Because as much as I want that, I want more than that. I want something that I see now he'll never give me. Something he can't give. I'm so fucking stupid.

He stares at me, his breath coming hard. "Then why the fuck are you out here? You don't need money. You don't care about anything but your family. I can't do anything else for you."

I stare at him, my heart thudding in my ears. Is that... frustration in his voice? He stares back at me expectantly. Like I should have something to say to that.

But I don't.

Devlin bends and scoops up the ball in one hand, turning away as he stands. "You broke my cousin's arm," he says. "You should know there will be retaliation."

"Me?" I ask, anger emerging from the swirling emotions inside me. "I didn't break his arm, Devlin. I didn't touch him. That's between you three and my brothers. You're the one who dragged me into the middle of it. I've never wanted anything to do with any of this."

He pauses, his back to me, his hand hanging by his side with the football still clutched in it. I watch his silhouette outlined by the pale glow of the light in the tree, frustrated that I can't see his reaction. "Yeah, well, like you said, there you are," he says at last. "Right in the middle of it."

"Why?" I demand. "Why can't you leave me out of it? Why can't you all just leave me alone?"

Devlin turns back slowly, his eyes glinting like steel as they fix on mine. "Don't you think I've asked myself that question a hundred times?"

I stare back at him, not sure what to say to that. Is he saying he's tried to leave me alone? That he thinks about me as often as I think of him? Does he lie in bed thinking about me just next door, untouchable, unreachable, completely off-limits?

"So… What?" I ask. "What are you going to do to us now?"

"I don't know," he says. "It's not my call."

Interesting. I figured he made all the calls. But of course he can't tell me anything useful. Just enough to keep me hanging on his every last word, begging for scraps.

"Then why are you telling me this?" I ask, gritting my teeth with frustration.

"I'm doing you a favor," he says, his eyes dark in the shadows of the night. "I'm telling you to watch out for yourself, Crystal. It's too late to tell you to leave us alone. You did permanent damage. They'll repay you in kind."

They.

He didn't say *we.* Maybe he's not the one running the show. I remember Chase telling me something about the Grampa knowing everything. And Nonna said basically the same thing.

"Do your worst," I challenge, holding out my arms. "You've already broken me. I'm your little dog now, right? Here I am, begging for scraps."

"This has nothing to do with the Darling Dog," he says. "You brought that on yourself."

"Oh, right. By standing up for some poor freshman you were humiliating."

Devlin smirks. "Exactly."

"Then why fuck with me beyond that?" I ask. "If it has nothing to do with that, why drag me into this shit with my brothers? Because I'm a girl? Is that why you pulled me into the middle of something that has nothing to do with me, just to get back at my brothers?"

He doesn't answer.

"That's bullshit." I spit out the words, too frustrated to care if I sound like a bitch.

"Yeah," he says, surprising me even more. "The most vulnerable one gets taken down first. That's just the way it is."

"That's not fair," I point out. "I didn't ask to be part of this bullshit war between our families."

Devlin lets out a puff of breath and shrugs. "Like you said, this is war. All's fair."

It's not fair, and that pisses me off beyond words. I want to cry at the unfairness of it. Not just that he used me, but that we couldn't be together even if we wanted to be. We've gone too far now—both of our families have. I feel the ache of unshed tears behind my eyes, in my throat. Fuck. I'm too vulnerable to be around a Darling right now.

"So, what now?" I whisper, forcing the tears back. "You fucked me and threw me away. You made your point with my family. You broke me, Devlin. And you got Royal. That's worse than we could ever do. So why keep destroying us? You've already won."

"It's not that easy," he says. "Not with my family. They won't stop until this town is rid of every one of you and the dirty money you brought with you."

"You want to drive us out of town," I murmur, halfway to myself. "Just like last time."

But last time, no one disappeared.

Did they?

Devlin hesitates, then says quietly, "Preston didn't take Royal. I don't know who did, but…"

"What?" I ask, my heart beating so hard I can't hear my own whispered word.

Devlin runs his palm up the back of his head. "I'll ask around," he says, avoiding my gaze.

Tears brim in my eyes, and I want to believe him. I want to believe so bad it aches. But I've been deceived by one too many Darlings. I'm not the trusting girl who climbed in the limo with Colt a week ago. Tonight, I won't be partying. I'll go home, and I'll replay every word of this night until morning. I'll read between the lines and decipher every word for hidden clues. I'll be the best damn detective this shitty little town has ever seen. Because I will find my brother. And when I do, they will fucking pay.

I blink, letting a single tear trickle down my cheek. I'm glad Devlin's not looking into my eyes, because he would see the burning fury of a thousand suns in mine instead of the meek little girl he believes me to be when I whisper, "Thank you."

eighteen

Devlin

Crystal turns, but I catch her elbow before she can walk away. I'm not ready to let her go yet. I want to play with my puppy, have a little fun with her first.

"I'm not going to find what you want," I say. And then, because I can't help being a dick, I add, "But if you want to thank me, you can do it on your knees."

"Why would I thank you if you can't find my brother?"

"You tell me," I say, stepping closer. Even in a hoodie and furry boots, she's cute as fuck. She's so short I could pick her up, toss her over my shoulder… And carry her off to do very bad things to her. "You were ready to thank me in your room yesterday morning."

"I did thank you," she said.

"How about a proper thank you," I say, letting my fingers skim lightly up the outside of her thigh. Her lips part, and her eyes widen just a fraction. It's enough to send a swell of that addictive power through me—and to send the blood rushing to my dick. This girl is dangerous as fuck.

"Thank you," she says. "For showing me exactly how much I mean to you."

I draw back and quirk an eyebrow.

"See, you could have just fucked me the way you fuck other girls," she says.

"You've been watching me fuck other girls?" I ask, smirking at her. "You really are kinky."

She smirks right back at me. "Like I'm nothing. At first, I thought that's what it was. Just another notch on your bedpost."

"Who says you're not?"

"You did," she says, leaning up toward me, laying a hand on my chest. I can tell she's fucking with me now, but I can't extricate myself from the spiderwebs she's weaving. "You said it wasn't personal. That I was just a pawn in your game to get back at my brothers. My brothers took your parking spot. So you wrecked Royal's car. He wrecked yours. So you wrecked me."

I scowl at her. "So?"

I wait, hating that I'm hanging on her every word like I'm the fucking dog here.

She wets her lips, her little pink tongue darting out and making me wonder what it would feel like on my cock. Maybe I just need to keep fucking her until I get it out of my system, because it sure as hell hasn't gotten any better since I fucked her a second time. And this time, I know she's doing it intentionally, that she's every bit as calculating in this moment as any other girl who's tried to lay a trap for me or one of my family. But fuck if I'll let her do what no one else has managed to do.

"So, everyone in this town knows how much you loved that car," she murmurs. "It was your most prized possession. If my virginity was worth your car, then you must think I'm worth a fortune, Devlin Darling."

I jerk my hand away from her arm. I hate this girl, the plotting little snake. This is a girl I have no problem destroying. I want to destroy her, to erase her, to bring her back to the girl she is when I'm inside her, the girl who whimpers helplessly with need. That's where she belongs— on her back, begging for my cock to wreck her. This girl… This girl is one who needs to be broken, put in her place.

"You're not worth shit," I say. "You couldn't even get someone to fuck you for a ride back to school."

"I didn't have to," she says, that conniving smirk all over her lips. "I'm not a whore, despite your best efforts to make everyone believe otherwise by telling everyone what happens between us. You want to call me trashy, but you're the one who goes around talking about what we do behind closed doors. All the money in the world can't make that anything other than what it is—low class."

"Says the girl who let me fuck her in a public bathroom."

"Says the boy who dragged me in there to fuck," she shoots back.

"I didn't drag you in there to fuck," I say. "I wanted to talk to you."

"Deny it all you want, but there were two people in that bathroom who wanted it," she says. "I didn't hear you telling me to get lost."

She's really pushing my limits, and I don't handle that well. Maybe I've got anger issues, but she knows it, and she's provoking me. She's about to learn what happens when she pokes the beast. I step forward and grab her by the back of her neck, pulling her close enough that our noses almost touch. "I've told you to get lost, but you just keep coming back like a fucking cockroach," I say. "So let me make it clear one more time. You're not welcome. Your family is not welcome. We don't want you here. And I don't want you, period."

Crystal's hand wraps around my dick, and I suck in a breath. "Could have fooled me," she whispers.

"Yeah, I'm a guy, and you're a hole," I say, stroking my nose along hers. "That doesn't mean I want you. I only fucked you because my grandpa was busy that day."

She tries to draw back, but I clamp my hand tighter around the back of her neck, keeping her in place. "What does that mean?" she demands, her playfulness gone.

Good. I knew she'd break first.

"He would have fucked you himself, but he had something better to do that night," I tell her. "So I did him a favor."

She wriggles around, and for a minute, we wrestle for control. She arches her back so her tits press right up against my chest, and I lose my concentration. Then she twists sideways and ducks under my hand, spinning away from me. "What the fuck, Devlin," she says, her hair all messed up from her escape, her eyes wild and her breaths coming in quick little puffs in the early November night. "You think I'd hook up with your *grandpa?*"

I shrug. "If he wanted you."

"You're disgusting," she says, spitting the words at me like bits of ice from a wintery sky.

"I told you it wasn't personal," I say, tucking my hands in my pockets like I don't want to reach out and touch her flushed face, run my fingers through her chocolate mane, smother her smart mouth with mine. "I didn't even choose you. It was just a job. You should know all about those, if you're the mafia princess you claim to be. Call it a hit. And trust me, Sugar, I might have enjoyed hitting that, but it was never payment for my car. Your ass wouldn't buy a tank of gas for my car."

nineteen

Crystal

I'm so mad I can't think straight. I can't think at all. I just turn and run because I know if I don't, I'm going to explode. Devlin's voice cuts through the night, a sharp command, but I don't stop. The next second, I hear his footsteps behind me, quick and light as he races after me like I intercepted the ball. But this isn't a game. Not anymore. There's too much at stake.

Devlin's hand closes around my upper arm, yanking me to a stop so fast I whip around and without thinking, strike him. My palm stings across his cheek, and Devlin's head snaps back. His eyes widen, and I cringe backwards, expecting a blow in return. Instead, he grabs me and wrenches me to him, his mouth smashing down on mine. For one second, I let myself have what I want so much, more than anything in the world.

And then reality crashes over me. What he's done to me, said to me, burns through the fog in my mind, stinging through my veins like acid.

I tear myself from him and throw my hair back, trying to collect myself. "No, Devlin," I say, hurling the words at him like missiles. "You can't just kiss me and think it erases everything you just said. You can't just—"

I don't get to finish, because he grabs me and kisses me again, his mouth claiming mine with the force of a hungry tiger. His teeth clash with mine, and I taste blood, and I don't care if it's his or mine. I want this kiss, his kiss, to last forever. This is the only place where we're good, and I don't want to ruin it. My body welcomes the kiss, swooning with relief against him, my thirst quenched at last.

"No," I say again, but this time, Devlin holds on tight when I try to break free. I struggle, yanking at my arms, but he holds fast. I lose my footing on the slippery dew and go down, and Devlin drops with me, rolling onto me and pinning my hands. My body awakens at the contact, and I writhe like a live wire, aching for the pleasure and pain of his brutality. I can't tell if I'm trying to free myself or rub myself against him until he's the one who breaks, until he can't resist the temptation of my body under his any more than I can resist him.

"Crystal, would you—"

This time, I cut him off. "Let me go," I bark, jerking my hands free. I buck under him, rolling us sideways. He grabs my hips, flipping us until I'm on top of him. I sit up, straddling his hips, and pull back. My hand blazes across his other cheek like lightning, and I relish the sting against my palm, the fury that storms his eyes and takes them over.

"You fucking bitch," he says, snatching my hand before I can hit him again. He flips us back over, grinding me into the ground as his hips pin mine.

"You fucking bastard," I snap back, my breath coming fast as I grab the front of his shirt and tear at it, pulling so hard the fabric tears down the middle. "I hate you."

"Ditto," Devlin growls, yanking my knee up around his hips again and grinding his hardness against me. I gasp, heat pulsing between my thighs as he pins me with his shoulders and reaches down for my pants. My feet find his hips, shoving his sweats down even as my hands brace against his shoulders to push him away. His breath is hot against my neck, sending a delicious shiver of weakness through me, and the smell of fresh sweat on his skin makes blood throb between my thighs.

"Wait." I freeze as the cold air hits my heated skin, my panting breaths heavy in the damp night. "I—I can't."

"What do you mean, you can't?" Devlin demands.

"Fuck," I mutter. "I… Have my period."

In answer, Devlin pulls my panties and pad aside and drives his hot, bare cock into me. I'm still sore from the last time, and though I'm wet and bleeding, he's so big that it hurts almost as much as the first time when he pushes himself up on his palms and buries himself to the hilt inside me. I don't care if it hurts. I want it to. I rip the front of his shirt further open, my nails raking down his bare chest and washboard abs. I want to hurt him, too.

"You're so fucking wet you make me want to cum like a virgin right now," he growls, drawing back and slamming into me a second time.

"Don't you dare," I hiss.

Devlin groans in response, jerking my knee up and driving into me with quick, angry thrusts. I scratch him again, and he grabs my hands and pins them to the ground, thrusting into me as I buck my hips. He uses the position to go even deeper, grinding his pelvic bone against me until I pant for more. He gives it to me, smashing into me over and over, fucking me into the ground.

I wrench my hands from his and wrap them around his iron biceps, digging my nails into his skin until I draw blood. Devlin grunts as I let out a soft cry with each punishing thrust, but I don't let go, and he doesn't relent. He slides his hands under me, gripping my ass with both hands to hold me still as he drives harder still, his chest crushing mine. I struggle to breathe, raking my nails down his back in protest.

Everything inside me is twisted inside out. I hate Devlin, but my body wants this, wants him. I'm fascinated by him, and terrified of him, and appalled by him, but my heart races his as our bodies crash and clash together. Pleasure takes me up, higher than I thought I could ever go. I try to hold back but I can't help myself, and his name tears from my lips as I cum.

Devlin's wordless growl meets my cry as he grinds into me one final time, his heat spilling inside me and his fingers squeezing my thigh with bruising force as he braces his other palm on the ground.

We fall together in a sweaty, panting pile. A cool breeze washes over us, chilling the wetness on my belly, my thighs, the sheen of moisture covering every inch of me. My heart is hammering in my chest, and I can feel his beating out the same rhythm against mine, as if we are made from the same whole, formed as two pieces of one being by some invisible, cruel god.

At last, my senses begin to return, and I realize what we just did. What I just let happen. Again. Even after he said those things to me.

"Get off me," I growl, shoving at him and struggling to free myself from under him. When he doesn't move, I punch at his shoulders until he rolls away, cursing under his breath.

"What the fuck is wrong with you?" he demands, sitting up and ripping what remains of his shirt off his muscular frame.

I jump to my feet, yanking my pants up, feeling the cold of my wet underwear hitting the heat between my thighs. Tears blur my vision, and I can't begin to explain to this boy my frustrations and anger, my pain and brokenness. Only one word comes, so I blurt it out, hurling it at him like an ax. "You," I spit out. "You're my fucking problem, Devlin Darling."

Without another word, I spin on my heels and run. I run across the lawn, past the lilac bushes with their lush green leaves that hide me once I'm beyond them. Shame burns through me, and fury, and so much emotion I can't contain it. It leaks out my eyes, down my cheeks, splashing onto my hands as I clamp them over my mouth to stop the sob from echoing across the space between our houses. They seemed so close once, but now the space expands as I run, and every step seems to take my house further from me.

At last, I reach the steps. That's when I make the mistake. That's when I look back, and before I even realize I'm doing it, I halfway expect Devlin to be there. To be standing between the bushes. Or following. Or calling after me.

But he's not there.

The lawn is empty except for my footprints in the dewy grass.

A sob catches in my throat, and it hurts to swallow it, but I do. I force my feet to move, to climb the stairs, one heavy step at a time. I force myself not to listen for his voice, for his footsteps that don't come. I force myself to tiptoe quietly past King's window, past Duke's, to my own. I force myself to climb through, and close the window, and lock it, and pull the curtain.

And then I let myself break. I let myself fall to pieces. I collapse onto my bed, pulling my knees to my chest and stifling my uncontrollable sobs in a frilly pillow that no longer fits the girl who bought it. I cry until my chest is a hollow cavern, until my body feels like it will turn inside out to purge itself of the unbearable ache. I cry until I'm empty, and there's nothing left inside me.

I'm not crying because he hurt me, or because the bruises on my thighs where he held me down are already blooming onto my skin. They do hurt, but I relish the pain. I press my own fingertips down on them, craving the ache. The ache of his touch, the proof that he'd been there. The proof that

Devlin Darling was inside me, that he loved me for a moment, that he gave himself to me as fully as I gave myself to him.

I cry because I'm weak. Because I don't want to crave his touch, but I do. Because I didn't want to give in, but I did. Because I can't help myself. When he touches me, I'm weak and helpless and broken, all the things a Dolce shouldn't be.

I shouldn't want the enemy. I shouldn't tremble at the thought of his hungry mouth on mine, of his tongue tasting me in ways too intimate to think about without blushing, of his thick, hard length demanding my submission.

I cry because what I said was true. Because he could have traded me for something cliché like a necklace or taken what he wanted without my permission. But he didn't. He made me want it, and that's so much worse than if he'd taken it by force. He showed me that he valued me, and that's worse than if he treated me like a cheap whore, another Darling Doll he could fuck and throw away. He may not want to admit it, but he respects me.

I sit up, clutching the soaked pillow to my chest.

Devlin Darling respects me. And the dangerous part, the part that can destroy him, is that I don't think he realizes it yet.

That's it.

That's my advantage.

I have to strike before he knows, before he realizes his own feelings for me.

twenty

Crystal

Day 5. How can you make someone pay when you have nothing they want?

We're sitting in the cafeteria at lunch the next day when I blurt out the question that's been frustrating me all morning as I mulled it over. "How do you get a guy to fall in love with you?"

"Anal," Duke says, stuffing a bite of sandwich in his mouth. My brothers all crack up, but I stare them down.

"Threesome," Baron says. "Nothing highlights the love between two people like adding a third person. It's the secret ingredient in all happy couples."

He and Duke high-five.

There are moments like these, where everything is so normal I forget that my twin isn't by my side. And then guilt twists around my heart like a strangling vine, choking off the joy before it ever really starts.

Dolly looks at me with big, sad eyes that say she knows exactly what I'm talking about even if my brothers are in too much denial to take my words seriously.

"If we knew that, don't you think we'd all have boyfriends?" Dixie asks, her longing gaze traveling to the Darlings' table, which is filled with their Dolls and their posse. Not a Darling boy in sight. It makes me jumpy, like they might appear from under our table and tell me they know what I'm scheming.

"Sing him 'Happy Birthday, Mr. President' and bake him a cake," King says. "Oh, and be Marilyn Monroe."

"I'm not talking about your freaky fantasies," I say. "I'm serious."

"Oh, it's not a fantasy," Duke says, adjusting himself under the table and hanging an arm around the back of Dolly's chair. "Anal is the answer."

"Then how come you're not in love?" I challenge.

"I will be when Dolly spreads that sweet ass and lets the anaconda in."

Dolly elbows him in the ribs, and he doubles over laughing, pulling her close as she shoves at him and giggles.

"I just threw up in my mouth," I say. "But thanks for the advice."

"Wait," King says, his eyes narrowing. "Why are you asking this?"

He looks so much like Royal when he wears that expression that my heart snaps in two. The twins fall silent, staring at me with open mouths.

"You're not…" King breaks off and shakes his head, his fists clenching on the table. "You can't mean what I think you mean."

"Look," I say. "Royal has been gone for five days. I can't just sit around and wait for the cops to do their jobs. They're not going to find him, okay?"

I stop, my throat too thick to speak, an ache gripping it like the savage fist of fate.

"We'll find him," King says. "Our family will find him. And you're not going to do anything stupid to make it worse." He wraps an arm around me and squeezes hard enough to make me catch my breath. He doesn't want me to fall apart in front of people, even when they're not looking. He held me together last year through the worst of it, telling me to be tough at school, not to let anyone knock me down from the pedestal they built for me. Royal was the one who held me when I cried, and Royal's no longer here.

Instead, there's Dolly reaching for my hand and squeezing, and King with his iron grip holding me together, and Dixie patting my knee, and the twins with the force of King's conviction magnified and reflected back at me. Because they believe in King, in our family, even when I'm starting to doubt that even they can make this one right.

"Let's take a potty break and fix our faces," Dolly says in her sugary, southern twang. "We'll be back in three shakes of a sheep's tail. You boys keep our spots warm."

King's hand closes around her arm, and he gives her a hard look. "Don't give our sister any stupid ideas. Understand?"

"Why, I don't have an idea in my pretty little head," Dolly says, deftly detaching his hand. "How could I possibly give your sister one?"

She walks off, leaving my brothers gaping after her, though I can't tell if it's because of what she said or because she looks like sex on legs. She turns to peer over her shoulder, snapping her fingers at me and Dixie when she sees that even we are too captivated by watching her walk away to have moved.

"Oh, okay," Dixie stammers, jumping up so fast she nearly knocks her chair over. Baron laughs and grabs it before it can crash to the floor, swatting her ass and making her yelp as she scurries after Dolly. I follow, my heart thudding in my chest as I join the girls. I don't know if I want to hear what Dolly has to say to me. She and the Darling boys have some relationship I can't begin to comprehend. She's known them all their lives. She might be his first kiss. His first time. His first love.

Which means maybe she knows how to make him fall in love, and I have to just suck up the way it makes me want to puke when I think of them together, of how I'm the opposite of his type, how when he sees me naked, he must think I look like a little girl compared to her breakneck curves, or at least homely and plain. No one could see her naked and then be satisfied with me. But I need this information, and if I have to suffer her story to get it, I'm going to do it.

By the time I get to the bathroom I'm shaking with dread at what lies ahead. Dolly is already leaning over the sink, applying another coat of baby pink lipstick to her plump lips when I step inside on Dixie's heels.

"So?" Dixie squeals, as excited as I've seen her since before the night of our shame. "Tell us everything. How do we get a Darling to fall in love?"

"You don't," Dolly says, dropping her lipstick back into her purse—today's is a tiny pink jeweled thing that won't hold much more than a phone.

"Wait," I say, turning to Dixie. "You want Colt to fall in love with you?"

"Well, yeah," she says, widening her eyes at me like I'm clueless.

I start to say he's a snake, but then I stop myself, because anyone would say that about Devlin, too. And really, I don't know Colt at all, do I? I'm assuming things about him, just like everyone else does. I don't know him any more than the next girl. He shows me what he wants me to see, just like all the guys do. I'm not special. I get the same as any other girl in school, despite being their dog.

I turn back to Dolly, my eyes narrowing. "He fell in love with you," I point out. "And if I had to guess, maybe Preston has, too?"

"You're so lucky," Dixie says on a sigh.

Dolly's eyes widen, her gaze flying to the door behind me. "Preston does not love me," she hisses, her tone fiercer than I've ever heard. "And don't go around saying stuff like that. You're going to get someone killed."

I plant a hand on my hip and raise an eyebrow. "Why would anyone care if you and Preston hook up? Unless Devlin still loves you…"

My heart hammers as I wait for her answer, sure that I'll fucking die if she says he does. Why else would Devlin kill his cousin for being with her?

"Shut up," she hisses, pushing past me to lean her back against the door to keep anyone from entering. "Let's just get this straight. I'm *not* hooking up with Preston, okay? Never have, never will."

"Okay," I say, raising both hands. "There's nothing happening between you. I didn't mean to get you in trouble."

"Okay," she says, eyeing me warily. "Now, as far as your question. Devlin doesn't fall in love. Neither does Colt. None of the Darlings fall in love. Grampa Darling still arranges all their marriages ahead of time."

"Annnnd you're Devlin's future wife?" I guess.

Explains why she doesn't want anyone to know she "skips class" with Preston every few days.

"Oh my god, are you really?" Dixie asks, her eyes rounding like saucers in her pale face.

"Look, the Darlings aren't like other boys," Dolly says. "They don't love anything but each other. Those boys… They'd die for each other. So if you think I'm coming between them, you're wrong. And you won't, either."

"I'm not trying to come between them," I say. I'd be lying if I said their devotion to each other doesn't impress me, though. I've seen the same thing in my own family. My brothers are ride-or-die for each other all the way. The only time a girl comes between them is when she's in the middle of a threesome. I can respect guys who are that loyal to each other and their family, even if that family wants to destroy mine. It's an admirable quality.

"Colt would never pick a girl like me," Dixie says with a sigh, back to the dejected girl she's been all week.

"Look, you need to just forget them," Dolly says, addressing both me and Dixie. "They don't fall in love. I dated Devlin, but he never loved me. I don't think he's capable of it. If there was a way to make him fall in love, don't you think someone would have done it by now? You can't think you're the first girl who wanted to make the Darlings fall in love."

"You're right," I say. "God, I'm so stupid. Of course he's not going to fall in love. I'm just like every other pathetic girl who wanted to snag them."

"You're not pathetic," Dolly says, her expression softening. "Trust me, I get it. I *so* get it, girl. But to those boys… They have football, and they have their family. That's all they're allowed. That's their life. Sex is nothing but a commodity to them. Like food. They do it because they need it. They'll eat you, shit you out, flush you down the toilet, and never think of you again. I'm not telling you this because I want them for myself, or because I want to hurt you. I'm telling you because you're both badass ladies who deserve better."

Dixie snorts.

"You are," Dolly insists. "You don't care what anyone thinks of you. I know how much shit you get for that. The mayor is my father. Believe me, I know how much pressure there is to be what they want. And you." She turns to me. "You made me see that being a Darling Doll is no better than a Darling Dog. It's all just bullshit to feed their egos, do their bidding, and support the hierarchy. I owe you for that, Crystal. I was so deep in it I don't think I ever would have seen that if you hadn't stumbled your drunk ass out onto Devlin's balcony after that party."

"You love him," I say softly, remembering what she said to me that night.

"I don't know how I feel anymore," she says. "It's complicated. Your brothers… It's like I was trapped in this tiny closet of a world, and I'd been breathing the same air for so long I didn't know the oxygen was gone from the room. I was suffocating until they opened the door. There's so much more out there than Willow Heights. So much more than Faulkner, Arkansas. Maybe I don't want to be the mayor's daughter and a pawn in Old Man Darlings' game all my life."

"What are you going to do?" Dixie asks, her eyes wide. "Where will you go?"

"I don't know," Dolly says. "Somewhere else. No one in this town is free. Not if you show up on Daddy Darling's radar."

"You're running away?"

"No," she says, shaking her head. "I'm not dumb. I'm going to graduate first. But then I'm out of here."

I think about her going off on her own, about how people outside this town will see her. Hell, how I saw her until I talked to her. Now that I know her… I have no doubt she's going to handle it just fine.

"You're a senior?" I ask.

"Yeah," she says. "Like Devlin."

Right. Devlin's not going to be here for the next two years of high school. The thought is strangely forlorn, like thinking of a football field after the lights go off and the stands sit empty. Like an empty throne in an abandoned castle.

My brothers can take that throne next year. It'll be easy with the leader of the Darling boys gone.

But that dream is hollow now. There's no longer four Dolce brothers. What does a metaphorical throne matter when the person who belongs on it is a ghost?

twenty-one

Crystal

Someone bumps against the bathroom door, startling me enough to scare away the tears before they arrive. Dolly steps away from the door, and a group of girls I recognize as Darling Dolls enters the bathroom in a cloud of perfume and giggles. As soon as they see us, the temperature around us drops. Their smiles turn to scowls, and they glare at us with open hostility.

"From the queen Darling Doll to sleeping with the dogs," Carmen says, crossing her arms and smirking at Dolly. "Or are you a dog, too?"

"You can't go from Doll to Dog," says a girl named Becca. She casts a disdainful look at me and Dixie. "Or the other way."

"Not interested," I say, turning to the mirror to check my makeup like I can't be bothered with her.

Carmen snorts. "Oh, please. We all know you let the Darlings run a train on you in the bathroom the other day. But if you think getting all three at once makes you special, don't even."

Dixie's face reddens, and she drops her gaze when I try to meet her eyes in the mirror. Well, that rumor escalated quickly.

"Good to know," I say. "So I guess all of you have been there, done that."

"We can have them any time we want," says a blonde girl with hours' worth of contouring trying to hide the fact that she has a horse face. "We're the Dolls, and I'm head cheerleader."

"So you've all let the Darlings run a train on you, and I'm the slut," I say, rolling my eyes.

"No, you're a *dog*," Becca says. "Don't forget your place in this school."

"Yeah," the Head Bitch says. "If they took turns all at once, that just means they're getting it over with quicker so they can go back to treating you like the dog you are. They just give you one taste so you'll beg like a dog for the rest of the year. How pathetic are you? You must have no class whatsoever to let them treat you like that."

I shrug. "Says a bunch of girls who let them collar you with a necklace and order you to do their bidding. I still don't see any difference between Dolls and the Dog. Think about it. Dolly has. I won't hold this against you if you want to come over to the other side."

"The difference is you're a dirty animal," Carmen says, her eyes flashing with anger. "You're a lap dog to them, and we're their queens. They respect us as equals. You're lower than the dirt on the bottom of their shoes."

I snort and look around their group as if searching for someone. "Didn't you used to have a friend named Lacey? Where is she now? I notice she doesn't sit with you since she ate dog food off the floor. You think the same thing can't happen to you? They can take everything from you with a snap of their fingers. And you know why? Because you let them. You play into the charade."

Carmen steps forward, getting up in my face. "It's not a charade. We're queens in this school. The top of the social ladder. You're yapping and running around the base of it because you can't even climb the first rung."

"You know, I feel bad for you," I say. "I've been where you are, and I wouldn't want to be there again. When you come around, talk to us. We'll be here for you. Now, if you'll excuse me, I have to go freshen up my lady bits. Gotta make sure the station's fresh and clean for that train coming through soon."

"Ugh, you really are an animal," Becca says with a scoff.

I turn to the mirror and pull my sleek pony forward over one shoulder, surveying the belted dress that skims over my hips and falls to the top of my kneecaps. I look as prim and proper as a girl on the WHPA brochure. I give the Dolls a sugary smile. "Must be why all three of your boyfriends fuck me like animals."

When they leave in a huff, Dixie stares at me in awe. "You really did used to be a mean girl, didn't you?"

"Yeah. I was." I smooth my skirt to wipe the sweat from my palms. I fucking hate cutting down other girls. I never wanted to do that again. But I'm not going to lay down and roll over when they treat me like a dog.

"Did you really let the Darlings… You know." Dixie's face reddens, and she drops her gaze again.

"Of course not," I say, trying to calm my racing heart and shaking hands.

"Why'd you say that?" Dixie asks. "You're just making it worse for yourself."

I snort. "I think we're past that. How can it be worse? Denying the rumors doesn't make them go away. People are going to believe them no matter what I say. I might as well embrace the fact that I'm now the school slut. Maybe I can get something out of it."

"She's right," Dolly says in her sweet lilting drawl. "You can't stop the rumor train. You just gotta ride it until someone more interesting gets on."

"I got off it," Dixie says quietly.

"You miss it, don't you?" I ask, cocking my head and studying my complicated friend.

"Yeah," she admits with a shrug. "But I knew it wouldn't last. A fat freshman is a boring target. It's predictable. Obviously, *I'm* a dog."

"Fuck that," I say. "No one here is a dog. Don't let me hear you say that again."

"Fine," she says. "But you have to admit it's more interesting for both the spectators and the Darlings themselves when they're picking on someone their own size."

"Maybe that applies if you're talking about my brothers, but I'm hardly their size."

"You're a challenge," Dixie says. "Ruining you is harder. In their eyes, I was ruined before I got here. They were just biding their time with me because they needed a dog. They always wanted someone spicier."

"Devlin does love a challenge," Dolly says, studying me critically.

"Who picks the Darling Dog?" I ask. "You said there's only one at a time. Do they only last one year?"

One year of this shit might do more than ruin me. It might kill me.

"The guys pick the Dog," Dolly says. "But from what I've heard, it's not just them."

"What do you mean?" I ask, my heart flipping.

"Grampa Darling has a finger in every pie when it comes to his family," she says. "He knows what's going on with all five of his sons and all their kids, too. At least the legitimate ones. I bet there's a dozen or more Darling bastards scattered around town, too."

"Doesn't he have seven sons?" I ask.

Dolly glances at the door and lowers her voice. "Yeah, but he disowned a couple of them. We don't talk about them. They don't even use his last name."

"Damn."

"Yeah," she says. "The grandkids that go here are obviously his favorites, though. I mean, their family helped found this school. I hear Grampa Darling and a bunch of the sons are still in the Midnight Swans. You'll see them up at school sometimes at odd hours."

"The Midnight Swans?" I ask, my own voice lowering with excitement despite myself.

"The secret society?" Dixie whispers, her eyes wide.

"Yeah," Dolly says. "I don't think I'm supposed to know about it, but I heard my dad talking about it once when I was a kid. They're super exclusive, and you have to go through some big hazing-type ceremony to get in. Once you're in, though… You're in for life."

Sounds a lot like the mafia, I think. I keep that to myself, though.

"Wow," Dixie breathes. "I wonder if my dad's in it."

"Pretty much everyone who's a member goes to an Ivy League school, and every big-shot here in Faulkner has been a member," Dolly says. "All the alums in the area come to the meetings, and of course the new initiates."

"Which are the three Darlings who go to school here," I guess.

"Yeah," she says. "They meet here at night. I'm pretty sure Grampa Darling is the head of the Swans, but I'm sure only the members know that for sure."

Realization jolts through me. Last night, Devlin told me he'd "ask around" about Royal. He had to mean he'd ask his grandfather, the guy who apparently knows everything that goes on in this town. I can't help the rush of adrenaline that races through me at the knowledge that he's going to take that risk for me. For my brother, who he hates.

Maybe I can make him fall for me after all. Maybe he's already starting to.

My pulse flutters at the thought, but I push away those feelings and turn to my friends. "Do you know when and where they meet?"

"No," Dolly says. "Crystal, you can't do whatever you're thinking about doing. If you spy on their meeting, they'll… I don't know what they'd do. But you don't want to do that."

"Maybe I do," I say.

Before she can argue, the bell rings. A group of girls enter the bathroom, and we walk out.

Both of Devlin's cousins are standing not two feet outside the bathroom like some sort of creepers. When Preston sees us, his eyes blaze with fury. His wrist and forearm are in a cast. I wince, swallowing hard. I didn't mean for him to get hurt like that. A milk shower is hardly worth a football career.

"You're hanging out with *her?*" he asks, his gaze burning into me.

"I told you, I'm tired of being your doll," Dolly says. "You don't get to pick my friends. Go to hell, Preston Darling."

She pushes past him and marches off, her tiny pink purse swinging from her wrist.

"Get lost, Winn-Dixie," Colt says, tossing his hair off his forehead and jerking his chin toward my other friend.

"Sorry," she whispers to me before scurrying away.

I look from one boy to the next, my heart in my throat, replaying what Carmen said. Was that a rumor that escalated, or a warning of what they have planned?

"You," Preston says to me, his tan cheeks flushed darker with anger. Everything about him is sharp as a blade—his eyes, his chin, his jaw, the spikes in his hair. He's all angles and cold fury. He takes one step forward, his broad shoulders menacing as he backs me against the wall. "Why the fuck are you still here?"

A shiver goes through me, and I swallow hard before speaking. "I'm sorry," I say truthfully. "I wouldn't wish that injury on anyone, Preston. Not even you."

His blue eyes pierce into me, and he crowds forward until he's almost touching me, just an inch of space between us. He speaks slowly, gritting out the words. "You better leave this school and disappear like your brother."

"Don't you dare talk to me about Royal," I hiss back. "Unless you're telling me where he is."

"The only thing I'm telling you is to go away," he says. "If you're not gone by the end of the day, you're going to be sorry you ever set foot in this school."

He turns and walks away, leaving me standing there shaking with Colt. He tosses his hair out of his eyes in that casual gesture, like what just happened is nothing to him. "If I were you, I'd listen," he says. "Why don't you go on back to New York where you belong? Wouldn't that be nicer than having everyone despise you? That can't be fun, now can it, Sweetie Pie?"

"Fuck off and die," I say, pushing away from the wall. "You know, every time I talk to one of you, I think that one has to be the worst."

"Now, don't be like that," he says with an easy grin, falling into step beside me. "You know we're warning you for your own good. Preston's going to rape your ass if you don't listen."

I stop in the middle of the hall, letting everyone else go around, though half of them slow and crane their necks to see what their prince is doing with me, the school dog.

"Seriously, what is it, Colt?" I demand. "Do you have a contest to see which one of you can be most psychotic every day?"

Colt steps closer, dropping his voice and touching my elbow. Our eyes meet, and for a moment, I see real concern. This is the boy who was my friend, the boy who joked with me in class, the boy who kissed me at homecoming.

And then I remember that's the same boy who organized a truce and took me to homecoming so his family could ambush my brother while we weren't around.

He leans closer, bending to speak into my ear. "Watch your back."

The next second, he's disappearing down the hall, his threat still sending chills through me.

twenty-two

Devlin

Other girls might chase me, but they'd never catch me. For Preston, that might have been a thrill. That was his game. Give them just enough to have hope. Make them chase it, make them degrade themselves. See how far they'd debase themselves for a chance to be his plaything, his Darling Doll. Half the time, he never gave them what they wanted. That's what really broke them.

They never caught me for another reason. I had no interest in being caught. I had no interest in being chased. I had no interest, period.

And then she came along. A girl who wouldn't chase me. A girl who didn't even hang around me, pretending she wasn't waiting for a cue, a sign that I might be interested. That's what they did with Preston. Even the girls who claimed not to want him, who played hard to get, they were just waiting for him to smile at them, to give them that seed of hope. And when he did, they were on him like .

Crystal didn't wait around giving me sidelong glances and hoping I'd look. She was smart. She avoided me. She stayed the hell away from me.

Even after what had happened between us, she didn't get clingy or needy like Dolly had. She couldn't be made to chase me. She respected herself too much for that. And that made me respect her. That made her the first girl who'd ever made me want to chase her.

twenty-three

Crystal

My heart hurts for people who go through life alone. The people who don't have a whole army of family to hold them up. Who don't have amazing friends to fall back on. Most of all, for the girl whose life I destroyed. Now I understand. I know how it feels to just be so. Fucking. Done.

"We're going to find Royal and take down the Darlings once and for all," Daddy says. He stands at a table set up in the living room, papers and maps strewn across it. "We all have a part to play. If you know your part because we already discussed it today, you can go ahead and get started."

Uncle Benny and Uncle Donny take a map and sit down on the couch, their heads bent together as they discuss whatever they're doing. King and Uncle Vinny join another group which includes a couple cousins, our grandfather, a great uncle, and a guy I call uncle even though he's no blood relation. Our family is complicated.

To be honest, I'm not sure I want to know what they're planning. I don't care. If it gets Royal back, and he's okay, it's worth anything.

"The whole county's looking," Daddy continues. "The mayor had a press conference today. The police force is on board, thanks to Vinny leaning on them a little." He raises a glass to the lawyer in the family, and a sober chorus of 'hear, hear' goes up before everyone turns back to their business.

"Your school is conducting their own investigation into anyone who might know anything. Remember, we want to get their focus on the Darlings and keep it there. Go talk to the administration at school. I'll do the same. Don't leave out anything about how much those boys were tormenting you."

Something funny twists in my belly. It's true that the Darlings have done nothing but attack and antagonize us since we arrived. But going after them like this feels somehow wrong.

I push the thought away. Anything that brings Royal home is right. If we have to step on a few toes to do it, that's just the way things are. They'd do the same to us.

"Where's Mom?" I ask, glancing around.

There's a beat of silence before Nonna takes my hand and squeezes. "Your mother's resting," she says.

"You mean drunk?" I ask, pulling away.

No one answers.

"Well, it's true," I say. "I'm tired of pretending. You don't have to shield and protect me. I'm not a kid. I know Mom's a lush. And I want to help find Royal. So, here's what I'm going to do. I'm going to make Devlin Darling fall in love with me, and he's going to tell me everything he knows about Royal, the Midnight Swans, and the Darling patriarch. And then I'm going to leave him like he left me."

The uncles shift and check Daddy's reaction.

"Crystal, we're not going to let him use you like that," King says. "You know Royal wouldn't want you to do that for him."

"No," Daddy says, holding up a hand to silence his oldest son. His eyes remain fixed on me, though. "I think that's a good plan, Crystal. Keep us updated as it unfolds."

I stand there, disbelieving. Most of me is relieved it went so well, happy that he so readily agreed, but a part of me is hurt, too. I really must be ruined in Daddy's eyes for him to let me use my body that way.

"Really?" I ask.

"They've halted construction on my new office building," he says. "I'm losing money on it every day. The slab was supposed to be poured a week ago. We need to get their focus off the business side of things and get personal."

"I say pour the slab, anyway," Uncle Donny says. "When has a little red tape ever stopped Tony Dolce?"

Donny is pretty much the adult version of Duke—loud, crude, and proud as fuck of our family name.

"You're right," Daddy says. Then he turns to my twin brothers. "In the meantime, one of you needs to keep the mayor's daughter happy. Buy her whatever she wants."

"On it," Duke says, lifting a hand.

"Good," Daddy says. "Baron, I want you to work your charms on the old bastard's favorite granddaughter. Show them if they want to get personal, we can play that game, too."

"Wait, what?" I ask. No one pays any attention. They've moved on to the next Darling they need to ruin. Well, I wanted to step out on my own a bit, to see what was beyond the little bubble my family so carefully maintains for me. This is a chance to do that. To be treated as an equal, or as close to it as they can manage. I'm not naïve enough to think my brothers treat girls with love and respect, but I don't want them to do to anyone what Devlin did to me.

"Mabel?" Baron asks, making a face.

"Yes, Mabel," Daddy says. "You think you can do that?"

Baron casts Duke a baleful look and then nods. "I'll try. But I'm pretty sure she's a robot."

"And King," Daddy says, addressing my oldest brother. "When you're not working with your uncles, you can work on Mrs. Darling next door."

"What?" I whisper, staring at my father like I've never seen him before. Whispers about the mafia are one thing.

Mom's paranoia about Daddy's leaving her for a younger woman is one thing. This? This is something else.

"You wanted to sit at the grownup's tables," Duke says with a grin, leaning back in his chair and hooking his hands behind his head. "Welcome to the adult version of the Dolces."

"Everyone clear about your assignment?" Daddy asks.

"Crystal clear," I mutter. "If only I can pull it off."

"You're a Dolce," Nonna says, smiling at me with a twinkle in her eye. "We women know how to make men fall in love with us."

"We do?" I ask. "I'm pretty sure I didn't inherit that trait."

"Let's take a little walk," Nonna says, giving me a wink. "I could use the fresh air."

"Now?" I ask, stretching my arms over my head. It's close to midnight, and I know she just wants to smoke. In truth, though, I just don't want to risk running into a certain insomniac football god out on the lawns.

"It'll give us some time to talk, woman to woman," Nonna says, tucking my hand into the crook of her elbow.

Her grip is stronger than you'd expect if you didn't know my grandmother has been taking martial arts lessons for years to keep herself in shape.

She drags me toward the door, only pausing to let my grandfather in front of us. He plucks her coat from the rack and holds it out while she slips her arms in. He leans down to give her a kiss on the lips, then opens the door for us. She slaps his ass on her way out the door. God, no wonder I'm such a horndog. I definitely inherited that trait from the Dolce side.

Once we're out on the lawn, though, I'm glad to be outside. The air is cool and crisp, and a silvery half-moon illuminates the grass, dried by a brisk wind tonight. Leaves tumble and swirl across the grass, ripped from the giant oak where Devlin's tire swing hangs and the lilac bushes between our properties. I pull my light jacket tighter around myself and hook my arm through Nonna's. She stops at the corner of the house, using it to shelter the flame as she lights her cigarette. Then, we walk out across the grass.

"So, you're going to tell me how to make a man fall in love?" I ask.

Nonna must hear the skepticism in my voice, because she laughs and bumps her hip against mine. "Don't sound so surprised. Your grandfather and I still have a very active love life."

"Ugh," I say. "Never mind. I'm sorry I asked."

"Don't be," she says. "I'm glad you're old enough for me to share my wisdom. You know, I tried to share it with your mother once, before she married my Tony. But she wasn't having any of the old ways. If you ask me, she'd have been a lot better off if she'd listened."

"Not that it's any of your business, and I wish they didn't make it mine, but my parents still have plenty of *love life,* as you so delicately put it."

Nonna laughs again, then drags on her cigarette. Leaves skitter by, scratching together with an eerie, papery rustle. "Well, in my youth, I was given a piece of advice from my grandmother. I promised to pass it on. Your mother found it very scandalous, but it hasn't failed me yet."

Mom may be a lot of things, but she's not uptight. If she found something scandalous, I'm probably not going like it too much, either.

"It hasn't failed you in what?" I ask. "Improving your sex life?"

"Oh, no," Nonna says. "That needs no help. When you have a foxy lady like me, and a besotted man like your grandfather, it comes naturally."

"Okay," I say slowly. "Then what's this magic love potion?"

"Exactly that," she says. "It makes a man fall in love with you. He can't help but fall once you've given him a taste."

"Of… What?" I ask.

"Your blood," she says. "You have to put a drop of your blood in his food."

"Well," I say. "That's a little… Crazy."

"Not just any blood," Nonna says, giving me a conspiratorial smile. "Your *special* blood."

"Your what?" I ask, then wish I hadn't. I pull my arm away. "Oh, gross! You better not mean what I think you mean."

Nonna throws her head back and laughs. "I'm afraid I mean exactly that."

"I'm telling Grandpa." I cross my arms and try to glare instead of laughing, because really, what else can I do?

"You wouldn't dare," she scolds.

"Nonna, please tell me you didn't really feed Granddad a drop of your period blood."

"I most certainly did," she says. "And I'm not sorry. It's kept our marriage strong for all these years. Your grandfather fell madly in love with me, and to this day, he'd do anything for me. If you want your fellow to do the same for you, to give you the information you want out of him, you're going to have to follow my example."

I squinch my eyes shut and try to imagine doing something like that to Devlin. "Maybe back in the seventies, that's something people did," I say. "Nowadays? Not so much."

"Just try it," Nonna says. "What's the worst that could happen?"

"I don't know," I say. "He could find out, and I could die of shame?"

"Oh, don't be ashamed," she says, waving a dismissive hand. "Women have been doing it for thousands of years.

Unless you have a better idea, you'd be wise to at least try. It won't hurt him. I promise. Your grandfather is healthy as an ox."

"I don't know…"

I think of last night. Devlin didn't run screaming when I told him I had my period. He didn't seem to even care. Nothing about our relationship is normal, or healthy, or conventional. Nothing about it is honest or open, either. If I want to feed him a little extra seasoning in his coffee, what's he going to do about it? Nothing, that's what. Even if it doesn't work, which of course it won't, it'll give me the satisfaction of knowing I fed him something disgusting.

"Fine," I say at last. "But don't be disappointed if we don't live happily ever after. I'm only getting him to fall in love with me so I can get information out of him."

And break his cruel, stone heart into a million pieces. If he even has a heart. At this point, I'd feed him magic beans if I thought it would make him fall in love. Desperate times call for desperate measures.

twenty-four

Crystal

We used to laugh at people who visited psychics, fortune tellers, and palm readers. We scoffed from atop our thrones at the peasants making idols of trinkets, clutching their rabbits feet and four-leaf clovers. How desperate, we said. Desperate, indeed.

"Here," I say, sitting down in science with two coffee cups. I shove one at Devlin before scooting in to hide my hands in my lap so he won't see them shaking.

"Now you're bringing me coffee?" Devlin asks, his eyes narrowing in suspicion. "I didn't think you were one of those girls."

"I'm not," I say. "That's so maybe you can stay awake all morning and go to fucking sleep tonight instead of keeping me up with your midnight football practice."

"It's a game day," he says. "I won't be home at midnight."

I try not to think about what that means. About what girl he'll go home with after the game, what cheerleader will attach herself to him and coo about his amazing performance, bat her lashes, and ask to see his tattoos.

"Then give it back," I say, snagging his cup. I'd forgotten about football, about what would happen in town tonight as it does every Friday. They don't really care about Royal. Sure, it was on the news when he disappeared. The mayor said if anyone saw "the runaway" to call the authorities. But no one thinks he's here.

I had forgotten that to the rest of the world, life is normal. All I was thinking was that it's the last day of the longest week of my life. If I don't do something to distract myself from the fact that it's been a week since Royal disappeared, I might implode, my heart turning to a black hole that consumes the rest of me.

"How do you know how I like my coffee?" Devlin asks, taking the drink back. A smile twitches at the corners of his lips even as he continues to eye me with wariness.

"I don't," I say. "So drink it black like a man."

Devlin deftly switches out my cup with his. "You probably poisoned mine."

"Or drink the fru-fru one," I say with a shrug. If I'm going to pull this off, I'm going to have to act like I didn't tamper with his coffee. I force my face to stay indifferent as I take a sip of his plain black coffee. I force myself not to gag as I think about what I put in it. I force myself not to search for a tang of salt or iron in the bitterness.

Thank fuck it tastes just like regular black coffee.

Devlin watches me take another sip of his coffee like he's waiting for me to fall to the floor and start foaming at the mouth. He takes one drink of mine and chokes. For a second, I think he's going to spit it back on the table. Then he shoves it back to me and snags the black coffee, taking such a big gulp it had to burn the fuck out of his mouth and throat. The guy doesn't even flinch. Either he's practiced the art of swallowing boiling water, or he can endure a shitload of pain.

"What the fuck are you drinking?" he asks.

"A cookies-and-cream cappuccino," I say. "It's delicious, in case you hadn't noticed. It has the perfect ratio of sugar, caffeine, and chocolate."

"Of course the candy-maker's daughter drinks sugar like it's water." He shakes his head and scowls, taking another drink of his coffee. I try not to stare. Not to act weird as class starts. But I keep watching him from the corner of my eye, waiting for him to taste me in his coffee. Some vicious little part of me thrills each time he takes a drink, knowing that I'm in that cup with the coffee, bewitching him with my feminine essence. A sick part of me wishes he'd notice, that he'd know he was drinking me.

He takes a drink and licks his lips, and a different kind of thrill runs through me. I press my knees together, a breathless ache growing between them as I watch his brooding, masculine profile. I imagine his tongue, his lips on me again, his strong hands pushing my thighs open, the stubble on his chin rasping against my delicate skin. Slowly, from the corner of his eye, he looks at me. And smirks.

I jerk my gaze away and duck my head. Fuck. He caught me staring. He's so fucking sexy I can't stop myself. Not two minutes later, I take another peek. This time, he's the one who looks away quickly.

I watch him drink from a cup that has a single drop of blood, like the drop I found on the driveway the morning after Royal disappeared.

This is for him. Not for me.

I drown my conflicting emotions in the sugar and caffeine of my drink, inhaling every drop and wishing I had more. There's not enough sugar in the world to make me forget about Devlin Darling.

twenty-five

Crystal

It's day 6. Is there any use in hoping?7

Midway through last period, I get a note from the office telling me to go to the gym to see Coach Snow after school. I don't even know who that is, so my suspicions are raised. At the end of class, I head for my locker. King meets me not two steps outside the classroom door.

"Again?" I ask, rolling my eyes. King's been following me around all day like a shadow.

"If those assholes were real men, they'd fight us like equals," he says. "They're three strong just like us now. But they're pussies who went after our little sister. Until I know it's safe for you at this school, you're getting an escort."

"Okay," I say. "But don't you have football practice today?"

"Yeah," he says. "You can come watch."

"Actually, I have this," I say, handing him the note. "Know anything about it?"

He scans it and hands it back with a smile. "Yeah. That's the cheer coach. Dad must have talked to her."

"Lovely," I mutter. I don't have the energy to fight Daddy right now. If he wants me to cheer, it wouldn't be the worst thing in the world. I kind of miss it sometimes. It'll take my mind off Royal, at the very least. Doing something physical that requires focus will get me out of my head for a while. And after all the bitches on the squad have put me down, I wouldn't mind showing up and blowing their small minds.

"I'll walk you down there," King says. "Come outside to the field when you're done."

We don't run into any Darlings on the way, but I spot Baron leaning against the lockers, his books tucked against his side in one hand. He's talking to the girl we saw outside the Darling's estate. She's studiously ignoring him as she digs in her locker.

"Wait a minute," I say, our conversation from the day before clicking into place. "*That's* Mabel Darling?"

"Yeah," King says, like I should know this. "Devlin's sister."

"What?" I ask, reeling with shock. Devlin has a *sister*? It doesn't make sense. I've never once seen her coming or going from Devlin's house, and I watch it more than I'd like to admit. Not to mention she blends into the crowd so well she's practically invisible. That's not something I expect of a Darling. I thought I'd blend in, but I couldn't do that for a single day at this school, and no one even knew me yet. She's from a family everyone puts on a pedestal, but I've never heard anyone so much as say her name at school. And she drives a Prius, for fuck's sake. How is this Grampa Darling's favorite?

But that's not what bothers me. What bothers me is the stupidest reason of all. Devlin never mentioned a sister.

Get it together, bitch, I tell myself sternly. I can't go getting all gooey over Devlin. I have a plan. A plan to destroy him. I have to remember that I hate him, that this is all for show. And why the fuck would Devlin tell me about his sister? It's not like we're dating.

And even when we are, when he's kissing my feet, I won't care about his sister. I'll only care that he loves me enough that I can break him and his family once and for all. I won't care that she might be a casualty in this war.

All is fair.

"She's nothing special," King says, bringing me out of my spinning thoughts. "Not like you."

"I saw her outside their house," I say. "I thought she was the help."

King laughs. "I hear she's the academic type. She's hot, though. Better than his mom."

"Are you really going to do that?" I ask, looking up at my brother as we continue down the hall.

He shrugs. "You gotta do what you gotta do. I don't mind cougars."

"Yeah, but…"

We arrive at the gym before I can articulate how I feel about that situation. King pushes open the door for me, then steps in and heads for an office off the side of the gym. A coach I've seen around campus stands and comes to meet us halfway across the gym. King reminds me to find him at practice when I'm done, then excuses himself after shaking hands with Coach Snow. When he's gone, Coach turns to me. She's short and muscular, skin tanned and tattooed below the rolled sleeves of her black polo shirt. Her short blonde hair is combed in a swoop back from her forehead, and she can't be much older than most of the students here.

"Thanks for stopping by," she says, motioning for me to follow her to her office. "I'm on my way out to my girls' practice, but I just wanted to catch you before you left for the day."

"Thanks?"

"As you probably know, I lost four of my girls mid-season, and I hear through the gossipvine you might be interested in a position on the squad." Coach sits down and kicks off her tennis shoes, reaching for a pair of canvas flats.

I'm sure she got a call from Daddy. I seriously doubt the Darlings are going to let me on the cheer team if they got Lacey and the other disgraced Dolls kicked off, but at least I can tell him I tried.

"Okay," I say slowly.

"I looked you up, and I'm impressed," Coach Snow goes on. "Your last school's squad was really something, and you're clearly talented. You interested in trying out?"

She straightens from her shoes and tosses the flop of bangs off her forehead, propping her hand on one knee and looking at me expectantly as she waits for me to accept her offer. Her voice is all business and her eyes are shrewd. I have no doubt she'll be a tough coach—the best kind.

"Yes," I say, shaking my ponytail over my shoulder to hang down my back and squaring my shoulders. "I'll have an original routine choreographed by next Friday."

"That's not necessary," Coach says, standing and gathering up a pile of pompoms and dropping them into a crate as she talks. Her sleeve slides up, revealing a pride tattoo that confirms what I already suspected.

"I don't mind," I say. "I want to try out and earn my spot, just like anyone else on the team. I don't want anyone to think you're giving me special treatment."

Coach Snow snorts and stands up, tucking the crate of pompoms under her arm. "Is that how things worked at your last school?"

"I just don't want the other girls to resent me," I say. "We're already taking their friends' spots. It's not going to make for a very cohesive squad if they hate us."

She quirks an eyebrow. "Us?"

"Oh, yeah," I say. "I have two friends who will be trying out with me."

She rubs her temple, and for a minute, I think she'll say no. I'm not going to cry about it if she does, but I don't want to be on the squad with a bunch of bitches who hate me. If I climb, I'm bringing my friends up with me.

"Okay," she says, lifting her head and nodding. "Next Friday."

She starts to turn toward the door, but I stop her. "Wait," I say. "Are you… From around here?"

"Born and raised," she says, her chin jutting just a bit.

"Are you a Darling?" I ask.

She laughs. "You're wondering how an out lesbian got a job at a fancy school in a small town like Faulkner?"

"Well…"

"The way I see it, if you want to make it around here, you can either be what they want you to be, or do what they want you to do," she says. "Most days, think I made the right choice."

She swings around and heads out, leaving me standing there to digest her words.

I start for the door that leads out to the football field, but just as I reach it, it swings open, and I find myself face to face with Preston. My heart does a little flip in my chest, and not for a pleasant reason. I freeze, and he pauses when he sees me, just staring for a long moment.

Finally, he steps inside, forcing me back a step if I don't want to collide with his broad, solid chest. He releases the door, letting it close behind him with a click of finality when it latches. His eyes never leave mine. "I thought I told you to disappear and not come back," he says, his voice a threat that sends a shiver cascading across my skin.

"I thought I told you I won't bow to your demands," I shoot back, forcing my tone to remain even, though my heart is hammering in my chest.

"You're not very smart, are you?" Preston asks, taking a single step toward me.

"Don't confuse lack of obedience with lack of intelligence," I answer. "I know what I'm doing."

I curse myself the moment the words are out of my mouth. I can see Preston latch onto them, his sharp eyes focusing in on me with more interest than I like.

"I bet," Preston says, cocking his head to one side. "I think you're more conniving than my boy gives you credit for."

"I don't know what you're talking about," I say, taking a step back, hoping to put distance between us without him noticing.

His eyes drop to my feet for just a second. I'm not pulling anything over on this Darling boy. "I think you do," he says slowly. "You like to play the innocent victim, but you've got venom in your veins, don't you, Dolce?"

"I think that's the first time you've ever called me by my name instead of that stupid dog name you made for me."

"You're more than a dog," he says, stepping forward.

I step back, quirking my head to peer up at him. "I am?"

Quick as a snake, his hand whips out, his fingers closing around my wrist. "You think you are, anyway," he says. "You think you're a honey badger. But I'm going to teach you different, little doggie. You're going to learn that if we say you're a dog, you're a fucking dog."

"Let me go," I say, yanking at my arm.

Preston's grip only tightens. "See, that's the problem with you," he says. "You keep thinking you have the power to negotiate. That you have something we want. But you don't."

"I have something Devlin wants," I blurt, digging my fingernails into his hand, trying to free my other wrist.

Preston lets out a snort of laughter. "No. We didn't take your virginity because we wanted it. We took it because we knew you valued it."

So, Devlin told them I was a virgin. Of course he fucking did.

"*You* didn't take anything," I point out. "Your family didn't fuck me, Preston. No one touched me but Devlin."

Preston lets out a snort of laughter. "No, baby girl," he says, his voice dropping. "Maybe Devlin's the only one who wrecked that sweet pussy, but when my family says you're fucked, you're fucked."

"Well, I'm sure Devlin will be happy to know his dick belongs to all of you."

"It sure as shit doesn't belong to you," Preston says, stepping even closer. "You think because he busted your cherry that he gives a shit what happens to you afterwards? I could throw you naked at his feet, and he'd just step right over you and keep walking."

"Well, he's given a fuck a few more times since then," I retort, anger pulsing through the hurt. Because he's saying the same things Devlin does, and after a while, I can't help but wonder if it's true. Maybe I'm nothing but a stupid girl, thinking it means something when all it means to Devlin is an easy fuck.

A flash of surprise crosses Preston's face, so fast I could almost believe I imagined it. But I didn't. He doesn't know that Devlin's been with me again.

I don't have time to wonder why Devlin hasn't told them that part.

"Liar," Preston says, his expression settling into a scary calm. "See, that's another problem with you. You're slippery as fuck. We keep putting you in your place, and you keep popping up instead of staying where you belong—under our bootheels."

"Maybe that's because that's not where I belong," I shoot back. "And you're just too proud to admit you made a mistake. I'm not a dog, and neither is any other girl at this school. Why do you have to keep people in line anyway, Preston? Is it so scary to imagine someone could be your equal?"

He snorts, dragging me across the gym as I balk and try to dig my heels in. "No one is our equal, Lassie. Least of all, you."

"Are you afraid all your dogs might go savage and eat you?" I yank backwards as he reaches a door, and I see the sign on it, and my heart stops. He shoves the door open with his shoulder and drags me through, into the boys' locker room.

"Every dog can be broken," he says. "You're just harder to train than a good dog. Dixie, she was a good dog. Just shut up and took it. You're a difficult bitch. But that doesn't mean you can't be broken. It just makes it sweeter to watch you crumble like a cookie when you do."

"My brothers will be in here looking for me any minute," I say, my heart racing and panic clawing inside my skin.

"I don't think so," Preston says, yanking me so hard my shoulder threatens to separate if I don't follow him. I stumble after him as he shoves me into a shower, still gripping my wrist so hard my fingers have gone numb. "See, they're going to be held a little longer than everyone else, since it's their first game tonight. They'll be out of the way. And the rest of the guys… Well, they deserve a little treat before the game. They've worked so hard."

"Let me go," I say, though I've been struggling so hard my arm is losing strength, tiring itself out. I'm not weak, but Preston's a guy, bigger and stronger than I am by a long shot.

But he only has one good arm. I don't waste any time thinking about it. I ball my free hand into a fist and slam it as hard as I can into his broken arm.

twenty-six

Crystal

Preston's howl of pain is music to my ears. I don't even feel bad for him as I duck around him and dart out the door of the locker room, leaving him hunched over his arm spewing curses. I'm halfway across the gym when I hear the door bang open behind me. I don't look back. I just run.

As I reach out to push open the doors of the gym, they disappear from under my hands, and I crash headlong into a man I vaguely recognize as one of the football coaches. I stumble backwards, pinwheeling my arms for balance. Before I can completely regain my footing, an arm clamps around me from behind, pinning me to a body that's hard with muscle and shaking with rage.

"Help me," I blurt out, struggling against him.

The coach frowns and looks from me to Preston as if weighing how much this will cost him.

"This is Darling business," Preston says, his breathing still labored from the pain. "Don't come back until after practice."

"No," I cry. "You have to help me."

The coach looks away.

My hope crumbles as he shuffles his feet and then backs out of the gym, letting the heavy door fall closed in my face. My rapid breathing echoes through the gym as I kick and struggle while Preston carries me across the room, my arms pinned at my sides and my legs pistoning, striking his shins with every step he takes. When he reaches the locker room, he hurls me against the door. I have no time to react, to prepare. One moment I'm straining to break free, and the next, he uses that momentum to throw me forward. I smash into the wood, my face connecting at the same moment as my hands. The door flies inward, and I topple to my knees, too stunned to move before he's on me, his hand fisting my hair. Blood drips from my nose onto the white tile between my hands.

"You had to be a bitch," he growls, dragging me across the tile floor. "Now, you pay for your sins and the sins of your father."

He lifts me by my hair and shoves me into the tiled shower stall where he had me before. My head knocks into the tile, and I struggle to hold my skirt down as Preston yanks my legs out from under me.

"No," I scream, kicking out at him.

He pulls out a knife, grabs my foot with the hand of his broken arm, sucking in a breath through the pain. I can't imagine how much it hurts him to use that hand right now, but I don't bother trying. Something primal takes over inside me when he reaches up my skirt with that knife. I just… Lose it.

I lurch to my feet, panic stealing every thought from my mind. I have no need for pride, for the pretense of poise. I'm an animal, trapped with my back against the wall. I fight. I knock the knife from his hand. I hit and scratch, kick, bite, scream. There's only white, blind panic. Preston shoves me back over and over, until my head connects with the tile hard enough to make blackness take over my vision. My knees give way, and it's through a fog of dizziness that I feel Preston yank my hands up. He's sitting on my chest, and I can't breathe. I'm drowning in my own blood. I struggle, and the world gets dimmer.

When it begins to clear, I feel him lifting me. Something cuts into my wrists, and my shoulders are yanked up. I struggle to gain my footing, grateful when I'm pulled upwards. I sway on my feet, unbalanced because my arms are pulled over my head. I yank at my hands, only to find them tied above my head, attached to the showerhead coming out of the wall.

"Let me go," I say, my voice strangled with a sob that hasn't made its way out.

I hear Preston behind me and twist around to see him picking up the knife I knocked away.

"The harder you fight, the worse you make it for yourself," he says, his breath coming fast from the fight. "But you have to be a cunt every minute of your life. You can't just break like a normal person. So, I guess we'll have to do this the hard way."

He steps up behind me, his hot breath on my neck sending shivers of cold terror through my entire body. His arm snakes around me, the clumsy cast grazing my other hip. I whimper in fear as the cold edge of his knife brushes the sensitive skin of my inner thigh. Preston's psychotic chuckle meets my ears as he leans even closer. Slowly, he slides the knife higher. I close my eyes. I can't do this. I can't. I have to die before he does this to me. The tip of his blade presses between my thighs, and a panting sob escapes me.

Preston's knife moves away from my skin, and violent shudders wrack my body. His clumsy hand grips my dress, pulling it tight as the blade tears through it.

"Did you think I was going to fuck you with the blade of my knife?" Preston whispers in my ear.

And then he laughs.

Another involuntary sob rips through me, wrenching my shoulders when my whole body convulses with terror. Preston makes quick work of the rest of my dress, stripping it from me until I'm standing there in a bra and panties, strung up like a sacrifice.

Strangled, uncontrollable sobs grip me as he makes quick work of my bra, then slides the blade of his knife down the back of my underwear, letting me feel the blunt edge of the blade against my crack before he cuts away the fabric. He yanks it free of me, leaving me completely bare.

Leaning forward, the heat of his body like a threat against my shivering skin, he chuckles. "I could fuck you right now," he whispers, his fingers landing on my hip. His touch is nothing like Devlin's bruising passion. Preston's touch is light, almost a caress.

"No," I whisper through trembling lips, my body going rigid at the promise in his fingers. It's the only word I can even think. The fight is drained from me, leaving me in a cold paralysis of dread.

"Yes," he says, his voice lilting as his mouth brushes my ear. "I could. Don't you see, Crystal? You don't get a choice. You never had a choice in any of this. You're just a pawn to us, the same way you're a pawn to your own family. There's no way to escape the game except to be taken out of play."

I squeeze my eyes closed, feeling the numbness in my arms from being pulled over my head so long. "Then just do it," I whisper. "Take me out."

"There you go again," Preston says, his voice taunting. "You don't get to decide that. Because we're the players, and you're the pawn. And we'll keep playing you, using you, to get to your family. And when you're not worth anything to us anymore, because we've used you up so well that you're worthless to your own family, then we'll stop. But *we'll* be the ones to tell you when you can leave the game. The sooner you realize that you have no say in any of it, the easier it will be on all of us."

"Fine," I say. "I have no say in it. Do what you want to me. Just please, untie me, Preston. My shoulders hurt. I can't feel my hands."

"A little pain never hurt anyone," he says, dragging his nose down from my ear to the hollow above my collarbone. His fingers tighten just a fraction, and his hips rock forward, skimming across my bare ass for just a second, just long enough for me to feel that he's hard.

I gasp, and he releases me, stepping away and surveying me. I have never wanted to hide more than I do when he steps back to look me over. A smirk curls his lips, and his heated gaze moves back to mine. "Damn," he says. "I can see why Devlin's been keeping you to himself."

Tears brim in my eyes, running down my face with the blood, dripping onto my chin and neck and chest. I plead with him again, but he only shakes his head and takes another step back. "This is called taking one for the team," he says. "Think about it while I'm gone. But don't worry. I'll be back with the rest of them. Even when I'm injured and can't play, I take care of my boys. I don't want to miss it when they find the delicious little treat I left for them."

He laughs and walks out, ignoring when I call and then scream after him to come back. I'm alone. I'm naked in the boys' locker room. I'm tied to the showerhead by what looks like a basketball net. I twist and pull, trying to free myself. My shoulders cramp, and my body shakes with sobs, but I can't break the chords no matter what I do. At last, I do what Preston wanted, what all of them have wanted since the moment I walked through the doors of Willow Heights for the first time. I sag against the cold tile wall, and I give up.

twenty-seven

Devlin

Game day practice is a joke. Ten minutes of scrimmaging just to get us together and get our heads in the game, and we all take a knee and listen to Coach trying to rile us up. This time, things are tense out there. Preston joins the huddle, though he can't play, and everyone sobers up. Coach seems intent on bending over and letting the Dolces fuck him in the ass, so now I'm supposed to throw the ball to those assholes.

Not fucking happening. Football means a lot to me, but not more than family, and not as much as it means to Preston. They fucked up his arm, and I'll die before I throw a single pass into Dolce hands.

Except hers.

"Dolces, stick around for a minute," our offensive coach calls, motioning them over as the rest of us start toward the back door of the locker room, which opens out to the field.

"I got a surprise for y'all," Preston says, slapping hands and asses as he jogs ahead of us and pulls open the door. We all stream in, and I head for the showers. I'm not interested in whatever cheerleader Preston's coerced into blowing half the team. Five or six guys are in front of me, gathered up around one of the shower stalls. They're nudging each other and snickering. I start to push past them, but Colt's hand falls on my shoulder and squeezes, hard.

"You're going to want to see this one, man."

I don't, but something in his voice gets my attention. I turn toward the blue, tiled shower stall for the first time, and that's when I see her.

She's huddled up against the wall, her eyes huge and her hair tangled, looking like a wounded animal. Her wrists are bound together, her arms not quite straight but pulled up above her head. And she's fucking naked.

It should be hot to see your girl all tied up and waiting, not a stitch of clothes on her, but there's nothing sexy about this. Her makeup is smeared, her hair is stringy and tangled, and blood is caked around her nostrils and trailing down her chin, droplets streaking the front of her torso. A huge purple bruise is swelling in the center of her forehead. She looks like a dog's so beaten it's crawled up under a porch to die.

"Who the fuck did this?" I ask, wheeling around toward the team, searching for Preston.

The guys fall silent, their eyes moving back and forth between me and my cousins. They know better than to step in and make a move before we say so.

"I did," Preston says. The shithead's smiling, calm as can be.

"This is my dog," I say, my hands balling into fists. I'm about to fucking lose it, and I don't even care.

"I thought she was *our* dog," he says.

The thought of him stripping her clothes off, touching her soft skin, makes me want to break every bone in his fucking body, starting with his other arm.

"Yeah, baby," Colt says, reaching past me to stroke his fingers down Crystal's back. She shrinks away, arching her back to put distance between them, and a terrified whimper escapes her lips. The whole team is eye-fucking this girl, this girl whose body that is mine alone to see.

"Get your own dog," I snarl, knocking his arm away hard enough that he swears and shakes his hand out. "This one's mine."

I step toward her, grasping the back of her neck.

"Prove it."

My head swings around, finding Preston standing there watching me, challenging me. At school, everyone wants one of us to be the leader, and that one is me. Preston doesn't challenge me at school, and outside of school, I know the truth—we're as close as brothers, all equals, the way it should be.

"What?" I ask, narrowing my eyes.

The other guys on the team stand frozen, not making a sound, barely even breathing.

"She says you didn't fuck her," Preston says. "If she's yours, she's yours. I won't touch her again. But I need proof."

"I fucked her," I say, my fingers trembling with rage around the back of Crystal's neck. She's shaking, her skin clammy and cold. "If anyone here doubts my word, I have the sheets to prove it."

I meet their eyes, and every guy in the locker room looks away. No one's gonna question my word. But the person I really want to look at is cowering beside me, trying to use my body as a shield between her and the roaming, hungry eyes of my teammates. I want to shake the shit out of her, to ask why the fuck she'd tell Preston we didn't hook up.

"She says you didn't fuck her, and her pussy's so tight I could hardly get a finger in," Preston says. "So if you really fucked her, then show us how it's done."

I can feel the vein in my temple pulsing with the red-hot blaze of my anger. I want to chop off his fingers one by one, making sure there's nothing left of him that's touched her. She's *mine*. Not his. Not ours. Every inch of her, inside and out, belongs to me and me alone. Only I can touch her. Only I can make her cum, make her cry, make her beg. Only I can break her and bring her to her knees, and when she's there, I want her sole focus, her worship, her obedience.

"Did you fuck her?" I ask, never once looking at the girl. My rage burns into my cousin. "If you fucked her, I'll rip your dick off, and the proof will be *your* bloody sheets."

Some of the guys mutter uneasily. They're not used to trouble at the top. We've always been a united front. There's the three of us, and there's them.

And now there's her.

"I didn't say that," Crystal mutters, pressing her body against the tile wall. "I told him we did it three times."

That's when I get it. Preston's not the one who broke the code.

I am.

I'm the one who broke the unspoken pact, the agreement between us. I let her worm her way in, let her wedge herself between us. I let him think she was still a dog to me. I didn't tell him I was still fucking her. But she told him.

Now it all makes sense. This isn't a challenge to see if I'll obey him in front of the team. This is penance for not telling him. He's shrewd as fuck. The second he knew I didn't tell him about her, he knew that's where he'd get me. This is the only way to make things right between us again. To admit that I fucked up, and to let him know I'm sorry.

"If you already fucked her," Preston says slowly. "Then it's no big deal. Show us how you fuck your dog, Devlin."

"Yeah, man, get the party started," Colt says, leaning an elbow on Preston's shoulder, a shit-eating grin on his face. He grabs his dick and adjusts himself. "I call next. I want to get my dick wet before the rest of them wreck her."

That asshole just wants to watch me fuck a bitch, and that fact pisses me off more than anything. Just because they're into that shit doesn't mean I am, and Colt knows it.

"No," Crystal whispers, her voice barely audible.

"No one touches her," I growl.

"Then you do it," Preston says. "Either fuck her, or we will."

"No," Crystal says, this time louder, but her voice is a pathetic quaver.

I turn to her. I know this isn't just about now. If I don't prove this to Preston, and even Colt, they're going to do it. If not now, then later.

I want to ask her which she would choose, but I can't. Not here, not with all of them watching.

I grab the twine holding her up and pull it toward me. Crystal gasps, her body turning slowly as she moves away from the wall. When her back is to me, I step in, pressing my body flush with hers. I pin her in front of me, flatten my hand on her smooth abdomen, and bury my face in her hair. The smell of her makes me start to harden, and the feel of her ass against my cock does the rest. When I'm not looking at her strung up like a fresh kill, or at them waiting like a pack of hungry dogs to devour the scraps, she's just Crystal, the girl I want more than I should. The girl who got under my skin and fucked my head all kinds of ways.

I wrap one arm around her chest, blocking the others' view. I don't want their eyes on her tits, on the hard points of her cold nipples. The sensation of them against my skin makes me nearly moan aloud.

"Is this what you want?" I whisper against her neck, where none of them can see it. The sound is buried in her hair, and I don't even know if she can hear it. "You want me to fuck you?"

In answer, she arches back, pressing her round ass against my cock. I don't want to want her like this, in front of a dozen other guys. I don't want to be hard, to have so little control over my own dick that it pulses against her ass when she moves against it even now, with an audience.

I want to fuck her alone, to be the only man who's ever heard her moaning cries of ecstasy when she cums. I don't share. When I'm inside her, I don't need anyone's eyes on me but hers. Standing here in a public locker room, I want to be too pissed to feel anything, even aroused. Too angry to do what Preston wants, what he knows I'll do because he figured it out before I was ready to tell even myself.

I'm disgusted with myself, with the heat that ripples through my veins, through my muscles, at the thought of being buried inside her again. I'm ashamed that when I slide my hand lower, burying it between her legs and covering her mound so our spectators can't see, that the thought of her tight, slippery cunt floods my mind, and blood races to my cock, now so hard it hurts.

The truth is, I'm blind with lust for her. I'm mad with the desire to sink my cock balls deep into her, to cum with my whole body, the way only she can make me. I'd rip my own dick off before I'd let anyone else fuck her. Before I can talk myself out of it, I yank open the laces on the front of my pants and shove the front of them down enough to free my cock.

The guys all cheer. I try not to hear them, but I can feel them watching, panting like dogs while this girl, who we called a dog, hangs her head forward, her hair obscuring her face, waiting for me to nail her for their enjoyment.

Suddenly, rage swells inside my chest, clutching it like a fist. I push my cock down, pushing the thick head against her entrance. I want to plow into her, to pound her for all I'm worth, to show them what they want to see. Not for their entertainment, but to show them what they can never have. And most of all, because Preston thinks I won't do it.

I grab a handful of her hair, pulling her head back, and they whoop louder, yelling for me to fuck her hard.

"Are you wet?" I growl into her hair. She shakes her head, and I remember the last time, how she tightened up and cried out in pain when I didn't get her ready, and that time, she was plenty wet.

I spit on my fingers and slide one into her, my cock throbbing at the stretch of her cunt around a single finger. I work another one in, pumping them a few times. The guys are going crazy, and I fucking hate them. I don't want to give them this view of her, but I don't want to hurt her, either. Gritting my teeth, I spit on my hand and smear it over my cock with the precum that's beading on the head. Then I guide it down and push it past the achingly tight grip of her entrance.

She gasps, widening her stance and dropping her head forward between her shoulders again. I don't hear the guys anymore. I don't hear anything except her soft gasps of breath as I grip her hip and push deeper into her slick, bare cunt. I grasp her shoulder and begin to move, slow at first and then faster as she gets wetter. A streak of blood smears my cock when I draw back, and I bury myself deep, glad she's still bleeding enough to lube her up. She gasps when I reach her depths, and I'm already close. I don't try to hold back or make myself wait for her. I fuck her hard and fast, pounding into her with the strength of the fury raging inside me, just like they want me to.

I learned a long time ago that being at the top doesn't make my life any more mine than the guy at the bottom of the shit pile of life. Probably less. This isn't for Crystal, but it's not for me, either. It's for Preston; for the asshole who spawned my father. It's for the team, who stand clapping and hooting when I grab her hair and pull her head back. She straightens, throwing her head back against my shoulder, and I grip her hip and slam up into her. She gasps aloud, a whimpering moan of pleasure.

I realize then that she's not just wet with blood. The slut *likes* it. Hell, for all I know she gets off on being fucked in front of an audience. Just because I hate that it feels good to me, that I can get it up for a girl who's hanging from the showerhead, doesn't mean she shares that self-loathing. I'm disgusted by my body's physical reaction, but I hadn't even considered that it might turn her on. Not until she arches her back and grinds her ass against me so I can go deeper.

I drive into her with bruising force, my strong fingers biting into her soft hip until I'm gripping the bone. She whimpers again, and I'm so fucking done with this show. I bury my cock all the way to my aching, full balls and let myself cum, releasing deep inside the stretch of her cunt. I do it because I'm a bastard, and my punishment is now her punishment. Because I'm a selfish asshole, and I don't want her to cum. Only I get to see that. Only I get to feel it pulse along every inch of my shaft, to hear her helpless, breathy cries as she cums with *my* name on her lips.

I press my forehead to her shoulder, cursing myself with everything I have inside me for doing this. I should have resisted harder. I should have fought Preston, not worried that someone might take a turn with her while my back was turned. Her body is shaking against mine, and reality begins to settle back into my body.

"I'm sorry," I mutter against her neck, my cock jerking as it spills the last pulses of cum into her depths.

She doesn't say anything. She hasn't said a word this whole time. All she said was no, and I fucked her anyway. I fucked her, and I liked it. There's no amount of self-loathing in the world that can change that fact.

I pull out, ignoring the jostling and hooting of the guys who still don't get it. Preston gets it. He knows what he did. He made me admit that I care about this girl who I shouldn't care about. That I kept something from him to protect a girl who should be nothing but a whore and a dog to me.

I put my dick away and turn to him, holding out an arm to block the others. I get right up in his face, close enough that I could choke the shit out of him. "Give me your knife."

Preston doesn't move, but his eyes lock on mine. Without breaking our stare-down, he takes out his knife and hands it to me. I could gut the bastard like a fish, but I won't. I won't hold the blade under his chin and threaten that if he ever touches my pet again, I'll slit his throat. I won't do anything because I've proved my point, and he's proved his. Anything else will happen behind closed doors and away from prying eyes.

I take the knife and grab the rope above Crystal. With one slash, I slice through it. She lets out a little cry and stumbles into the corner of the shower, holding her arms in front of her. I fold Preston's knife and tuck it into my pants before scooping Crystal up in my arms, ignoring the way she shrinks away from me. A couple of the guys grumble and boo quietly when they realize they won't be getting a turn. The fun is over. This one is off-limits.

"Get me a blanket," I say to no one in particular.

Colt appears with a huge towel, which he lays over Crystal. She huddles against me, burying her face in my chest as I cradle her body, one arm around her back and the other under her knees. Without another word, I turn and walk out, taking the girl with me. I know it's a mistake before I take a single step, that I'm going to pay for this. But I don't falter.

twenty-eight

Crystal

I keep my face turned to Devlin, away from Preston, away from Colt and the entire Willow Heights football team who witnessed. I don't move when Devlin carries me out. I don't look up until he's settling me into the passenger seat of his car, buckling me in. When he drives away, I turn my face to the window, away from him.

There's nothing to say. Every time I think they can't break me further, that I'm already shattered, they find a way. I'm done. I can't take any more. I want out. Is this how Royal felt? Was there something going on with him that he couldn't tell the rest of us? Did he really run away, like Daddy says? Is that the only way out? I want to leave the game and never set foot on their gameboard again. Why won't they let me out?

I lean my forehead on the glass, close my eyes, and don't think. When the car stops, I don't care. I still don't look. It doesn't matter where they take me or what they do to me now.

Devlin opens my door and lifts me out. My arms link around his neck. I don't care if it shows weakness. None of it matters. I won't play the game anymore. He carries me out of his garage, his feet crunching on gravel as he walks to the house. He enters through his back door and carries me up the stairs, through a room, and into a bathroom. After turning on the hot water and pulling the shower door closed, he finally looks at me.

"Are you okay?" he asks, his voice soft and sweet with that accent. I don't want it to affect me, but it still does.

I want to tell him no, that I'm not okay. Nothing about this day has been okay.

But I can't seem to muster the words.

Devlin's brow knits into a fierce frown. "Of course you're not fucking okay," he mutters, wrenching back the door of the shower. Steam billows out. He unwraps the towel around me, his hands rough and his mouth set in a grim line. Then, he pulls me into the shower and steps in, still fully clothed in his football uniform. The hot water washes down my back, thawing me from my frozen state. I start shaking again, as if my body's too confused to know what to do.

Devlin turns me away from him, so the water hits me right in the face. I splutter and turn my face away, then relax into the warm spray as it caresses my skin. For a minute, two, five, we don't move. I let the water wash away this day, wash away everything.

Devlin's hands rest on my hips, gentle yet firm and possessive. He presses a kiss to the back of my neck, his lips lingering. Slowly, his lips part, and his tongue meets my skin. An involuntary shudder of pleasure grips my body as he presses closer, his grip becoming more commanding and his chest brushing against my back with each breath. His mouth moves along my bare shoulder to the column of my neck, and I tilt my head, giving him access. He nips and sucks and licks, his tongue growing bolder with each stroke.

I stand motionless, my eyes drifting closed and a sigh escaping me. I can't deny the pleasure I feel at the sensations swirling through me—his commanding grip, his soft lips and tongue on my wet skin, the hot water coursing over my body. We stand there for a long time, until I lose all track of time, and all that exists is my body and this boy making it come alive again, making it ache for the familiar comfort of his touch and the pleasure it unleashes.

He turns me slowly, until I'm facing him. But I can't face him. Not yet. Maybe never. I can't meet his eyes, so I slide my tired arms around his neck and kiss him. He moans into my mouth, a rough, animal sound, pushing me back against the wall. He hooks a hand behind my thigh and drags it up, positioning himself between my legs. He grinds against me slowly, rolling his hips against mine as he pins me to the wall. His kiss is gentle, though, his nose angling away from my swollen one.

After a minute, he makes a frustrated sound and pulls away, dragging his wet jersey off his body and tossing it into the corner of the shower. I've never found football pads sexy, probably because I've seen my brothers in them so many times, but seeing Devlin standing there in a set of pads and his lace-up tight pants, I can't help but stare. His taught abs show through his soaked undershirt, the fabric clinging to his skin and revealing every ridge of muscle. His arms are bare, his tats on full display. I want to touch them, to run my fingers over them until I have every curve and line memorized.

I grab his hand when he reaches for his shoulder pads. "Leave them," I say, not even embarrassed that I'm panting at the sight of him.

Devlin's breath is coming as short and fast as mine, and he rips his eyes up from my body to meet my gaze. His eyes are swirling with some mix of anguish and lust, and his voice is husky when he speaks. "Can I go down on you?"

The madness in his gaze should scare me, but it doesn't. It sends a flare of heat straight to my core. I've never been wanted so much, so desperately. I don't know why he needs me, needs this, but he does. And god, I need it, too. I don't want to, but I do. I need him to prove to me that it wasn't all for show, that he really was doing what I thought he was in that locker room—tell the whole world that I'm his, that I'm off limits to every other man on this earth.

I swallow hard before nodding, feeling suddenly vulnerable as he stares at me. He steps forward, his body colliding with mine. His mouth crashes against mine roughly this time, his tongue sliding between my lips with commanding force. He pulls away, lifting my chin, his lips moving along my jawline, down the column of my neck again, gently this time. My fingers curl into his wet hair, and I drop my head back against the shower wall, the cold contrasting with the heat of the water and the desire pumping through my veins like blood.

Devlin drops lower, his hands gripping my sides and holding me up while his mouth devours the water sluicing down my chest. He buries his head between my breasts, then slides to one side, drawing my nipple into his mouth. He moans against my flesh, sending shivers of heat through me. Grabbing my breast, he squeezes and massages while his mouth sucks hard. Pain and pleasure spiral through me, and I cry out, the sound echoing around the bathroom. He moves to the other side, biting and sucking, licking and kissing, until I'm dizzy with want. He drops lower, mouthing my belly, flicking his tongue into my bellybutton before he's on his knees in front of me. My legs tremble as he grips my hips, holding me to the wall and pressing his nose to my mound and inhaling deeply.

He moans and opens his mouth, sucking at my flesh, opening my lips with his tongue. He works it deeper, lapping at me, stroking me, caressing me until I'm breathing so hard and fast I think I'm going to black out. I grip his shoulder pads, gasping out my pleasure in wordless little moans. The connection between us is different this time, both of us desperate for the moment of no return. Or maybe we've already passed that moment. Right now, I know there's no going back, that Devlin Darling has claimed me in a way no one else ever will, and I'm not sorry. I want to be his, want to wear the marks of his claiming proudly on my thighs and hips and neck where he's bruised me. I don't care if the whole world shows up to watch him fuck me next time. I want them to know.

I want them to know because I'm not the only one who's being possessed. Whatever this is between us, it's possessed us both. There's something between us that can never be broken, no matter how hard we try.

Devlin grabs me and lifts me, and I wrap my legs around his neck, resting my thighs on his shoulders while his tongue drives relentlessly into me. He slips a finger into me from below, working it deeper and then plunging it rhythmically as his tongue strokes at the very center of my pleasure, at the heart of me, until I break. My body goes rigid and then melts, and I spill over his fingers, his name tearing from my lips, stroking my tongue with the novelty of a first kiss and the finality of last words.

twenty-nine

Crystal

We lay on our sides in Devlin's bed, facing each other. He washed me clean before bringing me here, to the place where the devil himself sleeps. It's odd to think of this boy sleeping. I resist the urge to press my nose into his pillows, to inhale the scent of him collected there. Instead, I watch him, and he watches me. We're both naked, but we don't touch. We gaze into each other's eyes without words, without needing them. I don't know how to put it into words, but I feel the shift. Something's changed.

At last, when the sun creeps lower, slanting across the floor in hazy, pale strips of light, I speak. "What happened back there?" I ask, folding my hands together and sandwiching them between my cheek and the pillow.

Devlin's quiet for a long moment. I think he's going to refuse an answer, like he always does. But at last, he speaks. "I didn't tell Preston," he said. "Now, he knows."

I swallow hard, my pulse racing in my throat. "What does he know?"

"He knows you're mine."

He says it with such matter-of-fact certainty that there's no use arguing with him even if I wanted to. Like Preston said, I never had a choice in any of it. Why should this be any different?

But I don't want to argue. My heart soars at his words.

"Your dog?" I press, because I have to hear him say it. I have to know it's real.

"No," Devlin says, his turquoise gaze never leaving mine.

"What about Dolly?" I ask.

He draws back a bit, like he didn't expect that, and I watch the guards shutter over his eyes like windows. "What about her?"

"She's my friend," I say. "I don't want to get in the middle of anything."

The corners of Devlin's lips quirk up, but it's a bitter smile. "It's a little late for that, Sugar. You're already right in the middle of a lot of messy shit, and not just with her family and mine."

"Do you still love her?"

"No," he says simply.

I wait for him to go on, but he doesn't.

"But…?" I prod.

He rolls onto his back and covers his eyes with a forearm. "Our families meant us for each other."

"*Meant* you for each other?" I ask. "Like, an arranged marriage?"

Dolly already told me basically the same thing about their relationship, but damn. This isn't the 1800s.

"Don't sound so shocked," he says. "I thought you said the south was just like the mafia."

I don't know how to respond to that. My parents are far from perfect, but they definitely never picked a man I was going to marry one day. As far as Daddy's concerned, I'm pretty sure he hoped I'd join a convent and die a virgin.

For a while, we're quiet. This time, Devlin speaks first. "What did Preston do to you?"

"Nothing," I say. "I mean, he did what you saw. He didn't touch me. He just said that to get to you."

"It fucking worked," Devlin mutters. He moves his arm from over his eyes, using it to pillow his head instead. "And he better be glad he didn't touch you, or he'd be losing a finger."

I scoot closer, lay a hand on his bare chest. "I'm guessing he knows that, even if it hasn't been that way with your other… Dogs."

He scowls at the ceiling. "If he didn't before, he knows now."

"What happened to the last Darling Dog?"

"She's your friend. Ask her."

"You know that's not what I mean."

He sighs. "She moved back to Oklahoma."

"And the one before that?"

"Faulkner."

"She left school? Is she still at Faulkner High?"

"I… Don't know. Maybe."

"Was she from out of town, too?" I ask. "Is that how you pick? When someone new starts at Willow Heights?"

"No," he says. "It's not about being new. It's about not falling in line."

"Dixie didn't fall in line?" I ask.

He doesn't answer.

"Or she doesn't conform to what your version of a Willow Heights girl looks like?" I press.

"We don't pick them," he says quietly.

I let that sink in a minute. "You picked me," I point out.

"Yeah," he says, turning to smile at me. He slowly winds a strand of my hair behind my ear, sending a warm thrill across my skin. "I did."

He leans forward and places a gentle kiss on my bruised forehead. Now that my nosebleed has stopped, my nose is still tender, but my forehead is the only injury that really shows.

"So, your grandpa picks them?" I ask. "Or your secret society?"

He tenses, and I know I'm right, though he doesn't say a word.

"Why do you do it?" I ask.

"Don't you have to listen to the Don Corleone in your family?"

Devlin's phone chimes, and he reaches over to pick it up. He thumbs it on and stares at the screen for a long moment before sitting bolt upright.

"What is it?" I ask, sitting up, too. I lay a hand on his back, wanting to be back under the covers with him, safe and immersed in conversation. My heart is suddenly slamming in my chest. I can feel the difference in the air, in him. Something is wrong.

He turns to me and links his hand with mine. "I'm so sorry," he says, his fingers tightening and his eyes locking on mine.

I can barely force out a whisper. "What?"

"Crystal," he says. "They found a body."

thirty

Crystal

Devlin whips out of the driveway so fast I have to cling to the dash so I don't roll out the door. I scramble to buckle my seatbelt, my stomach dropping with the momentum as the car shoots forward down the narrow drive through our neighborhood. He rolls down the window far enough to reach out and flip off the reporter who's standing next to the gate before speeding away.

I can't think of anything, can't feel anything. I know I should. I should be screaming and keening like any sane person. Like a good sister, a good twin, would be doing. But there's no shattering, no tearing pain as my heart is torn slowly from my chest. There's only a cavity, a hollow space, where my heart should be. Because if Royal's gone, my heart is already gone, too.

It seems only a minute later when Devlin skids to a stop at a construction site. A handful of police cruisers crowd the curb, their lights flashing in the blue evening. An ambulance sits halfway on the street and halfway on the curb, the back door open. A backhoe sits off to one side, and broken slabs of cement litter the ground inside the site like fallen leaves. I'm out of the car and running before Devlin's even shut off the engine. I don't feel the ground under my bare feet, don't hear the cop yelling at me to stop. I only see the two men carrying a stretcher with a black bag on it.

An arm whips around my waist from behind, stopping me so fast that I fold in half. "Let me see him," I scream, fighting like a wild animal against the arm holding me. "That's my brother. Let me see him!"

I twist and hit at him wildly, my fist connecting with his jaw before I realize it's not Devlin holding me.

"Take a deep breath," Office Gunn says, still holding me in his crushing grip.

"I've got her," Devlin says, reaching for me.

Officer Gunn releases me warily, as if he thinks I might attack him again. "What are you kids doing here?" he asks. "You shouldn't be here, Dev."

Dev.

Fuck. This cop is BFFs with Devlin's father. Is he going to keep me from seeing what I don't want to see, what I have to see?

"Yeah," Devlin says, "You're probably right. I just got the text, and I came."

"This is a crime scene," Officer Gunn says, motioning to the torn up concrete, around which a handful of cops are stringing yellow tape like ghastly Halloween decorations.

"I don't need to go in there," I say, straining against Devlin's hold as the EMTs load the stretcher into the back of the ambulance. The lights are on, but the sirens are off.

Because this isn't an emergency. Because that black bag is zipped all the way up.

"I just need to see him," I say, my voice breaking.

"Can she?" Devlin asks, holding me against his chest and staring over my head at the cop.

"I don't think that's a good idea," Officer Gunn says. "If it's the missing boy…"

"He's my brother," I say, my voice rising. "I deserve to see him before you haul him away and chop him up for your autopsy."

"Just let her see if it's him," Devlin says. "Before the whole town gets wind of this."

Officer Gunn sighs and takes off his hat, running his hand over his shorn blond head. "I could probably lose my job for this…"

"Thank you," Devlin says, sounding relieved. He reaches past me to shake the officer's hand, but it's more like a squeeze. "You won't lose your job."

I've seen my father do this, telling people they'll be taken care of, but it's odd coming from someone still in high school. Maybe that's what happens when you're a big fish in a small pond instead of a big pond. My brothers had all the power in my last school, but the kids here have power in the whole town.

Suddenly, that seems like the most important thing in the world to think about. Anything but what's under that black shroud.

Devlin's arm tightens around my waist, and he starts for the ambulance. But suddenly, I know with stark clarity that I can't do this. I simply, unquestionably, cannot. My feet move automatically, over little chunks of broken cement and rocks and glass, but I don't feel anything. A whirlpool of panic has opened in my chest, sucking down every sensation, all rational thought.

"Devlin," I choke out, grabbing onto his shoulder when we reach the ambulance.

"Yeah, baby?" he says, looking down at me with a furrow of concern etched across his brow.

"I… I can't," I say, barely able to speak past the hyperventilating breaths that escape each time I open my lips. Everything seems far away, as if seen through a darkened tunnel.

"Okay," he says, cradling my face in his hands. "You don't have to."

"Hey," he says to the EMT. "I'd like to see who that is."

The lady, who doesn't look much older than us, frowns like Devlin's some kind of creeper with a corpse fetish. "We're not allowed to show people bodies," she says, turning her back to us as she crouches next to the stretcher.

I look away. I can't bring myself to look at what's on it. The way the bag fits around the shape inside it makes my stomach lurch sickeningly.

The ambulance driver comes around, stopping short when he sees us. "Devlin Darling," he exclaims, a smile spreading across his face. "Wow. I can't believe you're here. What's up, man? How's that arm?"

"Good," Devlin says, pulling me even closer, his posture stiffening. "I was hoping I could take a look at who you got there."

"Sure, of course," the guy says. "Anything for our big star. Hey, aren't you supposed to be at the game? I had to work but… You're not still in trouble, are you?" He gives Devlin a conspiratorial wink.

"Shit," I blurt. "You have a game. Why aren't you at your game?"

"Don't worry about it," Devlin mutters. "I'm going to look."

The moment he releases me to climb into the ambulance, my knees buckle. I brace my hand on the back of the vehicle, my head swimming. The EMT is staring at Devlin like he's holding a gun, and I can see a thin layer of sweat that's broken out on her lip in the last two minutes.

"I'm sorry," she mutters, wringing her hands and pressing her back to the wall. "I didn't realize who you were."

"Don't worry about it," Devlin says again, not even sparing her a glance before turning to the bag. And suddenly, I know I can't stand here and deny what's happening. A body was found on my father's construction site. And if it's Royal, the least I owe him is being the one to identify him. I may not be the sister he deserves, but I'm brave enough to look at him. I'm brave enough not to let his enemy tell me a truth I can't bear to look at. No matter how impossible it is, I have to do it.

"Wait," I gasp, dizzy but clearheaded. "Let me."

"Are you sure?" he asks.

I nod, and he grabs my hand and pulls me in. My hands are shaking so hard I can't hold the zipper. Devlin takes it and slides it down, lacing his fingers through mine and holding on tight as I kneel beside the stretcher and part the fabric to reveal the face inside.

thirty-one

Crystal

A pale face stares up at me, dirt and bruises covering every inch of his skin. I've been to my share of funerals, but it's different seeing someone battered and bloody, as if I can still see the remnants of the pain he felt in his last moments.

"It's not him," I choke out, and then collapse into Devlin's arms.

He catches me, his body rigid. "I know. I saw."

The screech of tires interrupts us, and the next second, I hear a familiar voice yelling. "Who the fuck tore up my slab? I just had this laid! It hadn't even finished drying!"

"Daddy," I say, jerking upright, a knot forming in my chest. I hadn't moved beyond the relief of knowing it's not Royal. But who is it? Why is there a dead guy under my dad's foundation? Someone must have set him up, and I have a pretty good guess who might want to frame him. But who is this dead person? Is his family looking for him, as sick as we are about Royal? If someone is willing to kill to keep us out of town, we're in more danger than I imagined. Are my other brothers safe? Is Daddy going to be arrested?

We don't know people here the way we did in New York. I don't even know if my uncle's license to practice law is good down here. Are they going to take away my family, one member at a time?

I jump out of the ambulance and run to my father, who wraps me up in his protective arms, turning us away from my uncles and the cops, who are getting heated.

"What are you doing here?" Daddy demands, not hiding his surprise. "What happened to your face? Your brothers were worried sick about you."

I feel an immediate pang of guilt. I know what it's like to have someone disappear on you. And after Royal disappeared, my brothers must be even more on edge. I was supposed to be waiting for them after their football practice. Instead, I disappeared without a trace, just like Royal. I don't even know what happened to my phone, so they couldn't contact me, either.

"I'm so sorry," I say. "I was with Devlin. I forgot my phone."

"He did this to you?" Daddy thunders, his eyes flashing murder.

"No," I say quickly. "I… Ran into a door at school."

Not technically a lie, and I don't want him to go into Papa Bear mode and murder the boy I'm just starting to understand, to unravel. I didn't do all this to gain his trust only to have Daddy screw it up with his temper. I give Daddy a meaningful look, so he'll remember the plan we devised. It seems so long ago now, even though it was only days. I can tell by Daddy's nod that he's not about to forget the plan. But to me, it doesn't even matter. It all seems so meaningless now, in the face of a murder. Thinking that was Royal in that bag… Something changed in that moment. If the stakes are life, then that's what we have to play for. Ruining some other family seems petty and trivial compared to that.

"And why were you two at my building site?" Daddy asks.

"I came to see if it was—" I break off and swallow the ache in my throat. "To see if it was him," I finish in a whisper.

"Your brother's gonna be fine, sweetheart," Daddy says, slinging an arm around me and squeezing me to him. "He's tough. Now, you get on home. Daddy's got some business to take care of. Let your mother know I'll be out late."

"Can I use your phone?" I ask. "I need to let the guys know I'm okay."

"Sure, sweetheart," he says. "But don't be long. I've got some calls to make, too."

"Are you going to be… Arrested?" I ask, whispering the last word.

"No," Daddy says, giving my shoulder a squeeze before turning me toward Devlin. "Now, go on home. I'm sure you kids have somewhere better to be on a Friday night."

I shoot a quick text telling King that I lost my phone and then hand Daddy's phone back. Officer Gunn stands off to one side, watching our exchange, obviously waiting to ask my father some questions.

"And get changed if you're going out somewhere," Daddy calls to me as I join Devlin. Since I wasn't exactly thinking about how I looked when we left the Darlings' house, I'm wearing a pair of Devlin's sweatpants and a WHPA hoodie. Going home to change was the last thing on my mind, which is how I ended up out here barefoot in the first place.

"Okay," I say, then slip under Devlin's arm. He threw on jeans and a T-shirt, which he's wearing with his letter jacket. Even though he had the same thirty seconds to dress that I did, he somehow manages to look freaking perfect while I look like a total scrub.

Devlin quirks an eyebrow at me but doesn't speak as he leads me back to his car.

"What?" I ask, sliding into the passenger seat and tucking my hands under my thighs.

"Nothing." Devlin closes the door behind me before circling around and climbing in his seat.

"Tell me," I insist.

"Didn't you say something about my family being more controlling than yours?" he asks, pulling out onto the street.

"Yeah, because they pick out who you marry," I point out.

Devlin gives me a skeptical look. "Your father tells you what to wear."

"Exactly," I say. "That's hardly in the same realm as picking your wife."

The word makes a funny feeling settle in my chest.

As we make our way through town, I can't help but marvel at how empty the streets are. And it's not just because this is some nothing town in the south, not New York. It's because there's a game going on.

"Devlin," I say, turning to him. "Thank you."

He glances at me from the corner of his eye but doesn't speak.

"Really," I say. "You didn't have to do this for me. You were here for me tonight, and you didn't have to be. Not to mention you're missing your own game for me. And judging by the last game you missed, you could really use a better second-string QB."

"Some things are more important than football."

"Like what?" I ask. I know it's stupid of me to want this, to want him to say something to show he gives a shit. He's already done so much. I shouldn't need more. But the emotional trial of the evening has me needing some reassurance.

"Family," he says flatly.

"Even my family?" I ask, a bit of teasing entering my voice as I try to get him to show a peek of the real Devlin. "If I didn't know better, I'd think you had a heart in there somewhere."

"Yeah, well, don't go thinking that," he says, his voice gruff.

"Why not?" I ask, biting my lip as I reach over, inching my hand onto his thigh.

For a long moment, he doesn't react. Then he slides down in his seat, spreading his knees and angling his pelvis so I have no control over my gaze moving to his crotch. Even through his jeans, I can see what he's packing. I swallow hard, my cheeks warming. When I tear my eyes away, a knowing smirk twists Devlin's lips.

"You wanna thank me by putting that mouth to good use?"

I marvel at how fast he can deflect when my questions get too personal. In some ways, I know Devlin Darling better than I know anyone else in the world. But I barely know a thing about him. At least, not anything he's told me. What I know about him comes from gossip and secondhand sources, and it's as much about his family as it is about him. But I know how he changes the conversation, makes crude jokes that are meant to shock or distract me from the topic at hand.

"Okay," I say. "If you don't want to talk about it, that's cool. Your business is your business. I can respect that."

He glances at me for a beat too long, like he's trying to figure out if I'm fucking with him, using reverse psychology.

"You need to go home and change?" he asks at last, moving on to safer topics.

I shrug. "I'm getting used to wearing your clothes."

"Good," he says.

I'm dying to ask what that means, but I guess I've gotten as much of the real Devlin as I'm getting tonight. I'll take it.

It's sure as hell more than I've gotten before. It seems greedy to ask for more.

Besides, I'm distracted by the fact that he just passed the road that leads to our neighborhood. "Oh, so we're really not going home," I say. "Okay, then. Might have been nice to have some shoes, but I suppose I'll manage."

"Shit," he mutters, glancing at the clock on the dash. "Need me to turn around?"

"Would it really matter if I did?" I ask.

He scowls and checks the time again. "No."

Sighing, I cross my arms and stare out the windshield. "I'm going to go out on a limb here and guess you're not going to tell me where we're going, either."

Devlin doesn't answer for a minute, long enough that I start to get a little nervous.

"Crystal," he says slowly, adjusting his hands on the wheel and glancing sideways at me. "I think… I think you were right."

Warring urges spring to life inside me—whether to ask what he's talking about and ignore the fact that he just admitted he was wrong for maybe the first time in his life, or make a big deal out it. Deciding I don't know him well enough to tease him yet, at least not right now when his voice is so low and intense that it makes my heart skip a beat and my fingers tremble, I choose the first option.

"About… What?" I ask, my voice barely above a whisper.

"About my family having something to do with your brother," he says. "I think I might know where he is."

thirty-two

Crystal

I can't breathe. My pulse flutters like a dying moth. *Royal.* He might be safe. He might be alive. Suddenly, I feel faint, and I have to grip the door handle to stay upright.

"I asked around, like I told you I would," he says. "I didn't know before. I swear it to you."

I didn't want to believe it. I mean, I always said Preston had done something, knocked him out and kidnapped him or left him somewhere in a ditch. But I didn't want to believe it. I didn't want to believe it could be true, that his family could be capable of something so heinous, so unimaginably cruel.

Not when I'm falling for one of them.

No. *No.* I cannot think those things about Devlin. Not when I was scheming on him, and definitely not now, when I know his family is responsible for Royal's disappearance.

"Where is he?" I ask, my teeth clenching with fury. At him, at myself for not trying harder, sooner. For not looking in the right place. "He's at your grandfather's old house, isn't he? The one where we saw your sister acting all shady. That's why she's his favorite? Because she'll help him take care of a body?"

I'm seething by the time I stop, venom lacing every word as I shoot them at him like poison darts.

"No," Devlin says, his voice calm. "I already looked there."

That surprises me back from my anger a bit. He's been looking for my brother?

"When?" I demand.

Devlin pulls up at Willow Heights, the school dark and quiet now. An eerie feeling crawls along my spine, and a chill races along my arms at the sight of the school so empty and lifeless on a Friday night.

"Where is everyone?" I ask, adrenaline pumping through me as blind panic tries to claw its way back into my chest. I've been to a game. This place should be packed.

"In Ridgedale," Devlin says. "At the game."

I recognize the name I've heard a few times this week, and realize it's an away game, which makes me feel only marginally better. Why are we here? Did he bring me here to tie me up again? Lock me in some closet where no one will find me? Dispose of my body in some convenient way that makes it look like I did it to myself?

"This is the only time when no one will be around," Devlin says. "Everyone goes to the games. No one will drive by and see a car in the lot, and no one will be here tonight. But I've gotta do it now. The game will be over soon, and I don't want to be here when the team gets back."

I shudder and wrap my arms around myself, suddenly cold despite his hoodie. The memory of Preston's hands on me, of the knife between my thighs, of the team's animal frenzy watching Devlin fuck me, thinking they'd be next…

I drop my head forward and take a deep breath, trying to calm myself.

"Stay here," Devlin says. "I'll be back in a minute."

"Wait, what?" I ask, my head snapping up.

His jaw is hard, and he sits up straight, leaning in to loom over me, dominating the space like he knows I'll cave. "Stay. Here." He delivers the words slowly, deliberately, so there's no mistaking the command in his voice.

And like the dog he's trained me to be, I instinctually want to obey.

But fuck if I'm going to sit here while he goes to find my brother, or whatever clue he needs. "He's here?" I ask.

"Stay in the car," Devlin says, turning to open his door and step out. He leans down and fixes me with that gaze that's impossible to disobey, so full of masculine command and dominance. "Don't move."

He slams his door and starts off across the lot with long, purposeful strides, nothing like the slow strut I've seen before, the one that fits him so well.

It takes me a second to realize I'm just sitting here watching him go. I jump out of the car, my feet hitting the cold pavement with a shock. I run after him, catching up before falling into step beside him.

"Go back to the car," he snaps, not bothering to look my way.

"That would be a no," I say.

"Go back, or I'm not helping you."

"Then I'll call the cops and have them crawling all over this place," I say. "If I tell them he's here, they'll have dogs sniff him out no matter how hidden he is."

"Crystal, I *can't* bring you in here," he says, his voice a mixture of frustration and annoyance. He stops at a discrete side door to the building, crossing his arms over his chest and staring down at me. "Go back to the car before you get us both killed."

"No." I mirror his pose and stare up at him, refusing to back down. "This is my brother, Devlin. I'm not going to sit in the car while you find him. Fuck that. *Your* family did something wrong. Whatever you're afraid I'll see, their secret hiding place for dead bodies, or your secret society, it's not as important as his life. As *our* lives, if your family would really murder us for rescuing someone."

"You're a fucking pain in the ass, Dolce," he snaps, turning and shoving a key in the lock. He doesn't say the words in an endearing way, either. He sounds like he hates my guts.

I couldn't care less.

"I'm not about to let you go in there and do whatever you might do to Royal when I'm not there," I shoot back. "What are you going to do that you can't do with me there? Finish him off? Threaten him to silence?"

His family did this. I can't trust any of them, no matter how kind he was to me tonight. I have to remember the other side of Devlin. Sure, he was nice to me, but only because he fucked me in front of his entire football team before that. He's also a boy who held me down and threatened to disfigure me if I didn't obey him. A boy who took my virginity as part of a plot to destroy my family and told me it was nothing personal. For all I know, he was in on Royal's kidnapping the whole time, a decoy to keep me and my other brothers occupied while Preston and his dad pulled it off.

I shove through the door after him, so close on his heels that I run into him inside the door. I'm not even surprised he has the key. But he takes me by surprise when he spins and tucks his shoulder, slamming it into my solar plexus like he's taking down an offensive lineman. I go flying backwards, the shock of how painful it is hitting me as hard as the pain itself. I barely feel it when my ass hits the ground, my elbows hitting the concrete so hard I can't even scream with the pain of it. By the time I realize I'm on my ass outside the door, it's closed, and Devlin is gone.

Bastard.

It takes me a minute to recover enough to drag myself up. I sit on the ground and try to breathe through it. At least my head didn't hit the ground. But it could have. Fucking Devlin didn't even stick around to see if I was knocked out cold. He thinks I'm just going to stand out here throwing a fit, seething about what an asshole he is. Yeah, fuck that.

All I can see through the window in the classroom to my right is the eerie, dim security lighting of the halls inside. I search around, scanning the small stretch of pavement between the small door and a row of trees. It takes me a few minutes, but at last I find a decent sized stone under one of the trees. I pick it up and hurl it with all my might at the window of the classroom. I saw enough to know the door opens into a hallway, not into some secret chamber where the Midnight Swans meet, but that doesn't mean I can't find him.

The glass shatters, and shards rain down around me. Ignoring the pain when I step on them, I yank off Devlin's hoodie, wrap it around my hand, and punch out the glass at the bottom of the window, which is about even with the top of my head. I have to turn away and close my eyes so I don't blind myself, but after a minute, I've cleared a spot for myself. I grab the sill, gritting my teeth against the pain as shards of glass bite into my palm. I may be small, but I'm not weak. I was a cheerleader, and I have pride. I'd be damned if I was going to stand there shaking when I was holding up another girl's weight.

I grip the sill with both hands and jump, using the momentum to shove myself up and in. I lock my elbows, a little breathless as I struggle to get a knee onto the sill. From there, it's smooth sailing. I grab the window above and swing through, dropping down into the classroom. Cursing under my breath, I have to stop and pull a few pieces of glass from my bleeding feet after only a few steps. But once I get the big pieces out, I can ignore the smaller ones as I step out into the hall and run on tiptoes down the long, empty corridor lined with lockers. It's eerily silent when empty, with only the dim security lighting casting shadows around every corner.

I hear a soft footstep somewhere to my left, and I freeze, my heart beating so loud I can't tell if I imagined it. Then I hear another one, and I turn and race down a side hall, searching for Devlin. He must have heard the window shatter, but he didn't come to see what I'd done. Instead, he went on without me.

I stop in the hall, listening hard. The seconds tick by. Just when I think I've lost him, I hear the soft squeak of a door opening. I run back a few steps and duck into the library. Willow Heights' library looks more like something you'd find in a movie than a school. Sure, there are rows of modern books in the middle, but wall shelves stretch to the ceiling, leather-bound classics lining each one. In one shadowy window nook, behind one of the plush recliners set around the library for students to sit and read, I spot a sliver of light coming from beneath the shelves.

I run across the library, grateful of the carpet under my battered feet. I grab the shelving and pull, praying Devlin didn't lock the door behind him. For once, luck is with me, and the section of shelves pulls out, swinging open the hidden door. My breath catches in my throat as I stare down the stone steps.

Willow Heights is old, but this looks like an ancient cavern that might have been around for centuries. A set of rough stone steps leads down, each one about two feet wide and precariously non-uniform in width and height, as if someone made them from stones they found in nature. A single, incandescent bulb hangs over the stairs, which have no railing. My heart slamming in my chest, I descend after Devlin, trailing my hand down the wall. It's made of natural stone, too, and my fingers come away gritty with dust. My mangled feet welcome the cold of the stone steps, though I don't even want to know what grime I'm getting in the open cuts.

Devlin stands at the bottom of the stairs, not moving, though he must hear me coming. I stop behind him and wait, my heart pounding so hard in my ears that I can't hear anything. Did I just make a horrible mistake, walking into a trap? I know how fast Devlin can turn from a decent man to a monster. I know how callously he can betray me, like he did upstairs.

"Devlin?" I say, barely able to speak past the sick shaking that's taken over my whole body. He could lock me in here alone, treat me like a dog until I believed that's what I was.

"He should be here," Devlin says, his voice not cruel or angry but distracted, disbelieving. "Dad was sure of it."

"Is there another place the secret society meets?" I ask, wrapping my arms around myself and glancing around the creepy stone room, lit only with the bulb above the stairs. I can see chairs set around the room, though, and lamps on small tables between them. This must be where the Midnight Swans meet. At school. Probably at midnight.

"Shit," I blurt. "What time is it?"

Devlin pulls out his phone, and when he thumbs it on, I freeze. There, just a few inches in front of my bare toes, is a single drop of blood.

My mind spins back to that first morning in the driveway, when I stood shell-shocked and empty, seeing that drop left where my brother had been taken.

"Royal," I breathe.

"Dad!" Devlin cries, spinning around and nearly running me over. He catches my shoulders, his eyes boring into mine with desperation and panic. Releasing his grip, he grabs my hand and charges up the stairs, dragging me after him. It's all I can do to keep my feet and scramble up behind him, catching myself on my hand a few times when I stumble. He shoves the door closed behind us, not bothering to switch off the light. And then he's racing through the library, back down the hall. Splinters of glass bite deeper into my feet with each step, but I don't have time to stop. I know if I pull away, Devlin won't wait for me.

We fly down the hall, bursting out the door and into the parking lot. Devlin releases my hand, and I have to race to keep up with him as he sprints for his car. He dives in and fumbles the keys, dropping them to the floorboard and cursing savagely as he grabs them up. I'm barely in the door when he slams the car into drive and floors it. My door slams closed with the momentum, and I'm thrown back against my seat.

"Devlin," I cry, grabbing the dash and casting a wild glance in his direction. "What the fuck is going on?"

Another car turns onto the road past the school as we pull out of the lot, and Devlin curses again, glancing in his mirror and then slamming on the gas as we approach the stop sign at the intersection near the school. We fly through it without slowing, and I stop trying to figure out what's going on as Devlin tears through the streets, ignoring all traffic signs and signals. I yank my seatbelt out and buckle it, gasping for breath as we shoot forward so fast I feel like I'm on a rollercoaster about to drop from under us.

A pair of lights blurs by, and a long honk fades behind us, already far behind. We skid around a corner at breakneck speed, but Devlin spins the wheel into it, correcting his course and shooting forward along the road to our neighborhood. My mind is blank, my heart hammering with blind terror as we fly through the gate and along the narrow drive toward our houses. Devlin swings sharply into his driveway, the tires spitting gravel as we rocket down the long drive. He skids to a stop in front of the garage, the car sputtering and then dying before he spills out the door and sprints for the house.

I jump out and follow, not sure what we're after. Walking on gravel with bare, injured feet is not fun, and by the time I get inside, Devlin's already in a far room. He's not hard to follow, though. He tears through the house, calling his Dad as he throws open every door. I don't know why we need to find his dad, why he's in such danger, but I assume it has to do with ratting out the Swans. And even though I don't know how much Mr. Darling knew all along, I know that Devlin loves his father more than anything in this world. I can feel the anguish and terror in his every footstep, his every call for his father, and I know how it feels to lose someone who is your whole world.

So I go along, starting up the stairs for the second floor. Devlin passes me before I reach the top. We run along the hall, opening the doors until we reach the end.

No sign of Mr. Darling.

"What do we do?" I ask, grabbing Devlin's hand, trying to calm him. "Is there anywhere else he could be? Do you have a basement?"

He turns, yanking his hand from mine, and runs down the hall. He opens a door at the end and starts up a set of steep, narrow wooden steps that's more like a ladder with wide steps. I stop at the bottom, staring at the edge of the one that's just above eye level. There's a smear of blood on the edge. Suddenly, my heart is racing again, and I don't want to go up those steps. I don't want to see what's at the top.

"Devlin," I call, scrambling up behind him. Because he was there for me when I opened that body bag, when I was prepared for the worst thing I'd ever imagined. Devlin is not prepared.

We tumble out onto the attic floor together, my hands tangling with his legs before he can stand. It's dark and dusty, but there's a scent in the air that stops my heart, though it's faint. It's a putrid, dirty animal smell, like piss and copper pennies, body odor and greasy hair.

Somewhere far away, I hear sirens, but it's distant, in the back of my mind. Devlin's on his feet, smashing into something that clatters to the floor and shatters. He curses, and a box falls, and then a light blazes on, blinding us. I blink away the darkness and stare, uncomprehending, at a body laid out on the floor. His ankles are bound in duct tape topped with a thick rope which leads up to his middle, where his arms are bound straight down at his sides. As my eyes move up, my stomach lurches, and my knees give way. His face is swollen

and bruised and caked with so much blood I can't make out
his features. The tangle of black hair is all that gives away my
twin's identity.

thirty-three

Crystal

Devlin grabs me before I hit the floor, but I dive out of his arms, falling to my knees beside Royal. Tears splash onto his cheeks before I know I'm crying, and I know I'm saying something, but I don't know what words come out. I cradle his face, pleading for him to wake, to answer.

One of his eyes moves under the lid, but his lashes are glued shut with dried blood.

"Dad?" he whispers, his voice a dry rasp, like the dry leaves scraping against each other as they tumbled across the lawn outside.

"Royal," I cry, a hysterical laugh mixing with my tears, choking me as I try to speak. "It's me. I'm here."

And then I register the sound of the siren is outside this house, that Devlin is standing back just watching us, his face blank, uncomprehending.

My mind races with questions. Was he here all along? Did the cop see him and ignore it? Did the cop believe Devlin and not check this room? Or was he brought here after that? Tonight?

"Devlin?" I whisper, hating how weak my voice sounds, how it pleads for this to be someone else's doing.

His eyes snap to me, and his mouth tightens. After making a quick 911 call, he strides forward, dropping to his knees at Royal's feet and pulling out a knife. Making quick work of the bonds around my brother's feet, he moves up to his middle. Then he sets the knife on the floor and kneels behind me, wrapping his arms around me as I sit there, silent tears streaming down my face for my brother. I can't even touch him because I'm afraid I'll hurt him, that there's no place on him not covered in bruises.

Outside, I hear car doors slamming, and lots of yelling. But I focus on what's here. At last, I grasp Royal's hand. "You're going to be okay," I whisper. "We're going to get you out of here. We're going to be good again."

I don't know what I'm saying, words tumble out haphazardly. Devlin holds me tight, holding me up. If he weren't here, I'm sure I'd have melted into a puddle on the floor. But he's strong, and he gives me his strength, even when we hear the doors open downstairs, heavy footsteps on the stairs.

"Dad?" Royal mumbles again.

"It's me, Crystal," I remind him, squeezing his hand gently. "We're going to get you some help."

"Don't make me move again," Royal mutters.

"Okay," I say, laughing through my tears. "I won't. You don't have to move. Just stay like that. Help is on the way."

I can hear footsteps in the upstairs hallway now, coming closer.

"Crystal," Devlin says, pressing his face to the back of my neck and inhaling once, long and slow. "Whatever happens…"

I turn to him, releasing my hold on Royal and taking Devlin's face in my hands. His eyes go wide with surprise at the ferocity in my gaze. "We'll get through it," I say fiercely.

Devlin's lips press together, and he nods. "I just… I'm sorry."

"For what?" I ask, my heart skipping a beat in my chest.

"For being such an unforgiveable bastard," he says, his hands falling to my hips and squeezing. "I'm sorry. You didn't deserve any of it."

I swallow hard, not sure what to say. That wasn't what I was expecting. Tears are still running down my face, but my words come out strong. "You're right. I never asked to be pulled in the middle of your fight. But if you want my forgiveness, it'll take more than words. You're going to have to earn it, Devlin. Show me I can trust you."

His gaze darts to the trap door in the floor as footsteps begin up the steps before it slides back to me. His fingers tighten. "I can do that. I… I think… I care about you," he says, wincing at his own words.

Holy shit. Is His Royal Highness Devlin Darling getting tongue tied? For *me?*

Maybe Nonna's disgusting coffee trick worked.

I lean forward and press my forehead to his, sliding a hand to the back of his neck. "Me, too."

Devlin leans in and kisses me once, hard and quick, before pulling away and standing. "Okay," he says. "There's something I have to do first."

I wonder if it's something to do with Dolly, and jealousy twists in my heart even though I am her friend. Because no matter what I am to him, I can never be what she was.

Before I can dwell on it, Officer Gunn's head appears. He jumps up into the room with surprising speed when he sees Royal on the floor. He kneels beside him and checks his pulse, and then he calls over a radio for backup.

Then he turns to Devlin. "Where's your father?"

Devlin shakes his head. "It wasn't him," he says, kicking the knife away and holding up both hands. "It was me. I did it."

thirty-four

Devlin

Crystal's different. I'd tried to figure it out, but it all came down to the challenge. It wasn't that it was a challenge to get her. She didn't play hard to get. I'd fucked her with barely any effort. It only took one night of showing up for her, and there she was, putty in my hands. Maybe not enough people had shown up for her in her life.

But that isn't my business.

Or maybe now it is. Maybe now I know more than how to get her in bed. That wasn't hard, but then, I hadn't expected it to be. What I really didn't expect was that even after I fucked her, she kept on challenging me. She challenged my authority.

My place in this school. She challenged me as a person. And no one's ever done that before.

Somehow, she figured out how to get me before I figured out how to get more than her body.

And now, all I can do is prove to her that I can be the man she deserves. I just don't know how I can be that and the man my family wants me to be at the same time. I have to choose, somehow, between my future and my past, between everything I've ever known and counted on, and an unexpected, terrifying unknown.

I know what I should choose. But I also know I can't let a person who helped me take the fall for doing the right thing. Dad's the best man I know. If going to jail to protect him makes me half the man he is, I'll do it. Even if it means turning my back on a future I'd only just dared to imagine. Even if it means walking away from her.

thirty-five

Crystal

"How is he?" Mom asks, sweeping into the waiting room, looking as out of place as a tropical bird that's escaped the zoo and landed itself in this godforsaken town in the middle of Arkansas. Her yellow cocktail dress shows off her olive skin, and her lipstick if freshly applied.

"Oh, my, what happened to your face? You look positively hideous."

"Where have you been?" I demand, my voice angrier than I meant. "We've been here for hours."

"I was having cocktails with the neighbor," Mom says, pouting like a child. "It would have been rude to have my phone out."

"Come 'ere," King says, scooting over to leave a seat between us. "Sit down. Royal's stable but unconscious right now. Dad's in there with him."

"Well, thank God," Mom says, folding herself into the vacated chair. "I thought I'd be stuck in this backwards town longer. At least I've discovered a new cocktail. I can't wait to share it with the ladies when I get home."

Rage swells inside me, but Nonna takes my clenched hand and unfolds my fingers, smoothing my hand between hers. My other hand stays fisted around the icepack I've been holding on my bruise. My nose is red and swollen slightly, but compared to Royal, it's nothing. No broken bones, no concussion.

"Are you drunk?" I ask Mom, narrowing my eyes at her.

"Well, I wouldn't go that far," she says, waving a dismissive hand and giggling. She lowers her voice and leans in with a conspiratorial smile, and a cloud of boozy perfume surrounds me. "Have you had a mint julep? They're positively divine."

"In case you forgot, I'm sixteen, Mom."

I lean back in my chair and close my eyes, too exhausted to deal with his. Trying not to think about the cops swarming Devlin's attic, and what he said to me before that. The EMTs coming up, how hard they worked to get a stretcher through the trap door and back down a glorified ladder. The cops taking Devlin away in cuffs.

That's the part I try not to think about the most.

I'm half asleep when I hear the door open, and Daddy steps out with Dr. Swift, the doctor monitoring Royal. They talk for a minute, shake hands, and then part ways, Dr. Swift heading for the coffee machine in the corner and Daddy coming over to us.

All the uncles and cousins stand to greet him with hand clasps and sympathetic slaps on the shoulder. Uncle Vinny, who lost a son a few years ago, hugs Daddy and murmurs in his ear.

"We're going to get them back for this one," Uncle Donny says. "Don't you worry, Tony."

"There will be justice," Vinny says quietly. Looking at my favorite uncle, thin and bespectacled and soft-spoken with a somewhat jumpy manner, you'd think he was a tie salesman or telemarketer—anything other than the vicious, cutthroat lawyer that he is.

"Dolce justice," Donny mutters.

"Go get me some coffee, would you, sweetheart?" Daddy asks.

I get up and head to the coffee machine, not really wanting to hear them plotting their revenge, anyway. I spent the first few hours here picking glass from the soles of my feet, and now I'm bandaged and wearing fluffy new socks inside a pair of designer kicks. Apparently someone told my brothers what a mess I was, and they brought me a whole outfit along with the high tops.

Returning from the coffee pot, I hand the cup to Daddy. "Is he awake?" I ask.

Daddy shakes his head. "They gave him morphine. Knocked him right out."

"That's the good stuff," Uncle Benny says. "I'm going out for a smoke break. Anyone else?"

"I've got a cigar," Uncle Donny says.

"I might just step out for a breath of fresh air," Nonna says, standing and stretching her arms over her head. "All this sitting's making me crazy."

"Is that what it is?" Duke asks.

She swats at him before turning to Grampa Dolce. "Are you going to let him talk to me that way?"

"Mind your manners," Grampa growls at Duke, wrapping a thick arm around my *nonna* like she's fragile. She leans down and plants a big kiss on his lips before pulling away to trail after the smokers.

"Can we see him?" I ask, sitting down beside Daddy.

"I don't think he's ready for all this mess just yet."

I know what he means. My family has taken over the waiting room. I smile and lean my head on his shoulder. "He was asking for you when we found him."

"Was he?" Daddy asks, tensing. "Did he say anything else?"

"No," I say. "He just said not to make him move."

Daddy finishes his coffee and hands me the empty cup. "I'd better get back in there," he says. "I want to be there when he wakes up."

When he's gone, I yawn and get up to stretch, then decide to join Nonna and the uncles outside. I find them sitting on an old iron bench with an outdoor ashtray thing beside it. Donny gets up, but I wave away his offer of a seat. It's late, closer to morning than evening, and I've been sitting in a cramped hospital chair for too long. There's only one small hospital in Faulkner, and it's definitely not just for the rich and famous. It's an old, ugly brick building with tired staff, scorched coffee, and cracked plastic chairs.

"We were just talking about going home to get a few hours of sleep," Nonna says. "There's nothing we can do here, and we could all use it."

Yesterday was probably the longest day of my life, and I'm tired as fuck, but I can't bear the thought of being so far from Royal. We've only been apart for a week, but it feels like a year. I don't want to leave him again, not yet.

"I'll stay," I say, stifling another yawn.

Nonna's in the midst of trying to convince me to get sleep when a figure strolls out of the parking deck, one hand in the pocket of his ripped, light-wash jeans. Even from a distance, I recognize the lazy strut, the fringe of blond hair that he shakes out of his eyes with a toss of his head.

Fuck.

"Is that who I think it is?" Uncle Donny asks. "Is that one of them?"

My uncles both puff up like a couple of Papa Bears, but I hold up a hand to stop them and walk over to meet Colt halfway. "You've got a lot of nerve coming here," I say, glaring at him.

"I didn't know you owned the hospital," he says with an easy grin.

I cross my arms and narrow my eyes at him. "What do you want?"

"You look hot in jeans," he says, looking me up and down. "You should wear them more often."

"Thanks," I say, rolling my eyes. "But I can't possibly look hot right now. I look like Rudolph if his nose stopped working and he flew face-first into a tree."

"Maybe you just need someone to help guide your sleigh," he says. "I volunteer. I'll be Captain America. I'll slice down any tree that comes in your way."

"I thought you were Romeo."

He shrugs, that goofy grin still in place. "Every superhero needs an alter ego."

We stand in silence for a minute.

"Nice kicks, too," he says, nudging my toe with his. "You look kinda badass in that getup."

"Seriously, Colt," I say, glaring. "Why are you here?"

"I wanted to give you this," he says, pulling his hand from his pocket and holding out my phone. When I look from it to his face, his expression is serious. "I'm sorry about what Devlin did. I just wanted you to know that we had nothing to do with it."

"I don't think Devlin had anything to do with it." I've spent the entire night replaying everything in my mind. When Devlin saw that Royal wasn't in that school basement, he was surprised. When he ran out of there yelling for his dad, he didn't sound accusatory or shocked that his father would do something like that. He sounded scared. Scared for his dad, who betrayed their grandfather by telling Devlin where to find Royal.

"He confessed," Colt says, dropping his hand back to his side when I don't take the phone. He's looking at me like I'm a stupid, lovestruck idiot who won't believe the truth that's right in front of her. Maybe I am.

"I know," I say. "I'd think you'd need more than that to turn your back on your own family. Your boy, no less."

Colt hesitates, glancing around and lowering his voice before answering. "I didn't turn my back on my family. He did."

"So, it's your whole family against him?"

"He chose to do what he did," Colt says. "And yeah, I have family loyalties beyond him. I figured you'd understand that."

"Why?" I ask. "My *nonni* is a candy maker, not The Godfather."

"Oh," Colt says, looking surprised. "I thought…"

"What? That the mafia was here because a dozen Italians showed up at my house?"

He shrugs, his smile apologetic and slightly embarrassed, like a kid who just got called out and doesn't want to get in trouble. And maybe that's what he is. Maybe that's why he will be my friend one minute, and the next, he's doing what his cousins want. Suddenly, I understand him. I get it. Because of all the Darlings, Colt is the most like me.

He just wants to make everyone happy, and I get that. I really, really do. He's as lost and frustrated as I am, pulled in two or three or five different directions because he has to be the person his family wants all the time. He's never allowed to be the person he *is*, if he even knows who that is.

Still smiling, he holds out my phone again. "I put my number in your phone. So you can call me if you need anything. *Anything.*" He winks at me, and I feel a smile tugging at my lips. Why is he so damn hard to stay mad at?

"Thanks," I say, accepting the phone. "But I don't think Devlin would like that too much."

Colt tilts his head, giving me a curious look. "It's like that with y'all?"

"Yeah," I say, biting my lip to hide a smile. "It's like that."

We stand in silence for a minute, and I feel warmth creeping up my neck. At last, Colt lets out a chuckle and reaches out a hand to give me knuckles. "Okay, then," he says. "See ya around, Ru-liet."

There are too many missed calls and texts on my phone to look through, so I turn and walk back to where my uncles and Nonna are standing watching me. "What'd he want?" Uncle Donny asks.

"I think he's sweet on you," Nonna says.

"He's not," I say, rolling my eyes and holding up the phone. "He was just giving back the phone."

"Uh huh," Nonna says, sounding unconvinced. "How many of these handsome blond men can we count on seeing with you?"

"None," I say, my insides twisting at the thought of Devlin in a jail cell somewhere, waiting for his father to get back from wherever he is and post bail. I admire what he did for his dad, but I can't ignore the fact that his dad knew where Royal was. At least for a while. And Devlin knew. Maybe for only a day, but that day might matter.

"Well, as long as you don't use the secret ingredient on all the boys," Nonna says. "That's a recipe for disaster right there. You'll have 'em fighting over you for the rest of your life." She smiles, her small teeth slightly stained from the tobacco use, her eyes crinkling at the corners, but still looking as young and lively as ever.

I'm suddenly overcome by emotion, and I pull her into a hug. I can't help but wish she was my mother instead of my grandmother. She managed to raise a whole mess of kids without buying a ticket on the Nolet's Reserve and heading for Tipsy Town.

Nonna laughs and pulls away, swatting my arm. "None of that," she says. "Can't have any carrying on in the street, can we now?" It strikes me that maybe the Dolce image didn't start with my father making millions in the candy business. Nonna has the steel spine of a Dolce running through her every bit as much as the rest of us. Maybe that's where we all get it.

"I'm going in," I say. "I can't be away from Royal any longer than I have."

It's not until the next morning that Dr. Swift says we can go in. Duke and Baron are off raiding the hospital cafeteria and flirting to get extra chocolate pudding. I know they'd want me to wait, so we can all go in together, but I can't bring myself to wait any longer.

I stand over the cheap hospital bed where my twin lies, a tube up his nose and an IV running into the back of his hand, and hold back the flood of tears that wants to come. Last night, his face was caked with dried blood, but somehow, seeing it clean is even worse. I can see every bruise and cut and scrape on his battered and swollen face. Both his eyes are blackened and sunken, and the center of his lower lip was split so deeply it's now stitched up with black thread. More stitches are scattered over his face in various places, and I can't find a single spot on his cheeks that's normal skin color. They're yellow and green, blue, purple.

I gently take his hand in mine, careful not to jostle the IV. Royal's lids flutter open, and he looks up at me. The corner of his mouth tugs the tiniest bit. I can't tell if it's a grimace or a smile.

I smile, and the tears come.

"That ugly, huh?" Royal says, his voice slurred with sleep and the drugs he's on, raspy and hoarse from…

God, I don't want to know. Was he screaming? Denied water until his throat was too parched to speak?

"I'm so sorry," I manage to choke out.

"What're you sorry for?" Royal asks. "You found my carcass."

He smiles, but all I can think is that he used a word that's a little too close to the truth. How long would he have lasted up in that attic? A day more? Two? A week?

A sob wrenches free of my control, and I dive onto my brother, burying my face in his chest and letting them come. When I finally wear myself out, I get up and grab some tissues, clean up my face, and return to my twin. I can't bear to let him out of my sight. I slide onto the edge of the bed, wrapping my arms around him as well as I can while he's lying on his back.

"What happened?" I whisper.

"I was fucking ambushed," Royal says, his eyes falling closed again. "What happened to you?"

"Nothing," I say, touching the tender bruise on my forehead. "Do you know who attacked you?"

"I know who sent them," he says. "They were just a bunch of rednecks-for-hire."

"How'd they get the jump on you?"

"They had guns, for one thing."

"Shit." I shiver at the thought of Royal trying to fight his way out of a group of guys, only to be held at gunpoint. I swallow hard, forcing the bile down as it rises to my throat.

"They took me to this house first," he says. "But a couple days later, they took me out of there. I don't know where they took me. They put a fucking bag over my head and drove me somewhere. And then I sat in some basement for… I don't know how long. It felt like forever."

"Did they hurt you?" I ask, silent tears leaking from my eyes, falling onto his thin blanket.

"Yeah," Royal says quietly, his eyes still closed.

"Did they give you water or food or… oh, god… Let you go to the bathroom…" I choke on my words, trying to keep the sobs from returning. I have no right to cry like that. He's not crying. I wasn't there. I can only imagine how terrified he was, what he endured for a whole week at the hands of those psychopaths.

"At first," he says, his voice beginning to fade. "When I was in the house."

I remember Mabel leaving the house, how sketchy she was acting. So that's what she was doing. The psychotic little cunt was feeding my brother while he was chained up like an animal. Through it all, she knew where to find him. Devlin's dad could have found out, but he didn't. He didn't tell anyone. He lied to the cops, to Dad, to me. For all I know, he knew all along and didn't tell Devlin until he asked. He stood there and told me how sorry he was while knowing exactly where Royal was and what condition he was in. If I hadn't gotten to Devlin, if I hadn't convinced him to help me, Mr. Darling would have let Royal die down there.

Royal's body relaxes beside mine, and I think he's sleeping. But he keeps mumbling for another minute. "We're gonna get them, Crys... He saw me like that... Gave me water... Mabel... Can't let them hurt you...Dad's gonna make sure of it..."

"Shhh," I say, laying a hand on his chest and pressing my head into his shoulder. "It's okay, Royal. You can tell me later. Just rest."

"Can't," he mumbles, but the next second, he's snoring softly.

And for the first time in a full week, on a narrow hospital bed with a rail digging into my back and a mattress that must be made to discourage people from staying any longer than absolutely necessary, I sleep soundly, too.

thirty-six

Crystal

I wake when a nurse wheels a cart into the room. "Aw, look at y'all," she coos.

I scramble off the bed, ready to be yelled at for crowding her patient or breaking hospital protocol or something. "I'm his twin," I explain quickly.

"He mentioned he had a sister," she says, putting her stethoscope in her ears. "Twins, huh? That's pretty special."

"Yeah," I say, glancing around while she checks his heart and lungs.

"Looks like y'all have been though a lot."

Outside the small window, it looks like late afternoon. I've been sleeping all day in here. She's probably already been around and seen us and left us to sleep. I'm grateful but also guilty that I've been in here so long. The others must want time with Royal, too.

Not to mention the state I'm in. I'm starving, my arm is numb from lying on it, and I could use a long, long shower.

The memory of the last shower I took sends another spiral of guilt and conflicting feelings through me. Royal doesn't know I've been with Devlin, that I'm still with Devlin. He doesn't know Devlin's so much as touched me. He doesn't know that just yesterday Devlin bathed my naked body, savoring every inch of me inside and out. That he's tasted me and moaned with pleasure like I'm the most exquisite delicacy. That he's forcefully slammed his raw, bare cock into the depths of me and filled me with his cum.

He doesn't know that I'm falling for him. Not just the enemy family, but Royal's captors. I want to puke again, but instead, I make an excuse and escape before he wakes up, like the coward I am. It was one thing to face my other brothers after I slept with Devlin. I didn't have to tell them because he did it for me. And more than that, we had the shock of Royal's disappearance to focus on. Royal, who now I have to tell. And there will be nothing to take the focus off what I've done when Royal finds out.

My brothers are all watching TV in the waiting room when I walk in. They must have gone home at some point, because they've all changed into clean clothes, and Duke's wearing a backwards ballcap that he wasn't before.

"Sorry," I say, sitting down beside them. "I didn't mean to stay in there so long."

King gives me a distracted glance and hands me my phone before returning his attention to the TV. I try to turn on my phone, but the battery is dead. When I look up, I catch my breath. It's a local news channel, and though it's muted, the line scrolling across the bottom of the screen tells me what's coming before the earnest newscaster's face is replaced by a picture of Devlin.

"Turn on the sound," I say, balling my hands into fists so hard I feel my nails cutting into my palms.

"… In a prank apparently gone horribly wrong," the woman is saying. "Local authorities say the house was searched already in the week-long ordeal. They're still looking into how the victim could have been hidden during the search."

The screen cuts back to the anchorman in the studio. His forehead furrows as he adopts an overly solemn expression. "That sounds a rough time for everyone involved, Jackie."

"I'd say so," she says, the camera cutting back to her. In the background, the ugly brick hospital squats. "It can't be easy for either of the families. The missing boy is in stable condition, though, and reunited with his family right here inside Faulkner Regional."

"Sounds like a happy ending for everyone," the anchorman says. "We're always glad to see those."

"It won't be such a happy ending for the Darlings," King says. "That bastard's bail is set at a million."

"Are you serious?" I ask, turning to him. "How do you know that?"

He shrugs. "I looked it up."

"Can they even release that?" I ask. "He's a kid."

"He's eighteen," King says, his jaw tight. "He's not a kid, Crystal. You're a kid. Royal's a kid. *He's* an adult."

"Shit," I whisper, swallowing past the lump in my throat. Devlin's two years older than me. Than us. He's an adult who kidnapped a child.

Except… I know he's not.

With all the media attention this got, someone's going to have to pay this time. They can't cover it up or bury it the way I'm sure they do, just like my family does when someone commits a crime. But my brothers do things like joining illegal fight clubs, shoplifting liquor, maybe stealing a car for a quick joyride. They don't hurt people.

Kidnap is a serious crime. It's bigger than the local police. It's an FBI-worthy crime. A federal crime. It's not going to just go away, be swept under the rug because they're the Darlings and they can do no wrong in this town. This time, there will be serious consequences. There will be jail time in a federal prison.

I think of Devlin Darling doing hard time, and my chest tightens. He can't do that. Not even for his father. Whatever reason he has for covering it up, for protecting his family, he shouldn't be doing that. He shouldn't have to take the fall for the whole family for something he didn't even do. If it weren't for him, I might not have found Royal in time.

"No offense, sis, but you look like shit," Duke says, stretching his arms over his head. "Let me take you home for a while."

I hate the thought of leaving Royal, but I know I can't hover here forever. Besides, Daddy's still here, and I know my brothers all want to see Royal. So, I relent and let Duke take me home.

At home, I'm swept up in the whirlwind of energy in the kitchen as my *nonni* make food. Nonna pulls me into the kitchen and wants to hear all about Royal, though I didn't get to talk to him enough to tell her much. She's more interested in his welfare than what he said, anyway.

I'd like to slip away for a shower and a minute of quiet to brush my teeth, but those moments are few and far between when my whole family is around. Nonna enlists me to help set the long table in the dining room while she flits between helping cook, setting out candles on the table, and helping with the place settings. A few minutes later, the house is bursting with noise and the trod of heavy footsteps as my uncles, cousins, and brothers join us. There's so much masculine energy in the room it could smother a girl if she wasn't used to it.

"Pour Crystal a glass," Daddy says when Nonna reaches my place with the vino. "She's done her part, and done it beautifully. One more Darling behind bars."

"Hear, hear," Benny says, raising his glass and grinning at me. "Let justice be served."

"Wow," I say, scooting in at my place. "You're giving me wine? I really am at the grown-up table now."

"You're doing a woman's job," Daddy says. "You don't get treated like a kid anymore."

I don't know how to feel about that, and before I can respond, Uncle Donny changes the subject. "Your aunt Dottie's real sorry she couldn't make it to see her favorite niece," he says, scooting in and tucking his napkin into his collar. "Maybe she can make it at Christmas."

My other uncles check in with reports of their wives, kids, and friends who have heard about Royal and are so glad he's okay. For the next hour, we talk and eat. Every time a course is done, another makes its way to the table. I'm so hungry that for once I don't mind the excessiveness of my grandparents' cooking—even when Mom lovingly reminds me what pasta will do to my thighs and sugar will do to my skin.

"Everything's going our way now," Daddy says. "The police have the Darlings in custody, and we're well on our way to getting rid of the rest of them."

I set down my fork, remembering the pale, bloodless face inside that black bag. Suddenly, I'm sorry I ate all my nonni's food. "Who's the guy? The one at the construction site."

"One of the guys from the job," Daddy says. "He was working the forklift, and someone must have come up behind him when he stopped for a cigarette break."

"Smoking kills," Duke says, tipping his glass before taking a drink.

"Wasn't me," Donny says, then laughs that big belly laugh I've always found so warm. Now... I don't know. It sounds different when it comes after a statement like that.

"They were trying to frame me again," Daddy says. "Since it was my construction site. But I was at the bar when it happened."

"And so were we," Vinny says. "Lots of witnesses."

"Only Dad wasn't with us," Donny says, slapping Grampa's back.

"A doddering old man like me, I'm not capable of murder," Grampa says, making his voice all feeble and wavery. Then he gives a Cheshire grin, and everyone at the table laughs.

Oh god. I think I'll be sick. "Can I be excused?" I ask, pushing back from the table. "I think I ate too much."

They're all laughing when I exit the dining room and start the cleanup in the kitchen. It's dark out by the time I finish and have a chance to slip away to my room. It's the first time I've been alone in days, and though I love my family, I'm also an introvert, so it feels good to sink into a bath and close my eyes and be quiet. When I finally get out, I slide into bed, plug in my phone, and power it on.

I have dozens of missed calls, and ten times as many texts. I check the calls, mostly from my brothers yesterday evening, when they couldn't find me before the game. Dixie called three times, and Dolly called once, and a few random calls from unknown numbers.

I switch over to my messaging app.

The first one is from an unknown number. I scroll past to the next message.

Romeo(akaCaptainAmerica.Shh.Donttell): Hey, baby. I can fly in your window and rescue you any day. Just shoot me a text, and I'll be there.

I smile and shake my head, scrolling to the next text.

TheRealDollyBeckett: I heard they found your brother and he's okay. So happy for you!

It's followed by a bunch of kissy-face emojis. Past that are half a dozen messages asking where I am, saying my brothers are freaking out and can't find me, and asking if I'm okay.

I shoot her a message saying thanks, close her message, and scroll down.

DixieDog: OMG I heard what happened in the locker room. You okay?

I freeze, and my heart stops in my chest.

Fuck.

Of course that's going to get around school. I haven't had time to really process with all that's happened. My entire focus has been on Royal, with a few thoughts of Devlin being sent to jail. I haven't had time to think about myself, about the repercussions of what happened. The entire football team was there. Of course someone is going to talk, and by the time the rumor mill gets through with it, I'll have fucked the whole football team.

Oh, god.

I sink down in my bed and cover my face with a lavender, silk pillow. Royal thinks I'm still his sweet, innocent little sister. By the time he gets back to school, I'm going to be the town whore. Dolly's parents aren't going to let her hang out with me. Dixie's parents probably won't, either. And my family… Shit. I can't even think about what they'll do when they get wind of this.

My phone chimes, sucking me out of my anxiety spiral.

I pick it up and open the message.

Unknown Number: Please talk to me.

There are a dozen messages above that one, and it doesn't take a genius to figure out that Devlin has my number. I don't know where he got it, but I'm not surprised. No doubt they pulled it from my phone the night they stole it and led me around like a dog, or he threatened Dixie into spilling. It doesn't matter where he got it. I can't answer.

Still, I torture myself a little more by scrolling to the top and reading through them.

Unknown Number (11:06pm): Is he okay? Are you?

Unknown Number (11:40pm): I'm going to make it up to you. You don't have to believe me, but I will.

Unknown Number (11:53pm): I just remembered you don't have a phone. Well, you'll see these when you get it back. Call me? I need to talk to you.

Unknown Number (6:27am): You've probably heard by now, but Dad was arrested, too. And if you're thinking he's guilty, you're wrong. He didn't know anything about it until I asked him, and he asked around. He's not involved with those people. I wasn't going to let him take the fall alone, though. If that makes sense.

Unknown Number (8:30am): Well, you got what you wanted. My family is ruined.

Unknown Number (8:38am): That was dramatic. Sorry, haven't slept in over 24hrs. It's making me stupid. My family isn't ruined. No one can ruin the Darling name. It's just my immediate family. So, congratulations. And Long Live the Darlings!

Unknown Number (8:40am): That was sarcasm.

There's a long gap in the texts. The next one was sent this afternoon.

Unknown Number (4:58pm): Please answer. Just text me back and tell me to fuck off if you're done.

Unknown Number (6:05pm): Guess you're not talking to me, either. Theme of the day. I seem to have been disowned by the Darlings. Not sure I care. Except my cousins. Was not expecting that.

Unknown Number (7:08pm): I just wanted to talk. I don't have anyone else right now. But okay. I get it. I'm sorry, FWIW.

I close my eyes and hold the phone to my chest. This is what I wanted. This was the plan all along. And it worked. I don't even know how it did happen, but here we are.

My brothers would kill me for continuing to talk to Devlin now, when he's been arrested for kidnapping Royal. My parents would kill me, too, because imagine how bad it would look that I was dating the boy who nearly killed my brother? It's bad enough that I did it before I knew. What kind of monster would still love a boy after he did something like that?

I don't want to think about it, so I erase the whole thread and block his number. Because I'm that kind of monster.

thirty-seven

Crystal

I had revenge all wrong. I didn't need to dig two graves. I didn't even need to dig one. They had already dug them both.

A week later, Royal is home. The bruises have faded, and as far as broken bones go, he only had a few fractured ribs, which have to heal themselves over time. He had a concussion, too, but I know that's not the worst thing that happened to him. He's talked to the police and my brothers, but he hasn't talked to me about the week he was gone, and I haven't pressed. I don't want to make him relive that.

The day before I go back to school—Dad had me excused for the week, though my other brothers wanted to go back after a few days when they got bored of sitting around watching Royal sleep—I wander into the living room to find my twin staring off while the TV plays some NFL pregame show that would have once kept him glued to the screen.

I drop onto the arm of his recliner. "What's up?"

"When were you going to tell me?" Royal asks, staring out the window at the grey November afternoon.

I swallow hard, resisting the urge to play dumb, to ask, "*Tell you what?*" like I don't know.

I was going to tell him when he was all better, when things were back to normal. But I'm beginning to realize that will never happen. Our bruises have faded, but we've all been changed by this experience, this place. There's no going back. Every time I look at my brother, quietly fuming or staring off into space with a vacant expression, I know this is only the beginning of his healing. Like the broken ribs, which will continue hurting while he bears no outward marks, no bandages or bulky casts like Preston's, the greater damage is what cannot be seen.

"I was going to tell you," I say quietly, pressing my palms against my thighs to steady myself. I don't know what he's heard. We've both kept a low profile, not going online too much or posting anything about his recovery. But he must have seen something in his limited glances at social media.

"Is it still going on?" he asks.

"No," I say. I take a deep breath and say it again, forcing myself to accept the truth of it. "No. Nothing's going on."

I haven't seen Devlin all week. I halfway expected him to crawl through my window, but he hasn't contacted me. I haven't heard him outside at night, either.

"Does he know that?" Royal asks.

"I blocked his number, so yeah, I think he knows." My chest tightens painfully at the reminder of what I did. But it was what I had to do. He chose his family. I have to choose mine. It was ridiculous to believe we could ever be free of these bonds, of our names. There is no way off the gameboard until the players are done with us. For so long, I thought the Darling cousins were the players, the ones in control. But we're all the pawns of our parents.

"He posted bail," Royal says. "He and his dad should be on their way home."

"He hadn't posted bail?" I ask, my heart lurching into my throat.

Royal scowls at me. "No. Why?"

Part of me wants to lie, to keep one thing for myself, even if it's just a few text messages from a boy I can never allow myself to love. But nothing in this world is mine alone. Everything I do and say and see and wear… It all affects my whole family.

"He texted me a few times the first day," I admit.

"He's probably buddies with everyone down at the station," Royal says bitterly.

That means he probably hasn't had his phone while he's been staying in country jail, or wherever he's been until now. I guess they have rules there, even for the Darlings.

Royal turns to the window again. That's when I know he's not gazing off into nothingness. He might be lost in his own thoughts, ones I'll never be able to understand or share, but he's here for a reason. He's waiting. Waiting for Devlin and his dad to come home. Waiting to face the people who claimed responsibility for his imprisonment.

King and the twins appear in the doorway a minute later. Duke comes bounding in and leaps over the back of the couch, landing on his back on the leather before bouncing upright. "You ready for this, sis?"

I swallow hard. "I guess I have to be."

"It's showtime, baby," Duke says. "Payback starts now."

"You guys know it wasn't Devlin or his dad who did this," I say.

"Does it matter?" Royal asks, swinging around toward me, his eyes full of accusation and hurt.

"Well…" I cross my arms tightly across my middle, trying to fill the sick, empty feeling building there.

"It doesn't matter," King says, coming to stand behind our chair and laying one hand on my shoulder and one on Royal's. "You did your job, Crys, and you did it well. You should be proud. Now it's time to finish it."

"It doesn't matter which ones did it," Royal says, his eyes intent on me. "Their family did it. They did all of it. If it weren't for Devlin choosing us as targets, his family wouldn't have come after me."

I swallow hard and nod, even though I'm shaking with nerves at the thought of seeing Devlin. Does he even know I blocked him? That it's over?

"I'm with you, brother," King says, squeezing Royal's shoulder and locking eyes with him in some silent communication of solidarity. "We're going to make them all pay, every single Darling, down to the very last one. We won't rest until every Darling in Faulkner is running scared. Even the ones who changed their names and hid like the fucking cowards they are."

"That's not really fair," I mutter. "They were disowned by Grandpa Darling."

All four of my brothers stare at me. "They have Darling blood," Royal says at last. "What about you, Crystal? Do you have Darling blood now, too? Or are you still a Dolce?"

My throat tightens, and I can't swallow when I try. "Of course I'm still a Dolce," I say, my voice choked, pain twisting inside me. My twin is looking at me like a stranger. "How can you ask me that?"

We stay locked in a staring contest until Duke pops up from the couch. I glance up to see a car turning into the Darling's driveway. My heart flips, and I sway where I sit, my body threatening to tumble to the floor. I don't want to do this. I can't do it.

"Then let's go," King says.

"This is the best part," Duke says with a grin.

"He's right," Baron says, slinging an arm around my shoulders. "Finishing a job is the most satisfying part."

And suddenly, I know that this is my loyalty test. Devlin and I tried. We thought we could hide things from our families, but we both learned. He had to do what he did to me in the locker room to show his cousins that they came first. And I have to do this.

My legs feel numb and stiff as I walk out with my brothers. I can't seem to breathe, to swallow. I've been hiding this past week, unable to face anyone. I thought he knew I was done, that he had let me off easy. That I had let him down easy, and he was leaving me alone, and I wouldn't have to face him again. But I should have known. I should have known it wouldn't be that easy. Neither of our families would let us off that easy.

I swore I was done, that I'd given up, I wouldn't play anymore. But what choice do I have? Even if the Darlings stop forcing me to play, my own family will make me keep going until someone wins.

Or until we all lose.

I can't hide anymore. We're on the lawn between our houses before I can think of what I want to say. Duke throws an arm around me from the other side, and together, the twins half-carry me across the lawn. Every step takes us nowhere. The lawn has never seemed bigger, not even the night I met Devlin out here. But before I'm ready, we're stepping between the lilac bushes, bare and ugly now that they've dropped their leaves. A cold wind tugs at us, and the grey sky overhead is featureless and flat, witnessing with no emotion.

I try to draw inspiration from it, to pull the same glum numbness into myself. I'll be strong. For my family. I'll do what I have to do, just like Devlin did. I'll be hard as crystal.

Devlin steps out of the garage, where his dad parked the car. He stops when he sees us. He's wearing the same clothes he wore the night we found Royal. His dad stops beside him, and Devlin says something to him. His dad hesitates before heading toward the house.

Devlin starts toward us. I'm not going to be able to do it. I can't. I watch him walk across the expanse of lawn, wondering if it feels as long to him as it felt for me to cross our lawn. I tell myself this is what I wanted. I wanted him to want me. To like me. To fall for me. I wanted to break him the way he broke me. I try to summon the anger, the sense of betrayal I felt when I walked out of his bedroom the morning he took my virginity.

But it all feels empty now, hollow and meaningless. I don't hate him for that anymore. We've been through too much. This boy helped me find my brother, and I can never hate him for that. I felt his arms tight around me while I unzipped a body bag, thinking the worst thing in my life had come true. I drew strength from him as he held me upright while I knelt at Royal's side, waiting for help. I saw the fear in his eyes when he thought the person he loves most was in trouble. I watched this boy take the fall for that person no fear whatsoever, his face stoic as he silently held out his wrists and let a policeman handcuff him.

How can I hate a boy who would do those things, even if he's the same boy who did horrible things to me?

Duke and Baron drop their arms from around me as Devlin draws near. I have to do this on my own. They won't hold me up through this one.

"This is gonna be epic," Duke whispers in a sing-song voice.

"Be savage, like we know you can," King says, giving my shoulder blade a little nudge. I step forward on autopilot.

I realize now that this isn't just about destroying Devlin the way he destroyed me. This is about atonement. I did something unforgivable in our family—shamed them by being weak enough to fall under the enemy's spell. Now, I have to prove that I'm not weak, that I'm not naïve enough to believe the lies of a snake, that I won't do it again. This is how I prove to them that Dolce blood still runs in my veins, thicker than chocolate. This is how I show Royal that I didn't fuck his kidnapper for fun while he was locked in a dank basement without food or water, being beaten and… Whatever it was that put that haunted look in his eyes that hasn't gone away even now that he's home from the hospital.

"Hey, Crystal," Devlin says, stopping in front of us. He looks tense. He gives a little nod to my brothers. "You brought backup."

"Yeah," I say. Because that's my brilliant, savage response that's supposed to make Devlin die inside the way I did when he betrayed me. "You should appreciate the audience," I try again. "That's how you Darlings like to do things, right?"

Devlin swallows. His blue eyes are that frozen-lake color, the one that gives nothing away. But I know him now. I know enough to see the tiny cracks in the ice. I know I need to keep hitting until I break through.

After all, that's my assignment. That's how I prove that I'm worthy of being a Dolce, that I can be everything a Dolce daughter should be when she's not a little girl anymore. Now, I fulfill the expectations of a grown-up Dolce daughter. This is the real Crystal 2.0. Not just someone different at school, someone who doesn't need popularity, who has real friends, who stands up to bullies instead of becoming one. Crystal 2.0 is not Daddy's baby girl anymore. She's a snake, a woman who will seduce a boy, set fire to his heart, and watch it burn while she sits back and has a cocktail.

Devlin clears his throat. "Actually, I was hoping we could go somewhere and talk." His eyes are fixed on me alone, his expression intense, almost vulnerable. Now is when I have to strike. His weakness was right here all along. I should have known. We're the same, me and Devlin. We have the same weakness. Our family. The need for people to know that we're good, that our family is good. That we're not dirty mobsters or sadistic creeps.

"Whatever you got to say to our sister, you can say it right here," King says, puffing up and putting a protective arm around my shoulders. It used to make me feel all safe and loved when he went all Papa Bear on me, but now, a flash of annoyance goes through me. If they're going to make me do this, at least they can let me speak for myself.

"Look at him," Duke says, nudging Baron. "He used to be the big man on campus. One week taking it up the ass in the slammer, and he's turned into a little pussy."

"I bet they loved you," Baron says to Devlin. "Fresh meat with a pretty boy face like yours. Bet there was a line around the whole jail waiting for a chance to break you in."

"And don't worry about your mom," King says. "You can tell your dad that while he was away, I showed her what a real man can do for her. There's nothing like comforting a scared, older lady. She was so grateful she didn't even finish sucking down her drink before she was sucking down my cock."

Devlin doesn't even acknowledge them. His expression never changes, but his eyes do. A hardness closes over them like ice freezing over a pond in winter. His eyes bore into me like icicles piercing into the warmest places in my soft heart. "So that's it," he says. "I guess I made it easy for you."

This is my moment. I'm shaking, but I won't let him see. I shrug King's arm off. They propped me up, got it started. The train is moving, and it's too late to stop. I just need to jump on board.

I ball my hands into fists and squeeze until my nails bite in. Devlin waits. I wanted to make him fall, to hurt him like he hurt me. But I'm not like him in this way. He can decide

I'm an animal. He can humiliate me, use me, and torture me—with no remorse.

But I'm not a psychopath. Yes, I have to make him pay for what he did. And I want him to know how it feels, how much he hurt me.

But it's going to hurt me worse than I could ever hurt him.

When I feel Royal's quiet strength beside me, though, I know I can't go back. I know that it'll be a long time before that haunted look leaves his eyes, if it ever does. I know that Devlin is an inextricable part of the Darling machine, just as I'm part of my family's. And the whole machine has to be destroyed.

"That's the thing about dogs, Devlin," I say, my voice coming out softer than I intended. Somehow, it makes me sound even crueler. "They're animals. You back them into a corner and threaten them and hurt them enough, and they will fight back."

"Now you're going to fight back?" Devlin asks, quirking an eyebrow in amusement. The Devlin who walked across the lawn is gone. Now, there's only Devlin Darling, the school's king, their golden boy, their hero and bully.

"Oh, Devlin," I say. "I already did. You see, you tried to disgrace me, but all you did was disgrace yourselves. You showed how weak you really are. You said you were going to take down my family, but you couldn't do it the honorable way. You didn't fight fair, and we still won."

He gives me a haughty look and crosses his arms over his chest so his tats are on display. He tilts his head back and staring me down in that way that's meant to intimidate me. For some reason, it's hot as fuck. "I like you better on your back, when I can pound that attitude right out of you," he says with a smirk.

I shove that image away and plow onward. He doesn't know it, but he's making this easy. It's a lot harder to hurt a boy when he shows it. When he's being a dick, reminding me of all the reasons I hate him, I want to put him in his place. I'm going for the kill, and some sick and twisted little part of me loves it. Some part of me loves the thrill of the fight every bit as much as Royal does. Maybe he fights with fists while I fight with words, but I have no doubt he gets the same high.

I smirk right back at Devlin. "You played dirty, ambushing my brother instead of fighting him like a real man. And look at you. It took all three of you, three big strong men, to fight a girl. And face it, Devlin. You lost."

His eyes lock on mine, and his lips twist into a cruel smile. "I didn't lose anything worth keeping."

"Except you did," I say. "You can talk big, but I'm no fool. I know what you lost. You lost the respect of the school. You lost your place in the family. You gave it your best, but my family is stronger than ever, and yours is falling apart. And for what? We're still here, Devlin. In the end, what did you get out of trying to ruin us? You couldn't even ruin *me*."

He steps forward, his eyes darkening, his voice slinking out like a secret. "Sweetheart, if I wanted to ruin you, you'd already be ruined."

"See, that's where you're wrong," I say. "You think your family is better because they've had money for generations, but the truth is, you're just living in the past. Your family will never reclaim its glory because you can't go back in time. Everyone here is so enamored with the glory days of old, but the truth is, it's over, Devlin. And those stupid traditions and attitudes you hold onto aren't doing anything but holding you back. Because you think you can ruin a woman by fucking her, but I'll let you in on a little secret. We're not living in the 1800s anymore. A woman's worth isn't judged by the thickness of her hymen anymore, Devlin."

"I didn't say it was," he says, giving me a stormy look.

"Then you should know that fucking me won't ruin me any more than it ruined you."

"Your reputation probably says otherwise."

I shrug. "You think I care what all these backwards hicks think of me? So you tricked me into giving you my virginity. That shows what kind of person *you* are, not me."

"I thought we talked about that."

"And you thought I forgave you," I say. "That's cute, Devlin. You're not used to girls playing you, so I'll make it clear for you. I don't like you, Devlin. I don't want anything to do with you. You were nothing but a means to an end."

Devlin swallows, and I almost crumble, but I have to deliver the killing blow before he speaks.

I lean in and smile up at him. *"Don't take it personally."*

I take way too much pleasure in throwing his words back in his face, cutting him deeper with every word. Even as I know the blade is double-edged, and each word cuts into me with the same precision as a blade. I relish the pain. I want the pain. I want to hurt him as much as he hurt me, but I also want to hurt myself. I want to hurt so bad I can forget the look in his eyes, that I can't feel anything but my own pain, so I don't notice his.

"It sucks, doesn't it?" I ask, my voice soft again, almost apologetic.

Devlin lets out a soft, soundless snort of breath, his gaze incredulous. But I can see past that, can see a shadow of the boy inside there, the boy who carried me away and bathed me and lay in bed with me and held me. And I don't want to see any of that. I want to destroy that boy, to erase him.

I don't want to think about riding fast in his car, laughing, or the smell of him when he leans close, or the strong, dominating feel of his body against mine. I don't want to think about how close we've been, or about our bodies crashing together like storms determined to wreck each other. I don't want to think about the connection I feel with him, the certainty that we are the same, that I understand his cruelty because I'm just as cruel.

I don't have to remember how loved I felt when I let my guard down and let him in, and how dangerously, terrifyingly free I felt in those moments when it was just us, and I wasn't thinking about his family or mine.

And I don't want to think about how my heart is breaking more with each moment that passes. How it shatters slowly as he turns around without a word and walks away.

I wait, my heart quivering in my chest, praying he won't turn back. Hoping he will. If I see his face right now, I'll break in a way that can never be healed.

There are moments when being part of a family, of any family, is the best feeling in the world. A feeling of happiness and belonging, of knowing someone will have your back no matter how wrong you are.

And there are moments when being part of a family is the worst feeling. A feeling of being suffocated and trapped, of knowing that if you do the right thing, they will no longer have your back. That you'll become the enemy, and they'll turn their back on you and ruin you as quick as any rival.

Devlin doesn't turn back.

King puts an arm around my shoulders, and Royal puts one around my back, and we watch Devlin Darling walk across the endless lawn alone. I swallow back the ache of tears, the urge to cry his name, to run to him and wrap my arms around him in this moment when I have a whole army behind me and he has no one. But when I so much as twitch, my brothers' grip tightens, holding me together, holding me back. I am part of the fabric of the Dolce family, inextricably woven into it. I am a Dolce daughter. I am to remain poised at all times. I don't run after boys and beg forgiveness. I don't apologize for a well-played con.